John McIlraith

Life of Sir John Richardson

John McIlraith

Life of Sir John Richardson

ISBN/EAN: 9783337332846

Printed in Europe, USA, Canada, Australia, Japan

Cover: Foto ©Raphael Reischuk / pixelio.de

More available books at **www.hansebooks.com**

SIR JOHN RICHARDSON.

LONDON: PRINTED BY
SPOTTISWOODE AND CO., NEW-STREET SQUARE
AND PARLIAMENT STREET

H. Adlard, sc

John Richardson

LIFE

OF

SIR JOHN RICHARDSON,

C.B., LL.D., F.R.S. LOND., HON. F.R.S. EDIN.;

INSPECTOR OF NAVAL HOSPITALS AND FLEETS;

&c. &c. &c.

BY

THE REV. JOHN McILRAITH

MINISTER OF THE ENGLISH REFORMED CHURCH,
AMSTERDAM.

' The evenness and beauty of a strong and well-defined nature,
perfectly governed and balanced, is about the last thing one is
likely to meet with in one's researches into life.'—H. B. STOWE.

LONDON:

LONGMANS, GREEN, AND CO.

1868.

PREFACE.

Sir John Richardson has long been known as a most
intrepid explorer of the Arctic Regions, whose writings have largely contributed to the knowledge of
the Physical Geography, Flora, and Fauna of British
North America. To those who knew him intimately,
he was endeared by his high sense of honour, manly
courage, loving unselfish nature, and sincere yet
unostentatious piety.

In the belief that it can scarcely fail to be useful,
as well as interesting, the record of his life has been
compiled, and is now offered to the public.

My sincere thanks are due to Dr. J. E. Gray, of
the British Museum, Dr. Dalton Hooker, of Kew,
and many other friends of Sir John Richardson, from
whose contributions extracts appear in the course
of the work. I am especially indebted to Lady
Richardson for much valuable material and assistance; also to Mr. Carruthers, of Charlesfield, Annan,
who kindly placed at my disposal a large number of

letters and journals necessary in constructing the narrative. And though many of the letters could not be used, as referring either to family affairs or to matters of no public interest, yet they have enabled me to appreciate more fully the nobleness of his character. In a correspondence extending over upwards of sixty years, there does not occur an unkind sentence regarding a human being.

AMSTERDAM : *March* 1868.

CONTENTS.

CHAPTER VII.

CHAPTER VIII.

CHAPTER IX.

CHAPTER X.

CHAPTER XI.

CHAPTER XII.

CHAPTER XIII.

CHAPTER XIV.

CHAPTER XV.

CHAPTER XVI.

CHAPTER XVII.

CHAPTER XVIII.

a

CHAPTER XIX.

CHAPTER XX.

CHAPTER XXI.

CHAPTER XXII.

CHAPTER XXIII.

CHAPTER XXIV.

CHAPTER XXV.

THE LIFE

OF

SIR JOHN RICHARDSON.

CHAPTER I.

EARLY YEARS.

1787–1807.

JOHN RICHARDSON, son of Gabriel Richardson, Esq., of Rosebank, in the parish of Dumfries, and Anne Mundell, his wife, was born at Nith Place, Dumfries, on the 5th of November, 1787. He was the eldest of twelve children, of whom only the eleventh survives.

Mr. Gabriel Richardson, who was descended from an old and respectable family in Kirkpatrick Juxta, had settled in Dumfries some years prior to his marriage, and lived there to a good old age, universally respected for the rectitude of his public and private life, and beloved for his benevolence and kindly cheerfulness of disposition. He was a justice of the peace for the county, and many years chief magistrate of Dumfries. An old servant, who is still living, says, 'The Provost was a good friend to the poor, and never known to speak unkindly to any one.' His integrity and loving nature not only made him influential in the town and neighbourhood, but impressed his children, especially John, with no ordinary feelings of reverence and affection.

It is difficult to obtain information regarding a boyhood spent so long ago, but the few facts which have been gleaned are interesting. From his earliest years, John Richardson was always ready to do what he could for others, and carefully avoided giving any one pain. He was a stout, self-reliant, pleasant-looking boy, of a retiring nature.

Having made considerable progress in reading, he was sent, at four years of age, to a preparatory school. John owed much of his early training to his mother, daughter of Mr. Peter Mundell, a woman of vigorous understanding and clear judgment, frugal, independent, and generous. From her sons and daughters she exacted implicit obedience, and taught them, by precept and example, to love God and their neighbour. Her mother, Mrs. Mundell, who lived at Rosebank, a delightful country-house near the town, had also no small influence in forming the character of her grandson.

The few last years of Scotland's poet, Burns, were spent at Dumfries, and he was frequently a guest at Mr. Gabriel Richardson's hospitable table, the friendship then formed between the two families continuing unbroken as long as Mrs. Burns lived. From 1790 to 1796, the poet was in the habit of spending a few hours, each Sunday evening, in Nith Place, and among his admirers there was none more ardent, from youth to old age, than he who as a little boy attracted his attention.

Before this period, the metrical Scripture paraphrases, used along with the Psalms in public worship in Scotland, had been revised, and on one occasion, Burns pointed out some of those which he most admired, for John to commit to memory. In after life, he could only remember with certainty, as among the number selected, that beautiful hymn commencing :—

How bright these glorious spirits shine !
　　Whence all their white array ?
How came they to the blissful seats
　　Of everlasting day ?

Lo ! these are they from sufferings great
　　Who came to realms of light,
And in the blood of Christ have wash'd
　　Those robes which shine so bright.

Richardson was about six years old when this pleasant Sunday task was assigned to him. Two years later, he entered the grammar-school, on the same day with the poet's eldest son Robert, a boy of great intellectual promise. John never forgot Burns' bright smile and flashing eye, when he said to his father, 'I wonder which of them will be the greatest man ?' The boys were passionately fond of ballad poetry, **young** Burns excelling in **narration and recitation.** Spenser's 'Faery Queen,' borrowed from the Poet, was a special favourite **with** John Richardson, and the notice taken of him **by** Burns made **a** permanent impression on his **mind.** He always cherished **a** tender regard for **the** fascinating **bard** of Scotland, dwelling more on his manly independence and freedom from anything mean than on the one failing which destroyed him. The best poems **and** songs of Burns were stored up in his memory ready **to** be poured forth when his feelings were touched either by the pa**thetic or** the humorous. They cheered him with thoughts **of home, while** pacing the deck, during **his** life at sea, and afterwards amidst the solitude of the **North** American forests.

The teacher who had the most direct influence on **John Richardson was Mr. James** Gray, appointed rector of the Dumfries Grammar School **in 1794. He was a man of** genius and of great classical and literary attainments. **In 1801,** he was **chosen one of the** classical masters **of the** High **School of Edin**burgh, where, for upwards of twenty **years, he** held a prominent place **in** literary circles.

On November **3,** 1800, John Richardson was apprenticed for three years to his uncle, Mr. James Mundell, an eminent surgeon in Dumfries, who died during the following year, and was succeeded by Mr. Samuel Shortridge, under whom the engagement was completed. Meanwhile, by an

arrangement with Mr. Shortridge, he was enabled
to go to Edinburgh, in his fourteenth year, to begin
his studies at the University, during the winter
months of 1801–2. He attended Dr. Hope's lectures on chemistry, and the various classes necessary for the medical profession, delighting also to
study Greek under the able teaching of Professor
Dalzel.

On March 16, 1804, the young student thus
wrote to his father:—'I duly received your letter
mentioning that the directors of the Dumfries and
Galloway Infirmary wished me to engage for two
and a half years. After having considered the
arguments advanced by you in favour of that proposal, and others which presented themselves to
myself, I have decided that it will be well to comply
with their request, especially if they allow me to
accept of any situation which may occur, more to
my advantage, before my time is out.'

As house surgeon of the infirmary, Mr. Richardson fulfilled his engagement with great ability,
and, towards the close of 1806, returned to Edinburgh to pursue his studies at the University. He
was a conscientious student, and his insatiable
thirst for knowledge led him to read extensively
on the most various subjects. In December, 1806,
he wrote regarding his brother, who had accompanied him to Edinburgh, 'He pays great attention to his studies, and had the best exercise in
Professor Leslie's class. We have neither of us

occasion to be out after four o'clock, and spend the evenings in writing and reading on what we have heard through the day. Mr. Thomson has adopted the practice of examining his students on the Saturdays regarding what they have heard during the week, which will prove of considerable advantage to me.'

This absorbing love of study was fortunately counterbalanced by his love of nature and of exercise in the open air. His physical strength was great, and he delighted to take long rambles in the beautiful environs of Edinburgh. These excursions, either alone or in company with some swift-footed friend, extended far and wide. Through the glens of the Esk—over the Pentland Braid and Blackford hills—along the shore of the Frith of Forth from Musselburgh to Granton, he delighted to speed in the lengthening afternoon of a spring holiday. Thus he enjoyed some of the happiest and healthiest hours of student life, developing his powers of endurance and studying God's great book of nature.

CHAPTER II.

PASSES HIS EXAMINATION—ASSISTANT SURGEON ON BOARD THE 'NYMPHE.'

1807–1808.

In 1806, when acknowledging the arrival of a festal goose, sent by the thoughtful mother to her boys in Edinburgh, to remind them of the loving home of their childhood, John adds, ' I observe that assistant-surgeons are much wished at present for the navy'—a hint that the time was nearing when the active work of life must begin, and one of the family circle be too far off to share the Christmas cheer. He was beginning to think of selecting the Royal Navy as the most suitable sphere of duty.

Early in 1807, we find him preparing for his examination as surgeon, and planning to set out immediately for London to solicit employment in the public service. The brave honest youth resolved to push his way in the world instead of remaining at home to be a burden to his parents. In all his letters at this time, much delicacy and thoughtfulness are shown, in pointing out how few were his wants, and the encouragement **given by** Government, so as to **relieve his kind father from** anxiety about his **outfit** and other expenses. Thus early was manifested that **total** abnegation **of** self which, throughout **life, formed a prominent** feature in his character.

On February 17, he successfully **passed his** examination, and received a surgeon's diploma **and certificate for** the navy. '**The** examination lasted **only fifteen** minutes, and **was quite easy.'** There was **no necessity** for **lengthening** out the examination **of the young** student, who was favourably known **to** the examiners for his ability and diligence. **He had also** first-class certificates from the physician, surgeon, and directors of the Dumfries Infirmary, and **from** his former master, Dr. Samuel Shortridge, **which** proved of great service **to him. After** leaving Edinburgh, a few weeks were **spent at** Dumfries, many visits being made **to** the old surgery on the Plainstones, on the stout **oak** door **of** which **the** apprentices had for a century carved **their** names, **and to** the infirmary, **where he** had begun the practical **work of his** profession. **We may be** very **certain** that during this **brief visit to the** scenes of childhood, every spot **in the glen of** Kirkhouse of Kirkbean, where his maternal **uncle** lived, and which he always loved as the locality **of** his holiday rambles, was lingered **over; and that** the **prayerful** grandmother, the **kind** father **and** loving mother, the brothers and sisters, who were ever near to his heart, received assurances of never-dying affection.

On a Saturday evening, near the end of March, he arrived at Carlisle and went to bed early; but thoughts of the young life-world which he had left behind, and the duty-world about to be entered upon, kept him awake during the greater part of the night. Next morning the mail from Glasgow received the traveller, who, after a long and fatiguing journey, was set down at the 'Bull and Mouth,' St. Martin's-le-Grand, and took up his quarters in the Angel Inn until he could find suitable lodgings. He wrote to his father on March 25, 'I would have written to you yesterday, and actually began a letter, but from travelling three days and scarcely sleeping as many hours, the strangeness of the place, and one thing and another, I could not finish it, I was in such low spirits.'

This mood speedily passed away while striving to attain the object of his journey. Having brought letters of introduction to several young Dumfrisians who had gained a footing in the metropolis, the first day after his arrival was spent in delivering them, and the kind reception which he everywhere experienced made him cheerful and hopeful. He also renewed acquaintance with his former schoolfellow, Robert Burns, whom he found much improved in manner and appearance. The two friends were delighted to meet again. 'I begin to speak English and walk straight' is the playful postscript which the stripling adds to one of his letters, after an evening spent with several of his old school-companions.

Meanwhile, he takes lodgings at **No.** 11 Great **Queen Street,** Lincoln's Inn Fields—dines for a **shilling on** a plate of roast beef and **a** pint of ale. Having successfully passed examinations before the Royal College **of Surgeons,** London, and the Transport Board at the **Admiralty, Dr.** Harness, the medical superintendent, offered him **an** appointment, which he requested to be delayed for a week. **There was** something in the way in which the offer was made which hurt the young surgeon's sensi-**tive feelings.** Next day, Captain, afterwards Admiral, **Hope,** of Annandale, one of the Lords **of** the Admiralty, received **him** with much kindness, **and wrote to** Dr. **Harness,** requesting 'that Mr. Richardson be appointed **to** a frigate.' After presenting this letter at the medical department **of the** navy, he wrote to his father that Dr. Harness 'was much more **kind, and** went at once to see **what vacancies there were. He** then desired me **to call at** four o'clock **and I would** receive an appointment **to 'La** Nymphe,' frigate, fitting out at Deptford.'

This was all the more gratifying as great interest was, at that time, necessary to get into a frigate, many of the line-of-battle ships being in want of assistant-surgeons. The appointment to the

'Nymphe' was made on April 7, 1807, so that in
less than a fortnight after arriving in London, he
had met with several kind friends, talked Scotch
with five old schoolfellows, obtained a certificate
from the Royal College of Surgeons, and, through
Captain Hope's influence, the situation which he
wished. On April 15, he went to Deptford to take
a look at the frigate. One or two of the few men
on board were sick, and, as no surgeon had been
appointed, he thought it his duty to join her on
the following day. The 'Nymphe' was a favourite
and the young assistant-surgeon felt quite at home.
From Northfleet, where they went to ship a crew,
he writes : 'I believe I shall like the sea pretty
well, and the frigate is as good a vessel as I could
have wished. She mounts forty-four guns and sails
remarkably well. The officers are very civil. I
have formed a mess with two young midshipmen,
the captain's clerk, and master's mate. They are
genteel young men, and I dare say we shall mess
cheaply and comfortably.'

The anchor was raised on July 6, and the
'Nymphe' sailed for Spithead, where Captain
Conway Shipley immediately took the command.
From the first, the young seaman formed a high
opinion of his commander, and some months later
mentioned the comfort which he enjoyed and the
kindness of his captain, the surgeon, and his
brother officers, as reasons why he did not wish
to press for promotion.

At that time Napoleon was putting forth every effort to destroy British influence on the Continent, and the English ministry resolved not to allow the Danish fleet and naval stores to fall into the hands of the French. Denmark was critically situated. She was unable to resist the British forces; yet if she did not fight, Buonaparte would make that an excuse for seizing Holstein and Sleswick, alleging that the Danes had surrendered their fleet by a compact with his powerful enemy.

The destination of the 'Nymphe' was, therefore, the coasts of Denmark. On July 15, she took on board two large flat-bottomed boats, each capable of containing fifty men and a carronade, and two days later joined the fleet, commanded by Sir Samuel Hood, in the Downs. By August 23, he wrote, 'We are lying between the island of Samsoe and Zealand, in company with several other men-of-war, to prevent troops being conveyed from Jutland to Zealand. On the 24th we received news of hostilities having commenced by the Danes sinking one of our merchant-vessels. On the same day we got orders to join Commodore Keith, who was lying in the Belt with a large squadron blockading that side of Zealand. We accompanied him into the Baltic and then proceeded to our present station, about twelve miles from Stralsund, which is hid from us by the island of Rugen.' A few days later, the 'Nymphe' was off the island of Femern, to the south-east of

Sleswick.   Here the young surgeon, who was afterwards to gain his promotion by sharing in similar adventures, witnessed, for the first time, one of the skirmishes of the war.   On Sept. 1, he writes :

We espied three Danish galliots at anchor in a creek, stood in, and anchored about five miles from shore. Next day, one of our boats armed with a carronade was sent to fetch them out, but the enemy, being aware of our intention, had assembled a large party of volunteers on each side of the creek, which was not more than a musket-shot in breadth, who kept up a well-directed fire upon the boat when it approached the vessels. Our people, however, got possession of one, and were bringing it out when, perceiving six boats with volunteers putting off from the shore, they quitted the vessel, and fired the carronade with grape. This unexpected salutation made the volunteers leap out of their boats and make for the shore. They were by this time, however, in such numbers, that our people came away to the ship, after twice or thrice firing the carronade. We observed the proceedings from the frigate, and thought a great number of the enemy must have been killed, as whole troops of them fell down every time our men fired, but to our astonishment they immediately got up again. Some shots struck our boats, but fortunately no one was hurt.

While the 'Nymphe's' boat was thus engaged, the first shells began to be thrown into Copenhagen. Towards the end of September, a galliot ran foul of the frigate, carrying away her foremast and bowsprit, so that she had to run into Copenhagen for repairs. The effects of the siege and bombardment were still seen in all their repulsiveness. 'It is needless,' he wrote, 'for me to give you any account of the bombardment, especially as I was not a witness. It is, however, difficult for one who has not been in Copenhagen to conceive the devastation which the shells and rockets have made. There is a whole quarter of the city completely destroyed, not a single house standing.'

The 'Nymphe' resumed her station off Rugen, after her temporary repairs, and at the end of November arrived at Spithead. But there was no time for rest: Russia had joined the enemies of Great Britain, and Sir Sidney Smith was expected to secure the Russian fleet which had got into the Tagus. On December 20, the squadron of Sir Charles Cotton, to which the 'Nymphe' was attached, sailed from Portsmouth with a large convoy of transports. Encountering severe gales, the ships were scattered, Admiral Cotton, in the 'Minotaur,' with a part of the convoy seeking shelter in Falmouth, the 'Nymphe' and others proceeding to Cape Finisterre, the first place of rendezvous, and joining the fleet of Sir Sidney Smith on January 13, 1808.

'There are here,' he writes, 'nine line-of-battle ships and some small craft blockading the entrance to the Tagus, and it is reported that the Portuguese and Russian ships will attempt to get out, but if they do, I hope we shall give a good account of them.' The blockaded ships numbered nine sail of the line.

On Sir Charles Cotton's arrival, the swift-sailing 'Nymphe' was despatched to search for the missing convoy ships, which were eventually found at Gibraltar, getting ready to sail for Sicily. After a brief stay at the Rock, the 'Nymphe' returned to her station off the Tagus, and he became acquainted with the horrors of a military occupation, which he thus describes : 'The melancholy state of Portugal is, I observe, mentioned in the English newspapers without any exaggeration. Every morning, crowds of the better sort of inhabitants come off to our vessels wishing to remain until an opportunity occur of sending them to the Brazils, while numbers of the Portuguese soldiers and poor people enter into our service. There are some English among the refugees, who give very sad accounts of the country. "The roads," they say, "are covered with dead bodies, all provisions and property are in the hands of the French, and there is every prospect of famine in a short time." The boats are permitted by our fleet to fish, but the inhabitants receive no benefit by what is caught, the French seizing the whole, and giving paper money in exchange.'

The dull monotony of blockading duty was from time to time enlivened by a dashing episode. Early in March, one of the guard boats of the fleet, with fifteen men, made a rush up the Tagus, and brought out a cutter carrying three guns. This bold and successful enterprise so much alarmed the enemy, **that** they moored their ships farther inland, scarcely thinking themselves safe, though **seven** miles of river, lined with batteries, had to be passed before the British tars could come to close quarters. He shared in the enthusiasm of his gallant **captain** and brother officers. Impatient at the tedium of lying at anchor within sight of the **hostile** ships, he writes, 'There is no likelihood of the Russian fleet coming out **for a long** time.'

But if the enemy's ships **would** not come out, Captain Shipley determined to **go in for** them, and **a** party of volunteers from the **'Nymphe,'** including **the** assistant-surgeon, attempted to cut out a Portuguese vessel manned **by** Frenchmen. Some of the boats, however, having gone astray in the darkness, the bold adventure was abandoned. Another and still more unfortunate attempt **re**sulted in the loss of brave Captain Shipley, and several men. **Mr.** Richardson's coolness and bravery as a volunteer, on these occasions, were reported to Vice-Admiral Sir Charles Cotton, and **with a** favourable recommendation from Captain **Hope, led to** his being transferred to the flag-ship 'Hibernia,' **as** senior assistant. **Writing** to his **father** on April 25, he mentions **the** lamented death of Captain Shipley, but says nothing about his own adventures.

I have been removed **from** the 'Nymphe' into the 'Hibernia,' in consequence of Captain Hope's application to Sir Charles Cotton, and being in the flag-ship, I stand every chance of promotion on the first opportunity. I have only joined the 'Hibernia' to-day, so that I cannot say how I like her. I am senior assistant, the duty is easy, and I have very agreeable messmates—the other assistant, and the Captain of the Fleet's secretary.

On the 23rd we had the melancholy loss of Captain Shipley, who fell gallantly endeavouring to cut out a vessel from the Tagus. His loss will be generally felt and much lamented, as very few captains in the navy are more generally loved. His extreme bravery was the cause of his death. He boarded in a light boat containing only six men, while the rest of the boats were unable to pull up, on account of the current. His brother, Mr. Charles Shipley, was in the boat with him.

The vessel against which Captain Shipley was operating with the boats of the 'Nymphe' and of the 'Blossom' sloop-of-war, when he fell, was the 20-gun brig 'Garotta,' fitted out by the French, and having a crew of 150 men. She was lying, ready for sea, close under the guns of Belem Castle, with a heavy floating battery for additional protection. To prevent separation, orders were given for the boats, in two divisions, to tow each other until discovered by the enemy, when they were to cast off and make the best way alongside. They gained the entrance of the Tagus near the top of high water, but Captain Shipley, anxious to secure a good tide to bring off the prize, waited until the tide slacked, hoping to board before the ebb made strong; but the flood had no sooner ceased than a fresh in the river, caused by the heavy rains, came down at

the **rate of** six or eight miles an **hour.** The boats,
however, at about half-past **two in** the morning, got
within hail of the brig, and **the signal** was given to
board.   Captain Shipley, **in his gig,** dashed from
his companions, reached the Garotta, and having
jumped into the fore-rigging, was cutting away the
boarding-netting when he received a musket-ball
in the forehead, and fell dead into the water.   The
boats then got **into confusion,** and the tide coming
down like a sluice, **the enterprise had to** be abandoned.   The body **of** Captain Shipley **was** afterwards washed ashore, and recovered.

Thus fell a brave and accomplished gentleman in
the ardent pursuit of glory, a shining example of
dauntless valour and British heroism.

'Captain Shipley,' says **the** *Naval Chronicle*, 'was **the**
second surviving son of the Rev. W. D. Shipley, Dean of
St. Asaph.   He entered the naval profession very young,
in 1793, and in the "Invincible," during the action **of** 1st
June, 1794, showed **rare** courage.

'**He** was a native of Flintshire, in North **Wales, in** the
26th year of his age, tall and graceful in his person, firm in
his attachments, an invaluable friend, and most engaging in
his manners.   Perhaps there **never existed** an individual
who more eminently possessed **the power of** inspiring all
whom he commanded with sentiments similar to his own.
What those sentiments were, his life, short, alas! as it was,
and his glorious fall, have revealed.'

Mr. Richardson's period of service **in** the flag-
ship was **of** short duration, Sir Charles Cotton ad-

vancing him to the rank of Acting-Surgeon of the
'Hercule,' 74, on the 17th of May, six months before he had completed his twenty-first year. This
rapid promotion was the reward of his gallant conduct and devotion to his duties, though no doubt
forwarded also by the friendship of Captain Hope,
on whose influence he chiefly depended for obtaining its ratification by the Admiralty.

CHAPTER III.

ACTING-SURGEON OF THE 'HERCULE,' 74—SURGEON **OF** THE
'BLOSSOM' SLOOP-OF-WAR.

1808–1809.

THE blockade **of the** Tagus **was** continued during
the summer of 1808, the **French** position in the
Peninsula gradually becoming more critical, being
harassed by the inhabitants **as** well as by the naval
and land forces **of** Britain.   **In** Spain, numbers of
the French soldiers were barbarously murdered,
and **all the scattered parties** in Portugal had either
been taken prisoners or effected a retreat to Lisbon.
At the beginning of **July** Mr. Richardson wrote:

We have **sent 250 Marines** from the fleet to assist the
Portuguese in attacking Panisse, a place about forty miles
to the north of Lisbon, which **is garrisoned by** 500 French
soldiers, who have already attempted **to retire to** Lisbon,
but found it impossible **from** the manner **in** which they
were harassed by **the people.**   The French here seem very
much alarmed, and are **quite** on the alert.   They have
formed a number of **camps** along the coast at the mouth **of**
the Tagus.   From **the rock of** Lisbon to the city, a distance
of twelve miles, the **forts** are within pistol-shot of each

other. We have been at anchor for six months past, about four or five miles from the shore, so that we see all their manœuvres.

In August, affairs were drawing near to a crisis. General Sir Arthur Wellesley had arrived, and was landing his troops at Figueira, about ninety miles to the north of Lisbon, the French meanwhile having frequent reviews, to keep their own men in spirits and the Portuguese in check. In the British fleet, the opinion prevailed that the enemy must ultimately capitulate, and Mr. Richardson expected that the 'Hercule' would not be much longer absent from England. Sir Arthur Wellesley landed on the 3rd of August, Spencer on the 8th, and the advance commenced on the 10th, none of the Portuguese joining the troops, so much did they fear the French. On the 20th, the right wing, under Crawford, had a bloody but victorious fight, and immediately after Anstruther landed, General Moore being also close at hand. The Russian Admiral now wished to claim the neutrality of the port, which the British Admiral, whose force numbered twelve ships of the line, would not allow. During the struggle, which resulted in complete victory to the British land forces, the Portuguese behaved badly. 'The accounts in the newspapers,' Mr. Richardson wrote, 'of the Portuguese having joined our army in great numbers are very incorrect. About 1,400 were present at the last battle, but kept in the rear, and even remained only till they came within shot; for on a shell falling among them they immediately ran off, and returned to plunder the dead when the danger was over.'

Junot, having been defeated by Sir Arthur Wellesley at Vimieira, retreated towards Torres Vedras and Lisbon, whither the British troops, under Sir Hew Dalrymple, who had just arrived and assumed the chief command, were preparing to follow, when the Convention of Cintra put an end to further movements. It was concluded on the 22nd of August, the French agreeing to evacuate Portugal on condition of not being treated as prisoners of war, and of being landed in France with their arms and effects. The terms of the Convention were strongly condemned both in the Peninsula and Great Britain. They were no doubt more favourable to the French than the position seemed to warrant, but they prevented the necessity of more bloodshed and a protracted struggle.

The feeling of the officers of the fleet is given by Mr. Richardson, who thus wrote on the 4th of September :—

The French army has capitulated, but we do not yet know the terms. Sir Hew Dalrymple, however, is much blamed for having given too favourable terms, as from the force at his disposal they must have surrendered at discretion, and could not have ventured another battle. The 42nd and two other regiments took possession of the batteries on the 2nd of September, but the main body of the army does not advance, nor do we go into the Tagus until the French have embarked.

It is right to add that the court-martial, which the British Ministry was forced by public opinion to appoint for trying the officers who signed the Convention of Cintra, acquitted them of all blame, while both Napoleon and Wellington justified the terms agreed upon as being honourable and fair.

The tedious blockade of the Tagus was now ended, and the 'Hercule,' which stood very much in need of repairs, accompanied the Russian fleet to Spithead. On October 21, Mr. Richardson was gratified by learning that the Transport Board had confirmed his rank, and appointed him surgeon of the 'Blossom' sloop-of-war.

During the five months which he had spent on board the 'Hercule' his duty had been light, as he had two assistants and never more than from four to six on the sick list. And now, while the old ship is laid up to be repaired and fitted out for Channel service, he joins the trim little 'Blossom' for more active work. 'She is a fine vessel,' he writes, 'and was a good while in company with the "Nymphe," is frigate-built, indeed a complete frigate in miniature.'

He joined the 'Blossom' on November 1, 1808, and next day sailed for the coast of Africa with two merchant-vessels under convoy. The first place touched at was Madeira, which was reached on the 18th, and after a short stay they proceeded to Goree, thence to **Cape** Coast Castle, and finally to Prince's Island, **to** collect the homeward-bound ships. While lying in Funchal Bay, he wrote : 'I am extremely well pleased with the " Blossom," and the officers are very pleasant companions. Most of them are men of more knowledge and reading **than I** have met **at** sea before, and when we put our books together we have a very respectable **library.**' The estimate which he had formed of **his** brother officers was correct. They were accomplished gentlemen and scholars. Still the voyage was unfortunate for all.

Captain P——n, who seems to have been advanced in years, vain, suspicious, and overbearing, took offence at several of his officers, the ill-feeling, **if** not occasioned **by** the purser, being at least fomented **by** him. He acted as **a** spy upon their words and movements, and did not hesitate to tell falsehoods to increase the mischief. While the young officers were amusing themselves writing sonnets, the Captain thought they were plotting against his authority or enjoying **jokes at** his expense. His inability to share **in** their pursuits made them distasteful to him, and nothing **is so** irritating **to an** ignorant captain as to see those under him enjoying a book or cultivating literary tastes. Shortly after sailing for Madeira, the **first and** second lieutenants were placed under arrest, to be tried by **court-**martial when the vessel should **reach** England.

Even when sitting at the same table, these two officers **were** not permitted to **speak to each other,** the purser reporting **to** the captain everything which occurred. How **wearily the hours passed on board the little 'Blossom,' as she sailed further and further** away **from** England **and liberty, under** the burning suns of **Africa, can only be conceived** by those **who** have been pent **up in a small ship** whose commander imagined that all on board were mutinous and enemies.

The homeward voyage was fortunately not a long one, the 'Blossom' arriving in **the** Downs about the middle of April, when the lieutenants, who had suffered in health from **the** long confinement, and been obliged **to** go into the hospital, **were** tried **by** court-martial. They **were** both honourably acquitted, Captain Codrington, of the 'Blake,' saying, **in** full **court,** that **he** was **in** want of **a** lieutenant **and would** be glad **to have** either of those of the 'Blossom,' **as** their conduct appeared to have been thoroughly correct.

Mr. Richardson, **who had** escaped the horrors of confinement in **a** small vessel on the coast of **Africa** only because Captain P——n **was** afraid he might require the surgeon's assistance, was also accused, **tried on** April 26, and declared to be altogether **free from** blame. The day following **he** wrote **to his** father from on board **the** 'Blossom,' then in **the Downs** :—

I was prevented from writing in reply to your letter by

some unpleasant circumstances, now happily terminated. Soon after we left Madeira, the purser, who had been attempting to prejudice the mind of the captain against his officers, persuaded him that the two lieutenants were in a combination against him. The captain, who is a weak man, and of violent passions, instantly put them under arrest, and they remained so until our arrival in the Downs. Then the captain, knowing my intimacy with them, supposing that I must be guilty, and privy to a combination, also charged me with it. I was tried yesterday by court-martial, when the charges were so ridiculous, and my conduct proved to be so correct, that I was honourably acquitted without even the trouble of making a defence. The court stared at the behaviour of the captain, and the purser, the rascal, who was at the bottom of the whole business, on my looking at him became confused, sick, and fainted. No doubt his conscience pricked him. After that he could not say another word, and was obliged to be taken out of court. The poor captain, who is nearly deranged, will long have cause to repent his having listened to the purser's tales. The second lieutenant was tried to-day. The charges against him were trivial and ill-founded, and he too was honourably acquitted. The first lieutenant's trial is to-morrow, and I have no doubt that the result will be to his honour. On his acquittal the captain will be tried for oppression and abuse of power. I am almost sorry for him, although his behaviour to the two lieutenants has been most shameful. He is so weak and ignorant, that the purser's insinuations took their full effect. The two lieutenants, most excellent young men, suffered a great deal from their close confinement in the hot climate of Africa, and this business rendered the voyage more unpleasant than it would otherwise have been. I did not know of his intention to try me until our arrival in the Downs, so that I suffered no grievous uneasiness on that score, and indeed I have scarcely suffered any uneasiness, as I knew the frivolousness of the charges. It is no small mark of the propriety and correctness of my conduct that the captain himself was obliged to confess that it had been good. Never were charges so groundless brought before a court, and it was the evident opinion of every member and witness of the trial that the unfortunate captain was not in his right mind.

I like a hot country, and would have had a very pleasant voyage but for the affair which I have mentioned. Your letter arrived the same day as my indictment, and tended not a little to enliven me. I would have written immediately, but did not wish to make you uneasy by mentioning the business until it was settled, and I could not well write without doing so. I hope my silence has not made you in the least uneasy.

The officers having been acquitted, Captain P——n was suspended and ordered for trial, which began on May 16, and though he was not dismissed the service, his command of the ‘Blossom’ ceased. On May 20, Mr. Richardson writes: ‘The court-martial on the captain is just finished. He was tried for cruelty and oppression, unjust and un-officerlike conduct. The two former counts were not proved, and the two latter only in part, for which he was sentenced to be dismissed the ship. There is a very great difference between the trial of a captain and lieutenants, the court on the for-mer being composed of captains, who have a fellow-feeling for each other.’ The officers expected that their commander **would have been** dismissed the service.

Thus ended this disgraceful case of misrule. **It** shows how fraught with evil it **is for a** man **who** cannot govern his **passions, and is** weak enough **to be led away by anyone so** mean as **to** flatter him, **to be placed in command of a ship.**

Regarding Jonas Morris, the purser, Mr. Richard-**son wrote: 'He** perjured himself several times in **the court, and will be turned out of the** service in disgrace. **If we chose to try** him **he** would **be put** in the pillory, but such **a** wretch **is** beneath an honest man's notice. He has ruined himself, and is now, as vice always is when foiled, depressed to the lowest depths of meanness, and sits sighing in the gun-room in order to induce **us** to pity him, but does not dare to speak to us.'

Shortly after the trials, Mr. Richardson wrote:

I have applied to **Dr.** Harness **to** appoint me to **a** frigate, but he will have some difficulty in doing it, the Board, as **a** rule, keeping surgeons in sloops for **two** or three years **after** their first appointment. **If I** remain in the ' Blossom,' **there will be a new** captain, and a complete change among **the other officers.**

I enjoyed excellent health all **the time we were** on the **coast of** Africa, and **am** now as **well as ever** I was in my life. I like the sea **well** enough, but **do** not wish to remain longer than **to** entitle **me to** some situation on shore, as **sur**geon to a prison ship, **an hospital,** &c. That requires great interest, **and** cannot be obtained anyhow until after five **or six** years' service as surgeon.

On June 2, 1809, Captain (afterwards Sir Francis) Beaufort joined the 'Blossom,' which was again ordered on convoy service. The appearance and manner of the new commander, as well as the excellent character which he bore in the 'Woolwich,' 44, which he had just left, made the young surgeon feel assured that the voyage which was about to be made would be a pleasant one. He was right. Between Captain Beaufort and his officers perfect harmony reigned, and the friendship then formed remained unbroken to the close of the useful life of Sir Francis. Instead of discouraging the pursuit of knowledge, Captain Beaufort allowed perfect freedom of access to his excellent library—a privilege which proved of essential advantage to Mr. Richardson in pursuing his studies at this period, when cut off from many opportunities of improvement. 'I think we shall have a pleasant voyage,' he writes in June, 'as our new captain seems desirous to make all his officers comfortable, and is a very courteous sensible man.' Again, in July : 'Our purser is a gentleman, and Captain Beaufort is a very agreeable good man, who wishes to make everyone happy.'

The 'Blossom' was delayed some time by heavy gales. When these abated, she sailed with a transport laden with small-arms and ball-cartridges for Gijon, in the north of Spain, arriving there on June 25. Immediately after, she proceeded to Ferrol and Corunna, bringing home, at the beginning of July, forty men, women and children, who had been taken by the French during Sir John Moore's rapid retreat, and afterwards left to wander about the country.

The little sloop was now despatched to Quebec, the only drawback to the pleasure of the voyage being that, hampered with convoy, she could not give chase to the French vessels which were seen at a distance. In November, they were again in England.

On returning from this voyage he wrote to his father :—

We met with nothing interesting to you on our way out, as far as the Bank of Newfoundland, on which we arrived the 15th of August. In five days we crossed it and the small Bank, and got into the Gulf of St. Laurence. Thick fogs hang almost continually over the Banks of Newfoundland, the Gulf of St. Laurence, and parts in the neighbourhood, but luckily we had good, and frequently clear, weather.

The gulf and mouth of the St. Laurence abound in mackerel, and it is pleasant amusement fishing for them, as all that is necessary, when the ship is going three or four miles an hour, is to fasten a piece of red cloth, or (what is better) fish-skin, to the hook, and allow it to drag along the surface of the water, the fish biting with great eagerness. We saw several vessels belonging to the United States fishing for cod in the gulf. The fish which they take are smaller but firmer and better flavoured than those caught on the Great Bank. They are permitted by treaty to fish in the gulf, though possessing no territory on its borders.

Great numbers of large whales frequent these waters, and often came close to the ship.

On the 25th we cleared the gulf, and entered the St. Laurence. The island of Anticosti lies in the mouth of the river, dividing its entrance into two passages, the north and south. The island is very often involved in thick fogs, and is inhabited only by one family, maintained at the expense of the government of Quebec, to assist the crews of ships which are frequently wrecked here. It is low and rocky, covered with trees, and abounds in bears and wolves.

We entered the river by the South Passage, and kept along that shore which showed no signs of cultivation for 180 miles. On the north, or Labrador side, the lowest cultivated spot is 270 miles from the river's mouth. Where the banks are under culture they look extremely well. The houses are built of wood, painted white, and roofed with thin cedar boards or shingles, which when painted blue are exactly like slates. From the manner in which the land is sold, the houses are all built close to the river, and at nearly equal distances, seldom more than an acre apart, so that they look like one continued street. At Goose Island, twenty miles below Quebec, though the river is twelve miles broad, it is quite fresh at high water. At Quebec it suddenly narrows to a little more than a mile across.

The British troops composing the expedition to the island of Walcheren, at the mouth of the Scheldt, having been attacked by ague, terminating in a low nervous or putrid fever, and later by inflammation of the lungs, were about to be withdrawn from that place; and he writes:—

The affairs of the nation at present wear a very gloomy aspect. Buonaparte carries all before him on the continent.

He has a large fleet in the Mediterranean.   I hope they will
be induced to venture **to sea,** and fall in with one of our
fleets, which is equivalent **to** being defeated.   This would
serve to raise our drooping spirits.   You on shore can
scarcely conceive the anxiety with which we waited, on
seeing **a** strange sail, to obtain news from England, always
expecting **to** hear something great from **the** Expedition.
Alas ! how miserable the disappointment !

Here **is a** picture of life on **board :—**

You wish to know how I spend **my time ;** and as there is
a great deal of sameness in all my days, it will be easily
done.   At present I seldom get up before seven, in summer earlier, but whether sooner **or** later **my** time until
eight is generally spent on deck.   I breakfast at eight, visit
the sick at nine, which with writing **a** list for the captain,
and a daily report of each case for the Transport Board,
occupies me till eleven.   We dine at two o'clock, visit the
sick **again at** six, and if any are confined to bed, or particularly **ill, I** of course **do** it often.   At ten we generally go
to bed ; the intermediate time **I** usually spend reading or
walking **upon** deck, as we have not even a pack of cards or
backgammon-**board** amongst **us.**   The two lieutenants and
master dine with the captain, in turn, every third day.   In
the absence **of the** purser I dine with him about three times
a week.   In return, one **of the** midshipmen dines with us
every day, and the captain **on** Sunday.   Our **mess** costs us
at present from 60*l.* to 70*l.* per annum ; **the wine,** which
we are allowed duty-free, is twenty-six shillings per dozen,
each using a pint daily.

If we are stationed in the Channel this winter, something may be picked up **which** would be very accept-
able.   I received 20*l.* of prize-money for Copenhagen some

time ago, which nearly paid for a number of instruments which I had to purchase when last at Sheerness.

Captain Beaufort had the happy art of being on familiar and friendly terms with his officers without losing his position as commander.

On the 6th of December, Mr. Richardson wrote to his father :—

I do not think that I could advantageously retire from sea in time of war, and it is better to remain a surgeon in the navy than to practice in a small country town on shore, for I could not hope to meet with any encouragement in a city among able surgeons, without greater experience and farther attendance on the classes. To retire from the navy would be giving up a great deal without any adequate gain, and in a year or two I hope to be able to attend classes in London for six months at least, either on full or half-pay. Getting appointed to the flag-ship in Leith Roads would enable me to study at Edinburgh College.

This brave and independent spirit kept him steadily on the path to the prizes for which he longed, doing present duty well as the sure way to gain them. But although unable to gratify his parents by settling down as a medical practitioner at home, he prevailed on Captain Beaufort, early in 1810, to request the Transport Board to grant him a short leave of absence. This, however, could not then be given, unless his health rendered him incapable of service. The hope of seeing home, thus deferred, was, however, realised at the end of May, when his parents were gladdened by a short visit, during which he secured the interest of the Earl of Galloway, and hoped to be promoted to a frigate before requiring to sail again. In this he was disappointed, the 'Blossom' being ordered, at the beginning of July, to proceed with a large fleet of merchantmen and transports to the coast of Portugal, Spain, and the Mediterranean. Even thus early in his career, a spirit of contentment with all the turnings of Providence pervades his letters. 'If the "Blossom" remain in the Mediterranean,' he writes, 'I shall not be sorry at not having received an appointment to a larger vessel.'

Early in August they arrived at Gibraltar, having been three weeks on the voyage, with pleasant weather the greatest part of the way, but detained by some heavy sailers in the convoy. From Gibraltar, the 'Blossom,' in company with the 'Temeraire' and two Spanish three-deckers, sailed for Port Mahon in the island of Minorca. Here he exchanged with the surgeon of the 'Bombay,' 74, one of the ships belonging to the Toulon Blockading Fleet, and his connection with the 'Blossom' ceased.

Shortly after joining the 'Bombay,' he received sad news. The 'Blossom' had taken two prizes of little value; one of them a privateer carrying four guns, which had been attacked by the boats while lying becalmed. In this encounter, the first lieutenant, a very worthy, good man, and three of the sailors, were killed ; a master's mate, and eight others wounded. The privateer was boarded by only twenty-three men, who carried her, though the crew numbered fifty-six. His exchange into the 'Bombay' spared the young surgeon this sad sight.

CHAPTER IV.

SURGEON OF THE 'BOMBAY'—BLOCKADE OF TOULON—RETURNS
TO ENGLAND.

1810–1812.

WHEN the winter of 1810-11 was passed, the
monotony of Port Mahon was varied by a fruitless
run after two French line-of-battle ships which
had got out of Toulon. The 'Bombay' went in
search as far as Sicily, and on its return touched
at Cagliari, the capital of Sardinia. During the
following summer, the excitement of a chase was
frequently enjoyed. In May, the 'Bombay' pursued
two frigates, which were rapidly being gained upon,
when night fell and they escaped—all hopes of
prize-money vanishing with the dawn of day.
'However, I do not regret it,' the surgeon writes,
'as we did all we could. We next touched at
Algiers, and learned that the French frigates had
landed a consul there two days before. A brig,
which left Toulon in company with them, laden
with presents for the Dey of Algiers, has already
been destroyed by one of our cruisers.'

On the 16th of July, they are off Toulon, and he

writes :—' The **French**, after several unsuccessful attempts, **have at length** taken Tarragona by storm, and **their barbarity exceeded** everything **I ever heard of.** The **women and children were seen from** our **ships, stationed there,** leaping **from the walls, pursued by the** inhuman soldiers **with the** **bayonet.** None escaped but those **who were able** to conceal themselves till the next day.'

Thus Tarragona suffered for **the brave resistance** which it offered to the French army.

While the hostile fleet remained shut up in Toulon, the blockading ships giving **chase whenever** an **easterly wind** gave the Frenchmen **an** opportunity **of** getting out with safety for exercise, **a** letter to **his** brother Peter (who **occupied a** farm in Galloway) gives **us an** insight **into his dreams** of the future.

I never **trouble** myself with unavailing regrets, **and if at** any time **I do bestow a thought on** the subject, it **is** generally soon dismissed by a predestinarian saying, ' **it was** decreed so,' or ' c'est la fortune **de la** guerre.' Though, from the size of the ' Bombay,' I have every convenience which a life at sea affords, yet my happiness is merely of **the** negative kind. In all my reveries, waking dreams, or whatever name you give them, **a** retired life **in the** country, somewhere in the neighbourhood of my native town, stands foremost **in the** pictures which **I form** to myself of the future. **I** often **fancy** the happiness which a man must enjoy, living in the midst of his friends and possessed of a competency. These however are only dreams, never to be realised unless the ' lift should fa',' **or** what is just as likely, it should please that disturber of nations, Buonaparte, to grant us an honourable peace. Then, upon **my half-pay, I** might live **comfortably.**

Sir C. Cotton, our present commander-in-chief, **goes home soon, as he is to be** superseded by Sir Edward Pellew. **There will also be some** changes among the junior admirals. **We are at** present **in the** fleet off Toulon, and likely to re-main all the summer. **Next winter we** shall return to Port Mahon, **and after another summer** spent here, **we expect to go home.** Then, and **I look forward to the** time with im-**patience,** there may **be a chance of paying** you another **visit.** I hope you **will have your house in** better order **than when I saw you last. Perhaps there will** be some one **to look after it.**

My cabin is twenty-one feet long **and seven broad. I have spent all my spare cash in** adorning it. In that small **space, I have contrived to** stuff a sofa, a dressing-table, **a** chest of **drawers, and** book-case containing upwards **of a** hundred volumes; besides, **by** means of a curtain, it is divided **into two** apartments, **a** dressing-room and **a** sitting-room.

After a short visit to Port Mahon **and** Majorca, **with its pleasant** mountains and valleys, **the 'Bom-bay'·** returned **to** the station off Toulon. In No-**vember, he again** wrote **to his brother :—**

It gives me pleasure to **learn** that your agricultural pur-suits occupy so **much of** your time, **as by an** unremitted attention to them **you** will **not** only benefit yourself in a pecuniary way but also materially increase your happiness. A farmer possesses many advantages almost peculiar to his employment. The very exercise which is necessary for the proper superintendence of his affairs, preserves his health and keeps up a flow of spirits which sweetens all the events of life. Every day points out to his observing eye some progress which the plants are making. Nothing stands still, everything is changing. On the other hand, with me, the sun makes his diurnal revolution and sets in his western wave, without producing anything new, and returning in the morning he only serves to show the same dull succession of objects.

We have been constantly at sea, except one week spent at Mahon refitting, and have been trying for three weeks past to get off Toulon, but have been prevented by strong northerly winds, and at last obliged to take shelter under the island of Minorca, where we are at present. We are, however, getting under-way to go to Palma Bay, in Sardinia, for water. I think we shall continue at sea for the remainder of the winter, as our present commander-in-chief seems to have a great antipathy to being in harbour. The French fleet nearly captured the 'Perleu' and 'Volontaire' frigates a few days ago; a line-of-battle ship and two frigates having engaged the former ship in a running fight four hours, half-an-hour of that time within musket-shot. Our frigate disabled the line-of-battle ship and effected her escape in a very gallant manner.

I had the pleasure, a few weeks ago, of meeting my old schoolfellow, Mr. McGhie. He is at present hospital mate in a temporary hospital established at Mahon. You may easily conceive the pleasure our meeting gave me when I tell you that he was the most intimate of my acquaintances in Dumfries.

The Spaniards, notwithstanding their late discomfitures, are making head again in Catalonia. Although the French have got all the strongholds, the peasantry are in such force that **they cannot get** provisions into Barcelona except by sea, and our vessels render that difficult also.

Captain Cuming, **our** late commander, **was** invalided some time ago and we **have got** Captain Norborne Thompson in his stead. **We** have all great reason to be pleased with the exchange. Not that I have any cause to complain of Captain Cuming, for **he** and I agreed very well, but **it** was not **so** with **the other officers, and it is** unpleasant to be in **a ship where** everyone is **not** comfortable. Captain Thompson is one **of the pleasantest and** most gentlemanly **officers in** the service, **and uses** his utmost endeavours to **make** his officers happy.

The long-continued **cruise** before **the** harbour **of** Toulon, where the French fleet was nestled, became **very** irksome, **and** when **the** boisterous weather set **in, the** young **surgeon** hoped that it would freshen **into a gale** and send them **to** Mahon, where the winters were always mild. Before Christmas came, the ' Bombay ' **was at** Minorca, and he wrote with the prayer for many happy returns of the season to all the loved ones in Scotland. **A** walking excursion through the **island, made** during **the** winter, afforded **him much pleasure and** amusement. Nowhere **was anything** worthy **of the name** of ploughing **in use—a man** poking **between the** rocks with **a crooked piece of** wood being **the** only apology **for it.**

The officers **of the** ' Bombay ' maintained the strictest regularity in their mode of living—a habit which the surgeon maintained through life.

Our mess is as regular (says he), if not more so, as any in the fleet. It costs about fourteen dollars a month, which at present rate of exchange is 50*l*. per annum. We live well, but drink only Mahon wine, which is similar to good claret, but not so strong and costs from sixpence to a shilling the bottle. We have an allowance of a pint after dinner, which is never exceeded except when strangers are on board, and then only in a slight degree. I believe no people indulge less in wine than officers of the navy, and, on board ship, they must be careful from a regard to their character and situation, drunkenness never being pardoned at sea.

The long-continued active service at last told on his health. The leave of absence, which, during the heat of the war, could not be granted to any one able for duty, became a necessity. In the summer of 1812, he hastened to the home of his childhood, and enjoyed for a few weeks the loved society of the family circle at Nith Place, from time to time paying visits to his brother, Mr. Peter Richardson, at Disdow, and sharing in the genial hospitalities of the kind people of Gatehouse. This, however, was an opportunity for study which had long been wished for, and must not be neglected. He set out for London, and writing to his father, says: 'I have laid out 20*l*. in taking perpetual tickets for surgical and anatomical lectures, so that, in the event of my being in London for a week or two at any future period, I can attend them free of expense. I have very good lodgings, and **only** require to **go** through one street to reach the lecture-rooms.'

This quiet season of study was succeeded **by** one **of active** duty at sea, a warrant appointing him **surgeon of** His Majesty's sloop ' Cruiser,' then **lying at** Sheerness, being issued **by the** Transport **Board, on** December 5, 1812.

CHAPTER V.

1812–1814.

'THE weather is unusually cold,' he wrote from
Sheerness in December, 'and I think Boney must
find his quarters very disagreeable, if the winter
has set in as keenly in Russia and Poland as it has
done here.' Two days after these words were
penned, Napoleon entered Paris alone, and the
news flew through Europe that the Russian winter
had been destructive as well as disagreeable—that
the Grand Army was no more.

The appointment to the 'Cruiser' was a fortunate one. The officers were pleasant companions,
and though anxious to enjoy the comforts and
opportunities for study which a life on shore would
afford, he requested his father not to be in a hurry
in applying to Captain Hope, the more so as it was
understood to be the rule to give these situations
to surgeons who had been ten years in the service.

Towards the end of February, the weather, which had been boisterous, moderated, and the 'Cruiser' sailed from the Nore to join the Baltic fleet, which it succeeded in doing at Wingo Sound, after a fair run across the North Sea. Here were the 'Courageux,' 'Daphne,' 'Zealous,' 'Ulysses,' and several brigs, Admiral Morris, the Commander-in-Chief, having his flag in the 'Vigo.' The 'Cruiser' was ordered to get ready to sail, as soon as the wind was favourable, for the Scaw or Cape Skagen, the extreme northern point of Denmark, a station which her officers considered to be one of the best for taking prizes, unless the fates were unpropitious. While waiting for a fair wind he visited one of the islands which form Wingo Sound, of which he says:—

It is named Brauno, and consists principally of barren rocks. There is one village on it of about 120 families. The houses are small, consisting of one room and a porch, or at most two. They are built of logs, dovetailed into each other at the corners, and the interstices filled with moss. The roofs are of thin deals covered with turf. It is a poor place, and the inhabitants subsist chiefly by fishing. In front of the village lies a patch of arable land, which is ploughed at present, but there is not the least appearance of vegetation to be seen anywhere; and I am told that the ground will continue in this apparently barren state until the end of April, when all at once the spring becomes general and advances much more rapidly than in Scotland.

The 'Cruiser's' active operations, off Cape

Skagen, were speedily brought to a close. Having
taken four Danish vessels, she bore up for Wingo
Sound on March 19, but was forced to run for
shelter to the coast of Sweden :—

We put to sea several times (Mr. Richardson writes), but
were always obliged to make for one or other of the ports
which abound on that coast, and lastly entered Salo Sound,
on the 27th. During the night of April 1, it coming on
to blow hard, we drove from our anchorage and grounded
on a reef of rocks, where we remained twenty-eight hours.
The guns and shot were got out, and everything possible
done to lighten the ship, and then by heaving cables, made
fast to anchors laid out ahead, we got her off with the loss
of the rudder and false keel. Our people worked inces-
santly for forty hours, got the guns and shot in again and
hung the rudder, so that she was ready for sea the next
day. I do not think our bottom is injured, as we do not
leak, but it will be necessary to go into dock to get a new
false keel and rudder. I am afraid that should the damages
be greater than we expect, the 'Cruiser' will be paid off,
an event which I do not wish to happen, as I could not enjoy more comfort, the utmost harmony subsisting between
the captain and officers. However, if Captain Toker be
promoted, she will probably be paid off, having run for
fifteen or sixteen years without having been thoroughly
repaired. In that case I shall renew my studies in London, which can be done with little additional expense,
having made myself a perpetual pupil. I am uncertain
when we shall be ordered home, but will remain at anchor
here as a kind of guard-ship till that time. This harbour
is crowded with vessels, there being upwards of 500 sail of
merchantmen waiting for a fair wind, besides a good many
men-of-war.

While lying in Wingo Sound, he observed the peculiarity of climate referred to when describing the island of Brauno. At the end of April the rigging of the ship was covered with ice, and before the middle of May vegetation was rapidly advancing. Early in June the 'Cruiser' reached Sheerness, and was docked for repairs :—

I once thought (he wrote) of applying for leave and going down to Scotland, or remaining in London to attend lectures while the 'Cruiser' is in harbour, but have given up the idea, for the present, chiefly from motives of economy. We have been so much in port lately that our expenses have been nearly double what they would have been had we remained at sea. I shall, however, do pretty well at the end of the year, as I am then entitled to an increase of pay, and should the 'Cruiser' be paid off after that, I shall be a little more my own master.

Her repairs completed, the 'Cruiser' was placed under the orders of Admiral Otway, and sailed to the north of Scotland, to look out for privateers, which had appeared among the Shetland Islands. In July she arrived at Long Hope, about seventeen miles from Kirkwall, where a large fleet of merchantmen, under the charge of two brigs, was lying at anchor and in great fear of the redoubted American privateer, Commodore Rogers, who was reported to be in those seas. There is no thought of the little 'Cruiser' attempting to fight the enemy—the odds were too great; but her officers were anxious to get a sight of him, and felt pretty

certain that he could not catch them if they wished
to run.   Several weeks were spent among the
Orkneys, on which was seen growing here and
there 'a birch, scarcely big enough to make a
broom.'   Meanwhile the 'Alexandria' and a sloop
of war have chased Commodore Rogers as far north
as the seventy-fourth parallel of latitude, and the
'Cruiser' has little to do but roam among the
islands.

Towards the end of August she sailed with
despatches for Admiral Lord Amelius Beauclerk,
whose flag-ship, the 'Royal Oak,' was supposed to
be cruising between Iceland and the Lewis.   The
weather was stormy, and, on September 7, during
a heavy gale, the 'Cruiser' sprung a leak, which
floated the powder magazine.   This accident made
them bear up for Leith, but the wind fouling
again on the 9th, she was run into Long Hope, to
wait for a favourable change.   Here it was ascertained that the extent and position of the leak
would make it necessary for her to be docked
in order to be repaired, and the 'Cruiser' was
accordingly ordered to Sheerness.   'I am sorry,'
Mr. Richardson wrote, 'that the accident has happened at this time, for it is not convenient to be so
much in harbour, especially after an unsuccessful
cruise.   The four vessels we detained in the Baltic
have been liberated, contrary to our expectation—I
suppose from political motives.'

The voyages of the 'Cruiser,' in 1813, had been

unfortunate, and tended **to deepen** his dislike for the sea **and** intensify the longing **for a home on** shore, where he could gather his books around him. Dr. Shortridge, of Dumfries, had been thinking of giving up practice, and Mr. Richardson, who had been urged to succeed him, writes :—

I am sorry that the appearances **of** peace have vanished, as my half-pay is now six shillings a day, and I should like **to retire, but** I think **that too much to** throw away without better prospects than **even full** practice at Dumfries holds forth, and I could not **expect** constant employment until after the lapse of several **years.** **However,** as a life at sea becomes daily less **and less to** my taste, I believe that, in a year or two, I shall **be** induced to quit **it,** even though I do sacrifice my half-pay. If, however, there were a fair prospect **of** becoming surgeon to a Marine Division, Naval Hospital, **or** Dockyard, I do not think that **four or five** years longer would be ill spent in serving for it. **I** have determined, at all events, to remain in the 'Cruiser,' as it is probable she will **be paid** off, when I **may** have an opportunity of a season **in** Edinburgh **on** half-pay. This would be of much advantage to me, and what I wish before entering into private practice.

The 'Cruiser' **was** put out **of** commission at Sheerness **on** November 27, **and** Mr. Richardson settled down **to** his studies in London, while waiting for another **ship.** 'I am making the most of my time,' he writes, 'by attending lectures here, and have no idea of leaving the service at present, as it is possible that a general peace may take place **soon,** and **if I get** employed again before that event, my half-pay will be no contemptible addition to my income, should I begin to practise on shore.'

The winter of 1813–14 was one of those pleasant seasons of quiet study, intermingled with the amenities of family life, which he so much enjoyed. Innocent recreations and the sight of smiling faces were all the more keenly relished from his being a hard-working student. Though busy with his books, he, nevertheless, found time to join the circle of friends of the family with whom he lodged, and danced as heartily as his young sisters at Dumfries.

Several causes united in inducing him to retain his position as surgeon in the Royal Navy. The absence of any love for a life at sea would have led a man of less firmness of purpose and fore-thought to retire, probably to repent the step after-wards when struggling hard to gain the means of living from a country practice. It was to be ex-pected that one so young and youthful in appear-ance would only succeed by degrees in gaining the confidence of the public in a town where he would have to compete with able surgeons of long expe-rience and established character. It was also his fixed resolve, once more to attend his *Alma Mater* in Edinburgh, and obtain a physician's diploma before settling down permanently as a medical practitioner: while by continuing in the service till the restoration of peace, his half-pay would be secured; and if war continued, there was the prospect of being appointed surgeon to an hospital, dockyard, or division of marines. He was, therefore, content to bide his time, and the reward came, sooner than was expected, to the patient waiter and conscientious worker.

In February 1814, having finished his course of lectures, he was anxious to obtain employment. Receiving a hint from one of the clerks at the Transport Board that there might be some delay, unless a way of stimulating them was found, he wrote for leave to go to Scotland, if it was not their intention to grant him an immediate appointment, as the expense of living respectably in London exceeded his half-pay.

This was an honest, manly way of moving the Board, and, to the honour of the members, the appeal was at once responded to. The letter was written on February 9, and, on the 12th he was appointed surgeon to the 1st battalion of Royal Marines, then serving in North America.

'I am pleased with the appointment,' were his words, 'as there is a chance of its leading to a permanent situation as surgeon of a marine corps.' This anticipation was correct. The turning-point of his course of life had come, and with the paying off of the 'Cruiser,' his life at sea, except as a passenger, may be said to have ended.

CHAPTER VI.

SAILS FOR AMERICA——BERMUDA——CANADA——HALIFAX——COAST
OF GEORGIA——CUMBERLAND ISLAND——RETURNS TO ENGLAND.

1814–1815.

WITH his usual promptitude, Mr. Richardson set
out for Portsmouth to hold himself in readiness
to sail for Canada. Here a considerable delay
occurred ; but a battalion of marines, just returned from Holland, being under orders to proceed to the Bermudas, he was appointed by the
Admiralty to do duty on the voyage out. This
secured the advantage of being at once placed on
full pay, and receiving the allowances attached
to his position.

After a tedious voyage, he reached the Bermudas towards the end of May, and having taken
a passage on board the 'Lord Collingwood' transport ship, sailed for Halifax. On June 3, he wrote,
giving an account of the Bermudas :—

They are a range of islands extending from east to west
about twenty miles, but their greatest breadth does not ex-
ceed two. The largest island in the group is called by the
inhabitants the 'continent' and is about twelve miles long.

There are several others from three to four miles in extent upon one of which stands the town of St. George. This is the capital, and indeed the only town, if a straggling row of houses and stores, running along the harbour, can deserve that name. Besides these, which may be termed the principal islands, there are many others much smaller, having one or two houses on each.

The surface is very rocky and uneven, there being many deep valleys and swamps; but the hills, though steep, do not rise much above the level of the sea, so that the islands cannot be seen at a greater distance than four or five leagues. Their shores are beset with innumerable rocks to the distance of ten or twelve miles on every side, except the southwest, which is the only one on which they can be approached. Very little of the country is cultivated. Part of it is covered with cedar trees, but the greater number of the hills produce only wild sage, without the smallest appearance of grass in the summer, though I have heard that a little springs up during the winter. The cedar trees were formerly much more numerous, and they built with them many small schooners for sale, but the demand has been so great that few trees are to be met with of a sufficient size. The soil on the hills is light and sandy, and does not appear to be capable of much improvement; but some of the valleys are very rich and might be made to produce anything if the laziness of the inhabitants did not prevent their cultivation. The climate is warm enough to ripen the finest fruits in the world, but the idleness of the people can only be equalled by their rapacity.

The houses are built of soft stone, which is to be procured in great abundance, but very little attention is paid to neatness in architecture and still less to comfort. Even in the very best houses few of the rooms have ceilings.

Their dining-rooms look like barns and are little better
furnished. A few chairs, a table, and an old cedar chest,
make up, in general, the whole amount of furniture.

On June 6, the 'Lord Collingwood' reached
Halifax, the capital of Nova Scotia, and Mr. Richardson landed to wait for an opportunity of proceeding to Quebec. In a letter from Quebec,
dated September 5, 1814, he gives an account of
his movements during June, July, and August.

In June, I went to Montreal by the steamboat in order
to join the first battalion. On arriving there I had the
mortification to learn that the greater part of it had been
drafted for the naval service on the lakes, and that the staff,
with a few non-commissioned officers and privates, amounting in all to one hundred, had received orders to go to
Halifax, for the purpose, it was said, of forming a new battalion from a detachment of marines which had arrived
from England. It vexed me a good deal to see so fine a
battalion broken up, as they were universally considered
here to be the most excellent body of men in the country
and exceedingly well disciplined, having been five years
embodied under the command of Colonel Williams.

They are much in want of medical men for the ships on
the lakes, in consequence of which I was ordered up there,
but after some little trouble I got the order cancelled, and
was allowed to proceed with the rest of the staff of the
battalion. I joined them at St. John's, on the Richelieu,
a river which flows from Lake Champlain into the St. Laurence, and marched with them to Chambley, where we embarked in the steamboat for Quebec. We had remarkably
fine weather during our march, which lasted four days, and

the country through which we passed was delightful. Our route lay along the banks of the Richelieu, which is about four times the size of the Nith, when largest, but frequently subdivided **into several** streams **by its** numerous islands, which, from the quantity of fine wood on them, have the most picturesque appearance. The farm-houses along the banks are **so** thickly situated **as to** look **like a** continued village, **and** the tin-covered spires of the **neat** Roman Catholic churches, peeping through the trees, added greatly to the effect of the scene. All the churches and a great **many** houses in this country are covered with tin. It forms **a** durable roof and has **a** fine appearance, particularly by moonlight.

We expect to sail for Halifax in ten days or a fortnight, and shall most likely remain there during the winter, as the season for operations on the coast of the United States must **be** over long before we can reach it.'

They arrived at Halifax, October 28, after a voyage **of** three weeks, **from** Quebec, and were **to** sail, ' **in** the course **of a** few days for Bermuda, **to** join **Sir** Alexander Cochrane.'

Our ultimate destination, he wrote, will most likely **be the coast of** America, but active operations will not be recommenced until the forces expected under **Lord** Hill **will** be ready to co-operate.

The Americans make great exertions. **The** late attack on their capital seems to have united all the different parties in one cause, and any force we can land on their coast will not **be** able to retain possession of it for any length of **time.** We may, indeed, carry on that predatory system of warfare which serves to degrade the British character with out materially injuring **the enemy.**

In the late attack **on** Washington, our troops destroyed the **few** works of art which were found there, **and were barbarous enough to burn** the public library, so that our conduct will not bear to be compared with that of the half-civilised Russians, who, with infinitely greater provocation, respected the monuments of learning and **of the** arts, during their progress through **France.**

At present **the** Americans have **only** a small **number of** regulars, who are badly disciplined and **ill-paid.** They have, however, **a** numerous militia, who are good light troops, particularly adapted for bush-fighting; **and if the** war continue, will **no** doubt become excellent soldiers. There is no want of bravery among them.

In January 1815, an expedition, **of which the** 1st battalion **of Royal** Marines formed **a** part, arrived **off the coast of** Georgia, **and** sailing **south-ward from Savannah,** took and plundered the **little** town of St. **Mary's, which was then** abandoned, **and** Cumberland Island taken possession of. **The** manner in which the expeditionary troops **treated** the property of non-combatants was most **discreditable, and** viewed with disgust **by** Mr. Richardson, whose sensitiveness regarding the **honour of the British name was only surpassed by his humanity.**

On February **7, 1815, he wrote from Cumberland Island, describing the position of the British** forces **and the sufferings of the natives.**

I mentioned **to you the capture of the town of St.**

Mary's. We evacuated that unfortunate little place after plundering it of almost everything of value, and are at present encamped on Cumberland Island, occupied in constructing entrenchments and raising forts, so that it is likely we shall make a long stay upon it.

This island is low and sandy, similar to the whole of Georgia, for many miles back, and is frequently intersected with marshes. As only a small portion of it has been cleared, the greatest part of the island is covered with forests which are difficult to penetrate from the thickness of the underwood. It is about twenty miles long and scarcely anywhere more than two broad, and is of no value to us except from the facilities which it affords of cutting off the trade of the Americans to Amelia, thus shutting up the principal outlet for their cotton. On this account, I suppose, we shall hold it during the remainder of the war.

A small expedition has been sent from this for the purpose of collecting all the tobacco and cotton on several islands a little to the northward. I do not know upon what principle we deprive the unresisting inhabitants of their property, but so it is that everything under the denomination of merchandise is taken for the general account, and the greatest part of what remains is seized by private plunderers. At first this system was confined to houses which had been deserted by the owners, but that has given the most of the men such a taste for it, that few escape. Those who come last and find everything carried off by their predecessors generally break the windows. From what I have already seen of this mode of warfare I do not think the American accounts are much exaggerated.

We have met with a severe check at New Orleans and lost many men, both by the fire of the enemy and the severity **of** the season. The cold is so intense at times there that many of the men have been frost-bitten, and even here, where there **is no** severe service, we have had from seventy to eighty men ill at a time with chilblains.

The principal proprietor on Cumberland Island is Mrs. Shaw, the daughter of General Green, who **was** second **in** command to Washington in the Revolutionary war. When we landed, she was reputed to be rich. Her slaves alone were worth ten thousand pounds sterling, the whole of whom have deserted. The overseer, a black man, carried the keys of the outhouses to his mistress yesterday and told her he intended to join the English. We had a number of men quartered in her cotton-houses which, through carelessness, were set on fire and totally destroyed, so that she is now reduced to poverty. All the slaves who offer themselves as soldiers are received, if fit for service, and those who merely wish to quit their masters are sent to the Bermudas or Halifax.

Fortunately **for both** countries, peace was soon after concluded, **and** the Royal Marines left Cumberland Island, and returned by way of the **Ber**mudas to England **to** be disbanded. In America, Mr. Richardson had seen much **of** the world, and having had charge of the hospital for the troops employed in Georgia, enjoyed the most favourable opportunities **for** enlarging **his** experience as a surgeon, and developing his administrative ability.

CHAPTER VII.

1815—1819.

THE general peace which followed the battle of Waterloo, enabled Mr. Richardson to obtain a season of rest from active service. He was placed on half-pay, and the long cherished plan of resuming his studies at the University of Edinburgh was carried into effect during the winter session of 1815-16.

There are few materials from which to sketch the student life of this period. We only catch glimpses of it in some of his letters, and those of early friends. He always avoided speaking of himself and his doings. This sensitive modesty—abhorrence of anything like egotism—increases, in no small degree, the difficulty of tracing his early career. We know, however, that he assiduously attended the classes in the University till 1817, when he obtained the degree of Doctor of

Medicine, the subject of his thesis being, ' De febre flava.'

Towards the close of 1817, Dr. Richardson began to practise as a physician at 36, Constitution Street, Leith. In the letters which he wrote at this time, there is not much said about his own affairs. One, however, to his father, dated April 6, 1818, refers to an important event, his approaching marriage to Mary, second daughter of William Stiven, Esq., Leith, which was solemnised on June 1.

His private practice as a physician was not very successful. We have no doubt that this failure was permitted by the Supreme Ruler, to lead him into the sphere for which he had been, unconsciously, preparing, and the duties of which, from his well-knit frame, habits of life, and mental qualities, he was admirably fitted to fulfil. An overland journey to the shores of the Arctic Sea was, at this time, about to be undertaken, and early in 1819, Dr. Richardson was appointed surgeon and naturalist to the expedition.

On March 26, 1819, the Secretary of the Admiralty wrote :—

Commissioner Searle, having put into my hand your application to be employed on the Northern Expedition, I wrote to a friend in Edinburgh to make enquiry whether you were acquainted with any of the branches of Natural History. As the report is satisfactory, if you feel disposed for such an expedition, and think that your health and qualifications are suitable for the undertaking, and you could be ready to set out from England by the first week in May, I request you to state to me whether you could undertake to collect and preserve specimens of minerals, plants, and animals, in order that I may lay it before Lord Melville, for his consideration and approval.

Dr. Richardson promptly replied, and on April 3, received the announcement of Lord Melville's having concurred in his appointment. On March 29, he wrote to his brother, Mr. Peter Richardson, informing him of the offer which had been made by the Admiralty, and that he had written to signify his acceptance of it, adding,—

I consider this appointment as affording a fairer prospect of advancement than any I have hitherto held, and as it will bring me into acquaintance with many scientific men, and those at the head of naval affairs, I am much pleased with it.

He was the more gratified at having been selected for this honourable service, that Macvey Napier, the editor of the 'Edinburgh Encyclopædia,' had been directed to make enquiries regarding his abilities, and report to Mr. Barrow, before the appointment was made.

Meantime, Dr. Richardson devotes every moment he can spare, to the study of mineralogy, Professor Jamieson kindly allowing him the use of his museum, and to attend his lectures free. On April 7, he wrote to his father:—

I shall proceed, by sea, to London, next week, when I shall learn more fully the objects of the expedition, and inform you.   Mrs. Richardson will fix her abode at Dalkeith until I return; but it is possible that she will pay you a visit in the summer.   I expect the service will be pleasant, and consider myself fortunate in being selected for it by the Admiralty.

If rapid success had crowned his efforts in Leith, these loving hearts, so recently united by the closest of ties, might have shrunk from the long separation which must necessarily follow his acceptance of this appointment.   The young wife, however deeply she felt the breaking up of her new home, and the parting which was so soon to take place, never murmured or complained. Having gained the acquiescence of his wife, he followed the leadings of Providence.   In the wastes of the northern wilderness, the nobler points of his character were to be brought prominently out. He went forth, resolved to gain some share of fame, and prove himself worthy of his wife's love, and returned, as we shall see, with the foundation of a noble character firmly laid.

CHAPTER VIII.

VOYAGES OF DISCOVERY TO THE POLAR REGIONS—DR. RICH-
ARDSON IN LONDON—SAILS FROM GRAVESEND—ARRIVES AT
YORK FACTORY—SPENDS THE FIRST WINTER AT CUMBER-
LAND HOUSE.

1819–1820.

WE now come to the time when Dr. Richardson
became connected with those expeditions to the
Arctic American coast, during which were brought
out so prominently the high sense of honour,
bravery, self-denial, patient endurance, loving
tenderness—especially to the weak—and firm faith
in God's goodness, for which he was remarkable.

In 1818, renewed efforts were begun to extend
our knowledge of the Arctic seas, and discover
the passage between the North Pacific and Atlantic Oceans. The 'Dorothea,' under Commander
David Buchan, and the 'Trent,' Lieutenant John
Franklin, proceeded northwards to endeavour to
cross the Polar Sea; but between Spitzbergen
and Greenland, the 'Dorothea' received so much
injury in the ice, that they were obliged to return.
The 'Isabella,' commanded by Captain John Ross,

and the 'Alexander,' by Lieutenant William Edward Parry, were appointed to perform their voyage of discovery through Davis' Straits. This voyage was so far successful, that it established the accuracy of Baffin's survey of the bay which bears his name; but Captain Ross returned, without having examined Lancaster Sound. In 1819, therefore, the 'Hecla' and 'Griper' were commissioned for that duty, the former ship commanded by Lieutenant William Edward Parry, and the latter, by Lieutenant Mathew Liddon.

Meanwhile, Lieutenant Franklin was appointed to lead an expedition over land, from Hudson's Bay to the mouth of the Coppermine River, in order to determine the latitudes and longitudes, and trending of the northern coast eastward, to the extremity of the American continent. The officers appointed to accompany Franklin were Dr. John Richardson, as surgeon and naturalist, Mr. (now Rear-Admiral Sir George) Back, and Mr. Robert Hood, midshipmen, to make illustrative drawings, plans of the routes taken, and assist their chief in obtaining observations. A happier combination of talent and noble qualities of mind could scarcely have been formed, and the friendships, which were cemented by daring and suffering for each other in the snowy wastes, remained unbroken in after-life.

On April 24, 1819, Dr. Richardson wrote to his father :—

I arrived in London yesterday, after a passage of seven days from Leith. I have seen the officer who is to command the expedition, and am much pleased with his manners. He is a lieutenant in the navy, and his name is Franklin. I have also seen Sir Joseph Banks, and have a general invitation to his house. To-morrow evening, there is a general assemblage of literary and scientific men in his library, to which I mean to go for the purpose of being introduced to Dr. Leach and Mr. Koënig of the British Museum.

Our expedition will occupy a longer time than I expected; at least two years from the time we leave England. The plan is to land at York Fort in August, and thence proceed as soon as possible to Fort Chipewyan, an advanced post of the Hudson's Bay Company. It is doubtful whether we shall be able to get that length previous to the setting-in of winter, but if we do, it is intended to winter there, and proceed northwards in the spring, for the purpose of determining the north-east boundary of the American continent. This object may be attained in the course of the first summer, but it will be left in the discretion of the commanding officer to return southwards on approach of winter, and complete, during the following summer, any part of his survey which he may have left unfinished.

My duty will be to collect minerals, plants, and animals. The country has never been visited by a naturalist, and presents a rich harvest. My knowledge of these subjects is very limited, but I am endeavouring to extend it by the opportunities afforded me here, and if I succeed in making a good collection, I have no doubt of my promotion on my return.

My wife intends visiting you in the summer, when you

will have an opportunity of observing in her those domestic virtues which have rendered the last year the happiest in my life. The hope of acquiring the power of rendering her more comfortable, and the possibility of obtaining some portion of fame, and proving myself worthy of her affection, are the inducements which I have to undertake the expedition, and are the only motives strong enough to enable me to endure so long an absence.

During his brief sojourn in London, he became acquainted with many who were distinguished for their scientific attainments, and others who have since gained for themselves undying fame. The eminent naturalist, Dr. J. E. Gray, of the British Museum, thus mentions the commencement of his long friendship with the subject of our Memoir :—

When Sir John Richardson came to London, on his appointment to accompany Sir John Franklin on his memorable Overland Expedition, he brought with him a letter of introduction to Sir Joseph Banks. I happened to be then studying in the library in Soho Square, and Sir Joseph referred him to me, as a person who could give him information respecting the collection and preservation of animals. We had a good deal of conversation on this and other subjects connected with Natural History, and the acquaintance thus begun ripened into an intimacy, which lasted without interruption until the time of his death, and enabled me thoroughly to understand and appreciate his high and estimable character, both as a Naturalist and as a man.

On Sunday, May 23, 1819, the party embarked at Gravesend, in the 'Prince of Wales,' a vessel

belonging to the Hudson's Bay Company. A
week later, Dr. Richardson wrote to his wife,—

We have been detained, in the mouth of the Thames,
by contrary winds, and are now at anchor in Hollesly Bay.
I regret this detention the less as it will ensure my receiving
a letter from you on arriving at the Orkneys. After
quitting these Islands, I have no chance for at least twelve
months, but shall hope for the best, trusting to that Providence which is all powerful.

I have now had an opportunity of becoming better acquainted with the commanding officer, and have every
reason to consider myself most fortunate in being associated
with him. He is a steady, religious, and cheerful man, and
altogether an honour to the profession. The young gentlemen, too, who accompany us, are pleasant companions, and
I trust that our expedition will prove an agreeable one.
The recollection of home will, indeed, intrude, but I endeavour to console myself with the reflection that you are
in good hands. The coast of Sussex, near which we are
anchored, looks beautiful, but the views I have of it only
serve to remind me of the scenes about Newbattle, where I
trust my beloved Mary is enjoying the beauties of Nature,
and not allowing the sorrow of our separation too much to
undermine her happiness.

We shall have divine service every Sunday, both during
our voyage out and our after progress. How pleasant to
reflect that you and I, though in different quarters of the
globe, may be occupied, at the same time, in offering up
our thanksgivings to that Being whose bounties fill the whole
earth !

A letter, written while the vessel was approach-

ing her destined port, gives a graphic description
of the voyage, which had been stormy :—

After passing the southern point of Greenland, named
Cape Farewell, we met with much ice, but as it did not lie
thick, little difficulty was experienced in forcing a way
through it; nor did it prove so great an impediment as the
contrary winds that still continue to thwart us. Near the
coast of Greenland, the fields or streams of ice consisted of
a collection of loose and comparatively flat pieces, more or
less densely compacted together, according to the state of
the weather, but in approaching the shores of Labrador, we
fell in with many icebergs, or large floating islands of ice.
The variety of forms assumed by these masses afforded us
amusement, but occasionally, we saw some of such an
enormous size that every other feeling gave place to
astonishment.

One of these larger Bergs we estimated to be two hundred
feet high above the water, and more than half a mile in
length. Its surface was broken by mountains, with deep
valleys between. Enormous as these dimensions must appear, you will be more surprised when I inform you that
the part of an iceberg which projects above water, amounts
only to the ninth part of the whole mass, that being the
proportion of ice which floats above salt water. Arthur's
seat, clothed in snow, would have formed only one pinnacle
to this Berg. When these bodies became familiar to us,
from their frequency, we derived much pleasure from the
various shades and gradations of colour they exhibited. The
more compact parts were generally of a bright verdigris
blue; towards the base a fine sea-green colour prevailed;
here and there a tint of red was seen, and the summits alone
were snow-white. As the part of the ice which is covered

by the sea decays more rapidly than that which is in the air, it often happens that one of these islands becomes top-heavy, and tumbles over. We never saw one in the act of making this revolution, **but** most of them bore marks **of** having **overturned** twice or thrice, the old water-lines (intersecting each other in various directions), being still deeply engraved **on** their surfaces. These enormous masses would at first sight appear **to** block **up** all approach to the frozen shores of the North, but when we consider the manner in which they **are detached,** and carried southward to melt away under warmer seas and skies, it affords us a new reason to admire the ways of Providence, which by means of admirably simple agents accomplishes the most important **ends.**

Everyone was by this time tired of the length of our **voyage, and** extremely anxious to see the Island of Resolution, **which forms one** side of the entrance of Hudson's Straits, and is generally **the** first land which the Hudson's Bay traders see after leaving the shores of Britain. At length we saw it, but under such circumstances that we had great cause to bless the goodness of the Divine Being who protects **and** upholds **his** creatures when there is none else **to help.** We first beheld the land during a fog, which soon became **so** thick **that we** could **not** see the length of the **ship. In** consequence of this we got involved in a field of **ice; then** to add to our distress, it fell calm, **and,** although **we could** perceive that we were carried along by a strong current, yet the fog deprived us of ascertaining its direction, **and** the depth of water **was** too great to admit of our anchoring. After remaining **in** this situation for two or three hours, receiving occasionally some heavy blows from **the** ice, an alarm **was** given that we were close to the rocks.

We all ran upon deck and beheld a tremendous cliff, frowning directly over the mast-heads of the ship. It was perfectly perpendicular, covered in many places by sheets of ice, and its summit was so high, and shrouded in so thick a fog, that it could not be traced from the deck. We had scarcely time to make any useful exertions, for in a few minutes the ship fell broadside against the cliff, along the face of which she was violently hurried by the current towards a ridge of broken rocks, which in a short time would have torn the stoutest vessel to pieces. The heavy swell which prevailed, caused the ship, in her passage, to beat against various rocky ledges which projected under water. One of the blows she thus sustained drove the rudder out of its place, but it fortunately hung suspended by a tackling which had been employed to secure it on coming amongst the ice. At this instant, when all human exertions seemed perfectly fruitless, the current eddied off shore, a land breeze sprung up, a boat that we had put overboard succeeded in taking us in tow, and what appears almost miraculous, one of the last bumps the ship received caused the rudder to fall back into its place. By this combination of favourable circumstances, we succeeded in getting round the point which we so much dreaded, and setting all sail, steered from the land. Upon the first alarm of danger, the women and children, of whom we had a large number on board, going to Lord Selkirk's colony, rushed upon deck, and by their expressions of fear and despair added to the horrors of the scene. The officers, however, prevailed upon them to go below out of the way of the sailors; but scarcely had this been effected, when the current carried us against a large iceberg, which had grounded upon a ridge of sunken rocks that lay at some distance from the shore. The crash of the masts and yards, together with the grinding of the ship's side against the ice, terrified them more than ever; but **we** got speedily clear of this second danger without receiving further damage.   Our troubles were not, however, **at an end; the ship had** been so much injured whilst on the **rocks, that on examination a great deal** of water was found in the hold. **All hands** were **instantly set to** the pumps, but, to **our** mortification, **we** found **that the** water rushed **in faster than we could,** with every exertion, discharge it.

Affairs now wore a gloomy aspect.   The water in the **hold increased** to upwards **of five feet, and** the men were **getting** tired **at the pumps, when fortunately** the weather **cleared** up a little, and we saw the ' Eddystone,' one of the **vessels** that accompanied **us, at no great** distance, **so we bore down and** informed those on board of our situation. Every **assistance in their** power was promptly supplied. They sent **twenty men and** two carpenters.   The services **of** the latter **were invaluable, as our own** carpenter had died in the **earlier** part **of the** voyage.   **These** operations were, however, necessarily **slow, and** it **was not until the** evening of the second day that we **succeeded** in getting all the water out **of** the ship.   **During the whole of** this time, not only the officers and **men worked hard, but even** many of the **women, recovering** their spirits, proved eminently useful at **the pumps.**

On arriving at York Factory, **the expedition found the** Hudson's Bay Company and **the North-West Fur** Company waging with each other **a war in** which battles were fought, lives lost, prisoners **taken,** and the **Indians demoralised** by the **free distribution of** spirituous **liquors.** Having received important information regarding the country through which they had to travel, it was resolved to take the route by Cumberland House, on the Saskatchewan, which was reached on October 23, a distance of 650 miles, by rivers and lakes, having been accomplished in six weeks. Winter was rapidly approaching. Large flocks of geese and ducks were seen moving southwards, and the waters at Cumberland House began to be closed with ice. Any farther advance by boats that season was impossible.

From this station Dr. Richardson wrote to his father on January 6, 1820.

We have got thus far on our journey to the North, and fixed our abode for the winter amidst greater comfort and plenty than we could have hoped for. Before leaving England, we expected to have got much farther, but the tediousness of the voyage out disappointed our wishes, and may prove the cause of our remaining a season longer in this country than was at first contemplated. It will require a concurrence of favourable circumstances to enable us to reach the sea next summer, especially as we must retire to a suitable wintering-place before the season is too far advanced. From these causes, our survey of the coast can only be made during 1821. The cold we have already experienced is about thirty degrees below zero, but we are well provided against it, and find this degree of cold not so disagreeable to the feelings as many of the damp winter days in Britain.

I have avoided sending home any details of our journey for various reasons, but particularly that I may be able, on my return, to avail myself of the privilege of travellers, and amuse you, during the winter nights, with some long stories. Besides, I have hitherto met with no surprising adventures or hair-breadth escapes, in our progress up the country. Everything has gone on provokingly smooth, and I am afraid that we shall not meet with any difficulties sufficient to ornament a narrative.

That no delay might be experienced when the rivers and lakes became clear of ice, Lieutenant Franklin and Mr. Back, accompanied by John Hepburn, an Orkney seaman, set out, January 18, for the trading posts at Carlton House, Isle à la Crosse, and Fort Chipewyan, to secure the stores necessary for the advance of the whole party in spring. Dr. Richardson and Mr. Hood were left at Cumberland House to bring up the boats and stores, as soon as the weather would permit.

During this time, he employed himself in studying the manners and customs and language of the Cree Indians, the rocks, vegetable products, animals, and fishes of the country. From this period, the religious side of his character begins to be more clearly reflected in his letters and journals. There is a depth of truth in his saying regarding a tender-hearted Indian, whose own privations were forgotten in his grief at the loss of a child, ' Misery may harden a disposition naturally bad, but it never fails to soften the heart of a good man.' In this furnace, all the members of the party were to be purified and come out nobler—better.

In a letter to his wife, dated March 6, 1820, he describes the solitude of the winter residence at Cumberland House :—

At this season, your walks will be enlivened by the appearance of vegetation. The snowdrop and crocus have already peeped forth, and bedeck the trim parterres now so universal in front of the tasteful abodes of the citizens of Edinburgh. In my rambles round that good old town, I have often been amused to observe that the flowers were arranged so as to form the initials of the owner's name. In this remote country, art has done nothing amiss, because she has done nothing. None of her creations chequer the face of the land, and break the sameness which prevails, particularly in the present season of the year. The miserable log houses in which we dwell are scarcely to be distinguished, in their winter dress, from the fallen trees with which the woods abound. I could find in my heart to forgive the bad taste displayed in the erection of the most fantastic building that ever was constructed, for the sake of the contrast it produces. Where there is no art, Nature loses half her charms.

When I began my letter, I thought of the pleasure you must be feeling, as an admirer of the works of God, in perceiving the earth bursting its frozen bands, and vegetation putting forth her powers. The joy, the exultation I have felt on such an occasion, was fresh in my mind, and I could not but contrast it with the depression produced by a winter unusually extended Winter, in unspotted livery, surrounds us. The snow covers the ground to the depth of three feet, and the trees bend under their ponderous load. If we pass the threshold of our hut, and enter the forest, a stillness so profound prevails that we are ready to start at the noise created by the pressure of our feet on the snow. The screams of a famished raven, or the crash of a lofty pine, rending through the intenseness of the frost, are the only sounds that invade the solemn silence. When in my walks I have accidentally met one of my companions in this dreary solitude, his figure, emerging from the shade, has conveyed, with irresistible force, to my mind, the idea of a being rising from the grave. I have often admired the pictures our great poets have drawn of absolute solitude, but never felt their full force till now. What must be the situation of a human being, 'alone on the wide, wide sea !' How dreadful if without faith in God ! An atheist could not dwell alone in the forests of America.

I must not, however, go on writing in this strain ; there are yet two months of winter to come, and I must endeavour to acquire and preserve that contentment which can render every situation tolerable. A thousand consolations offer themselves to one who is disposed to look for them.

CHAPTER IX.

JOURNEY **TO FORTS CHIPEWYAN**, PROVIDENCE, AND ENTER-
PRISE—WINTER RESIDENCE **AT FORT** ENTERPRISE.

1820-1821.

DURING the **long** winter residence **of ten months**
at Cumberland House, Dr. Richardson **examined**
the structure **of the** various species **of fish** obtained
from under **the snow, many** specimens **of lichens,**
and **made himself acquainted** with **the mineralogy**
of the surrounding country.

Spring at last **opened the waters, and on July**
13, he and Mr. Hood, after **a rapid journey of 857**
miles, joined their chief at Fort Chipewyan. **It**
was now found that **the fur** traders could grant
but scanty supplies, and the expedition party,
amounting **to** twenty-five, started from the **chief**
northern post of the North-West Company, **with**
only one full day's **supply** of food. At Fort Providence, on **the north side of** Great Slave Lake,
they were **joined by a** band of Copper Indians,
under a chief named Akaitcho, and reached their
wintering place, at Fort Enterprise, August 19,

having travelled 1,350 miles from Cumberland House.

Before leaving Fort Providence, he wrote to his father, mentioning the route which they intended to pursue, and then gave expression to a burst of tenderness :—

I have not received a line from home since I left the Orkneys, and you may easily conceive what my anxiety is about you all. The separation from my wife, and the distance to which I have removed myself from my friends, are sacrifices which nothing could have induced me to make, except the prospect which the present expedition held forth of rendering me ultimately more able to be of use to those whose absence I so much regret, and whose advantage I value far beyond my own comfort.

We have thus a glimpse of the chief motives which impelled this good and brave man to face the Arctic wilderness—duty and self-denying love. His brother, Mr. Peter Richardson, had leased the farm of Disdow, near Gatehouse, when agricultural produce was at war prices, and the change which peace brought caused him to fall into financial difficulties, his father being the chief loser. There were other brothers to educate, and Dr. Richardson hesitated not to leave home and wife to face the rigours and privations of the snowy regions if he might thus be enabled to aid those whom he loved. Before the lines which we have quoted reached Nith Place, the beloved father, for whom

they were intended, **was lying** at rest **in the family**
burying-ground in **St.** Michael's churchyard, Dumfries.

On October 23, 1820, letters arrived at Winter
Lake with **the sad, though not altogether unex-**
pected tidings.   **Writing from** Fort **Enterprise, at**
the beginning **of December, he thus refers to his**
bereavement :—

I have lost **a** tender parent and indulgent friend, **whose**
approbation I courted as **a** sufficient reward for all **my**
toils.   His worth was acknowledged by the world during
his life ; **but** his merits, solid not splendid, will soon be
forgotten, and the public remembrance of **him will pass**
away as **if he** had never been.   **It was** only amongst his
most intimate **friends** and in **his own family, that** his
tender goodness **of** heart could be appreciated **and his** upright principles thoroughly known.   **His** memory **will be**
long cherished in their **hearts and his example** will have **a**
powerful effect on his children.   I trust that, **encouraged**
by the peaceful close of his life, they may **contemn all**
meaner aims and look to a world beyond the grave, **and**
that, having nobly run the race that is set before them, they
may die the death of the righteous.

To his mother, who **had lost both her** husband
and youngest son, the latter **having** gone to Ja-
maica, **where one of his** maternal **uncles was a**
planter, **he** wrote :—

When you receive **this letter, your** grief **for the loss of**
the **partner of your heart and tender father of your family**
will have mellowed into a grateful resignation **to the dis-**

pensations of Providence. The **troubles he** had to encounter are best known to **you, the partner** of his cares,
anxieties, and **paternal affections. Great as they** were, he
bore them without a murmur and manfully stemmed a
torrent of adversity which would have overwhelmed any
one whose exertions **were** actuated by a zeal less ardent
than **his.** Let **us be** thankful **to God.** It was his will
to try **him** with **calamities,** but **he granted** strength and
wisdom to surmount them. I **shall not** now conceal from
you that I left home under the mournful conviction that **I
should see him no** more—that **I** should **never** again con-
template his countenance beaming with kindness and
suffused with joy at **the return of** one of his children. I
knew the fatal nature of his disorder, **and** often in my
solitary moments in this country **has a** dreadful picture **of**
his sufferings harrowed my feelings. I bless God that the
close of his life was undisturbed by **mental** conflicts.

It has pleased **God to** try you with another severe afflic-
tion in the loss of the youngest of your sons. **Poor
Edward!** His span **of life** was short. He was **cut off**
before **the** ripening **of his** understanding could enable us to
judge **of** his probable **progress** through life; but all the
dispensations of the Almighty are merciful. My brother's
lot appeared to be **cast in a land** where the traffic in their
fellow-creatures **has** debased the nature of its inhabitants,
and where the lust of sordid gain **has snapped** asunder the
holy bonds of religion. In such **a** situation, his young
mind was exposed to contamination and his eternal welfare
endangered. God, of **his gracious** goodness, has early
removed **him** from temptation **and we** ought to rest in the
hope that the **merits** of his blessed Redeemer have exalted
him to mansions of perpetual rest.

He thus describes the winter quarters of the party at Fort Enterprise, on Winter Lake :—

We arrived here on August 20, and finding it a fit place for a winter residence immediately commenced the requisite buildings.' Beyond this spot, which is situated two and a half degrees to the northward of Fort Providence, the country is destitute of wood, its vegetable productions consisting solely of various species of moss upon which the reindeer feed. The abundance of this kind of food attracts these animals in great numbers to the barren hills in the summer season, but during the winter they retire to the woods, partly for shelter from the inclemency of the weather and partly because the snow being loose is more easily removed in their search after the moss. In fine weather, however, they pay occasional visits to their favourite pastures on the barren grounds.

That we may be as much advanced as possible when the return of summer permits us to resume our journey, we have fixed our abode upon the verge of the woods, and indeed we could not have selected a more convenient or beautiful spot. The surrounding country is finely varied by hill and dale and interspersed with numerous lakes connected by small streams. One of these lakes, which we have named Winter Lake, discharges its waters by a moderately sized river, whose sheltering banks are clothed with wood. Amidst this wood, on a small and rather elevated plain, we have erected Fort Enterprise, and the situation is such that while we have an extensive southern prospect down the wooded banks of the river, the nakedness of the northern country is hid by a clump of trees on the rising ground in our rear.

Winter Lake supplies us with fish, but our staple commodity is the reindeer. We are just in the track of their visits to and from the woods and some are daily killed within sight of the house.

We have managed, notwithstanding the diminutive size of the trees, to construct a stately dwelling. It is fifty feet long, and twenty-four wide, and consists of three bed-rooms and a common hall. We have besides a large kitchen behind, a storehouse on one wing, and a house for twenty men on the other. If to this you add a few Indian lodges scattered in the foreground you may picture to yourself Fort Enterprise, and conclude that it makes a very respectable appearance.

The buildings are framed of logs and plastered on the outside and inside with clay. With the latter material also the roof is covered and the chimneys constructed. The windows are closed with thin parchment made of reindeer skin, and our chairs and tables are formed by the hatchet and knife, tools which the Canadians use with great dexterity.

The party having arranged to winter at Fort Enterprise, Mr. Back volunteered to return for ammunition and other supplies to Fort Providence, and, if possible, also to Fort Chipewyan. He set out from Winter Lake on October 18, and returned January 17, 1821, having travelled 1,104 miles on snow shoes, with no covering at night other than a blanket and deerskin, the thermometer frequently indicating forty degrees below zero. The supplies which he was able to obtain at the trading posts were far from being adequate for the wants of the expedition. Spring found

them **destitute of any** store of provisions, and
under the **necessity of** relinquishing the undertaking, **or of making the** journey **to the mouth of**
the Coppermine **River on** the **casual and often**
scanty products of the chase, and 200 pounds of
dried meat, which Dr. Richardson, **aided by two**
hunters, prepared at Point Lake, some distance in
advance.

In April, 1821, he **wrote to his** brother, **Mr.**
Peter Richardson :—

Your **letter** of April, 1820, has just **come to hand,** and
although the news is a year old, it is **agreeable to learn** of
the welfare **of our** friends, even **at** that distant **date.**

We have **travelled** through a country where intrigue and
violence have a powerful sway. **The** contests of the rival
Fur Companies have been **carried on** in a disgraceful **and**
barbarous manner; **but we are** now **fortunately** beyond
their direct influence, **though we still hear of wars and**
rumours of wars at **the** posts below. **Next summer will**
carry us into the territories of the unsophisticated Esqui-
maux, and if we should be compelled to eat blubber and
drink seal oil, it will be at a distance from the turmoils
which agitate the other parts of the world.

We already enjoy a greater length of **day than you do**
at **the same** season, and the sun is beginning **to have** considerable power, but **we do not expect the snow to** dis-
appear **before** the middle of **next month, nor** that we shall
be able to move **hence previous to the** month of June. It
will probably be **near the end of July** before the **ice will**
be entirely gone from **the** Coppermine River. **Our** proceedings, after we reach the **sea,** will **depend so much on**

circumstances with which we are at present unacquainted, that it is useless to hazard an opinion on the subject. We are likely to start in good health and spirits, having fed well during the winter, and not suffered from the cold, though rum a little below proof froze in our bed-rooms.

Having volunteered to lead the first detachment to the Coppermine River, Dr. Richardson set out on June 4. The party 'consisted of fifteen voya-geurs, three of them conducting dog sledges; Baldhead and Basil, two Indian hunters, with their wives; Akaiyazzeh, a sick Indian, and his wife, together with Angélique and Roulante.'

At Point Lake he encamped, and found the snow deeper than had been seen at any time around Winter Lake. Through the kindness of Rear-Admiral Sir George Back, we are able to give a humorous description of the journey from Fort Enterprise to Point Lake, which shows that Dr. Richardson could enjoy a bit of real fun as heartily as any of his companions.

Point Lake, June 9, 1821.

My dear Back,—Gilpin himself, that celebrated pictur-esque hunter, would have made a fruitless journey had he come with us. We followed the lakes and low grounds, which, after leaving Martin Lake, were so deeply covered with snow that it was impossible to distinguish lake from moor, and frequently when I was congratulating myself, I was surprised by sinking to the middle through the snow, and sticking among the large stones which cover the valleys.

I have said this much that you may judge of the sameness of the views that occurred on our journey. The only variety that we had was in crossing two extensive ridges of land which lie at the distance of seven or eight miles from each other, and nearly half way to the river.

I should suppose them to form the height of land between Winter and Coppermine Rivers, as all the hills which I have seen in this country consist of sand. Amongst these hills you may observe some curious basins, but nowhere did I see anything worthy of your pencil. So much for the country. It is a barren subject, and deserves to be thus briefly dismissed. Not so the motley group of which we were composed. It afforded ample scope for the ablest pencil or pen, and whether character or humour were most kept in view, would, in the hands of genius, produce a picture not in many respects inferior either to Chaucer's Pilgrims or Hogarth's Guards. The party was composed of twenty-three individuals, all marching in Indian file, but variously grouped according to their physical strength and the heaviness of their burdens. Belanger 'le gros,' exulting in his strength, was foremost in the rank. Belanger 'le rouge' followed close behind; whilst little Perrault completed the trio, and formed the first triangle in the picture. Adam came next, but at a respectful distance. His over-loaded sledge could not keep pace with the others, and he had frequently to lug along another with the 'butin' of his beloved Angelique. I need not trouble you with an account of the rank maintained by the rest of the party. You know their various characters and powers, and can arrange them correctly. Roulante came tumbling along in the rear, the snow sometimes too deep to admit of her legs reaching the bottom, but the rotundity of her body was such that **she never** sank beyond **a certain** depth.   **In** such cases it was admirable to **see the dexterity with** which she drew her extremities into **her enormous** corporation, and came rolling like an avalanche along **the surface of** the **snow.**   Dumas, **from the love he bore to the northern, carried Ryer,** and Michel, for reasons unknown, carried her **' butin.'   The** most prominent **figure, however,** of the **whole, because the most unearthly, was mother** Adam. **She came striding along supported by** a stick which **towered over the heads of all the others; a** pair of **red** stockings and **various other articles of** her garb heightened **the** peculiarities of her **figure; and as to her gait, it** was **similar to** nothing **I** had ever **before** seen.   Sometimes I **was** tempted to compare her to Hecate, **sometimes to** Meg Merrilies.   Not that she had mind enough **to be a** powerful sorceress, or majesty sufficient for a commanding presence, but because she appeared **to** be rather **a** creature of the imagination than **a** reality.   Every member of her **body** seemed to have belonged to different individuals and **to** have **been formed** by a random association into a sort **of** semblance of the human **form; but** from want of proper animation the extremities **never acted** in concert, and the distorted **spine** which composed the centre, now bent to **this side, now to that,** according as the leg which described **the greater or the smaller circle** was in motion, while the **arms** played up and **down to** preserve something like equi- **librium,** but with the involuntary and convulsive motions **of the** most fantastic of Shakespeare's weird sisters in the height of her frenzy.

   There was another figure of a different gender, with an unwashed face, matted locks, and moustaches of the colour **and strength** of straw; equip **him** as you please and place him in any part of the file you choose.

A Canadian would have told you the whole story in few words :—' Beaucoup de misère, point de chaudières, assez de sacrés.' You see I am determined that you should have your share of it by engaging you in the deciphering of this scrawl. Adieu ! compliments to all our messmates.

Yours sincerely,

JOHN RICHARDSON.

CHAPTER X.

1821.

ON June 25, the expedition set out from Point
Lake for the sea, dragging the canoes and baggage
over the snow and ice, the sharp points of which
tore their shoes and lacerated the feet at every
step. This weary work is at last over. They are
afloat on the Coppermine, and carried along with
great rapidity, their safety depending on the skill
and dexterity of the bowmen and steersmen. The
trees begin to put forth their leaves, the mossy
ground to be dotted with flowers, the summer
birds to flit about the woods, and the ducks, gulls,
and plovers to frequent the river. How cheering
and full of hope must every opening bud, and
every note of the feathered warblers have been,

after ten months of weary winter in the wilderness!

On approaching the Esquimaux country, great care was taken not to alarm them. At this time, one of the many stirring incidents of the journey occurred, and is narrated in Franklin's narrative:—

Dr. Richardson, having the first watch, had gone to the summit of the hill, and remained seated, contemplating the river that washed the precipice under his feet, long after dusk had hidden distant objects from his view. His thoughts were, perhaps, far distant from the surrounding objects, when he was roused by an indistinct noise behind him, and on looking round perceived that nine white wolves had ranged themselves in form of a crescent, and were advancing apparently with the intention of driving him into the river. On his rising up, they halted, and when he advanced they made way for his passage down to the tents. He had his gun in his hand, but forbore to fire, lest there should be Esquimaux in the neighbourhood.

'On the evening of July 14,' says Franklin, 'Dr. Richardson ascended a lofty hill about three miles from the encampment and obtained the first view of the sea. He saw the sun set a few minutes before midnight from the same elevated situation. It did not rise during the half hour he remained there, but before he reached the encampment its rays gilded the tops of the hills.'

To Mr. Wentzel, the trading agent at Fort Providence, who had accompanied the expedition to the sea, despatches for England were intrusted, and the farther duty of making sure that the Indians would place a supply of dried provision at

Fort Enterprise, **the first** point which **the** party would fall back upon **when overtaken by winter.** Information regarding **the** direction where **Akaitcho and** the other Indians would be hunting in September **and October, was also to** be left at **their last winter quarters, for the** guidance of the expedition on arriving there.

On **July 18, Dr. Richardson wrote :—**

After travelling **upwards** of a month over the shoals and **rapids, we** have **at length reached the sea. The** islands **about the** mouth **of the river are so** numerous that **we** do not **know as yet whether we have come to a** deep inlet or arm **of the** sea running east and west, or merely a coast lined **by an** assemblage of islands, which, crossing each other, look, from a distance, like a continued **shore. The** good **people** of **England** may, perhaps, **not give us the** credit **of having reached** the sea at all, when they learn that the water **is** only brackish—a fact which we **have** ascertained, not by dipping the finger **in and** tasting it, but by swallowing several kettlefuls. The islands are **high,** but, as well as the main shore, **they are** destitute of wood. At **the mouth of the river and** round the islands there is a small **channel of open water,** but, farther off, the ice ex-**tends in a continued** field, although we **are led to** expect that it will soon **break up.**

On July 21, the officers, with **John** Hepburn, **the** Orkney seaman, **and the** Canadian voyageurs, **in** two canoes, commenced their voyage on the Arctic Sea. With **want staring them** in the face, **they bravely pressed eastward, until** August 16, surveying the coasts of Bathurst's Inlet and Coronation Gulf to Point Turnagain, having sailed over 555 geographical miles. To advance further was to risk the loss of the whole party, and after having been detained for several days by a heavy snow-storm, the canoes were turned again in the direction of Bathurst's Inlet. Crossing Melville Sound in a strong wind and heavy sea, they ascended Hood's River for some distance. The canoes were then reduced in size and a course taken over the Barren Grounds for Point Lake. The sufferings endured can scarcely be conceived. Game was scarce, and the strength of the party rapidly failed under the united influences of cold, famine, and fatigue. A scanty meal of a nauseous weed, called *tripe de roche*, with an occasional partridge, was their sole support while toiling wearily on in hopes of reaching Winter Lake and finding supplies. On September 13, it was discovered that the Canadian voyageurs had thoughtlessly thrown away the fishing nets. All books and instruments not necessary to finding the way were now left behind, and a week later, Dr. Richardson, unable to carry them further, also deposited the specimens which he had collected on the coast. Still they were not without hope. Firm faith in the Almighty supported them.

Their sufferings increased. Mr. Hood became unable to move on behind the first man to direct the way. Franklin was also in the rear, and Richardson took the lead. Back was in advance with the hunters, trying to obtain game. On September 22, the men, who, weak and dispirited, had fallen several times and injured the canoe, would carry it no further. To this abandonment of the canoe, and the consequent delay in crossing the Coppermine River, may be attributed many of the subsequent disasters which befel the party.

The river was gained on September 26, but there were no means of getting to the other side. Through despondency, the Canadians had ceased to dread punishment, or to be stimulated by the hope of reward, and four days passed before they would begin to bind willows for a raft, which was at last constructed, only to find that there was no way of impelling it to the opposite bank against a strong wind.

'At this time,' says Franklin, in his narrative, 'Dr. Richardson, prompted by a desire of relieving his suffering companions, proposed to swim across the stream with a line and to haul the raft over. He launched into the stream with the line round his middle, but when he had got a short distance from the bank, his arms became benumbed with cold, and he lost the power of moving them; still he persevered, and turning on his back had nearly gained the opposite bank, when his legs also became powerless, and to our infinite alarm we beheld him sink. We instantly hauled upon the line and he came again on the surface, and was gradually drawn ashore in an almost lifeless state. Being rolled up in blankets, he was placed before a good fire of willows, and fortunately was just able to speak suf-

ficiently to give some slight directions respecting the manner of treating **him.** He recovered strength gradually, and
by the blessing of God **was** enabled in **the course of a few**
hours to converse, and **by the evening** was sufficiently recovered to remove into the tent. **We then** regretted to
learn that the skin of his **whole** left side was deprived **of**
feeling in consequence of exposure **to too** great heat. **He**
did not perfectly recover the **sensation** of that side until the
following summer. I cannot **describe** what every one felt
at beholding the skeleton which the Doctor's debilitated
frame exhibited. **When** he stripped, the **Canadians** simul-
taneously exclaimed, "**Ah que** nous sommes **maigres!**"'
Franklin **adds,** ' I have omitted **to mention** that **when he**
was about to step into the water, **he** put his foot on a dagger,
which **cut** him to the bone, but **this** misfortune **could not**
stop him from **attempting** the execution of his **generous** undertaking.'

A little canoe, formed of **willows covered with**
tent **canvas,** was at length made, **and** after a
week's delay, **the** party, **one by one,** crossed **the**
river. Mr. Back was immediately sent forward **to**
Fort Enterprise, with **the** strongest **of the Cana-**
dians, **to** search for **the Indians** and **send** back
aid. Mr. Hood was **now** very feeble, **and Dr.**
Richardson, having attached **himself to him,**
walked with him at a gentle **pace.** Old shoes and
scraps of leather, everything **which possessed any**
nutriment, was **now** resorted **to in order to sus-**
tain **life, and death** began **his work. The men**
became **appalled, and could scarcely be** restrained
from throwing away all they carried and hastening

on to the Fort, in which case no one would have lived to tell the sad tale.

Dr. Richardson, therefore, volunteered to en-camp with Mr. Hood, who felt too weak to pro-ceed, the good old sailor, John Hepburn, offering to remain with them. At the first place which promised some days' supply of *tripe de roche*, their tent was erected, and Franklin, with the Canadians, proceeded onward in hopes of finding relief.

CHAPTER XI.

THE ENCAMPMENT—MICHEL RETURNS—MURDER OF MR. HOOD
—DR. RICHARDSON, JOHN HEPBURN, AND MICHEL SET OUT
FOR FORT ENTERPRISE—DR. RICHARDSON NECESSITATED TO
SHOOT MICHEL—REUNION AT THE FORT—FORT ENTERPRISE
IN RUINS.

1821.

IN Dr. Richardson's journal, published in the
'Narrative of the First Overland Journey,' he
says :—

After Captain **Franklin** had bidden us farewell, we remained seated by the fire-side as long as the willows the
men had cut for us before they departed lasted. We had
no *tripe de roche* that day, but drank an infusion of the
country tea-plant, which was grateful from its warmth,
although it afforded no sustenance. We then retired to
bed, where we continued all the next day, as the weather
was stormy, and the snow-drift so heavy as to destroy every
prospect of success in our endeavours to light a fire with
the green and frozen willows, which were our only fuel.
Through the extreme kindness and forethought of a lady,*
the party, previous to leaving London, had been furnished

* Lady Lucy Barry, wife of the Hon. Col. Barry, of Newton-Barry.

with a small collection of religious books, of which we still retained two or three of the most portable, and they proved of incalculable benefit to us. We read portions of them to each other as we lay in bed, in addition to the morning and evening service, and found they inspired us on each perusal with so strong a sense of the omnipresence of a beneficent God, that our situation, even in these wilds, appeared no longer destitute; and we conversed, not only with calmness, but with cheerfulness, detailing with unrestrained confidence the past events of our lives, and dwelling with hope on our future prospects.

On the morning of the 29th, the weather, although cold, was clear, and I went in quest of *tripe de roche*, leaving Hepburn to cut willows for a fire, and Mr. Hood in bed. I had no success, as yesterday's snow-drift was so frozen on the surface of the rocks that I could not collect any of the weed; but, on my return to the tent, I found that Michel, the Iroquois, had come with a note from Mr. Franklin, which stated that this man and Jean Baptiste Belanger, being unable to proceed, were about to return to us, and that a mile beyond our present encampment there was a clump of pine-trees, to which he recommended us to remove the tent. Michel informed us that he had quitted Mr. Franklin's party yesterday morning, but that, having missed his way, he had passed the night on the snow a mile or two to the northward of us. Belanger, he said, being impatient, had left the fire about two hours earlier, and, as he had not arrived, he supposed he had gone astray.

Michel now produced a hare and a partridge which he had killed in the morning. This unexpected supply of provision was viewed by us with a deep sense of gratitude to the Almighty for His goodness, and we looked upon

Michel as the instrument He had chosen to preserve all our lives. He complained of cold, and Mr. Hood offered to share his buffalo robe with him at night. I gave him one of two shirts which I wore, whilst Hepburn, in the warmth of his heart, exclaimed, ' How I shall love this man if I find that he does not tell lies like the others.'

Early in the morning, Hepburn, Michel, and myself carried the ammunition and most of the other heavy articles to the pines. Michel was our guide, and it did not occur to us at the time that his conducting us perfectly straight was incompatible with his story of having gone astray on his way to us. After we had made a fire and drank a little of the country tea, Hepburn and I returned to the tent, where we arrived in the evening, much exhausted with our journey. Michel preferred sleeping where he was, and requested us to leave him a hatchet, which we did, after he had promised to come early in the morning to assist us in carrying the tent and bedding. Mr. Hood remained in bed all day. Seeing nothing of Belanger to-day, we gave him up for lost.

On the 11th, after waiting until late in the morning for Michel, who did not come, Hepburn and I loaded ourselves with the bedding, and, accompanied by Mr. Hood, set out for the pines. Mr. Hood was much affected with dimness of sight, giddiness, and other symptoms of extreme debility, which caused us to move very slow, and to make frequent halts. On arriving at the pines we were much alarmed to find that Michel was absent. We feared that he had lost his way in coming to us in the morning, although it was not easy to conjecture how that could have happened, as our footsteps of yesterday were very distinct. Hepburn went back for the tent, and returned with it after dusk, completely worn out with the fatigue of the day. Michel too arrived at the same time. He reported that he had been in chase of some deer which passed near his sleeping place in the morning, and although he did not come up with them, yet that he found a wolf which had been killed by the stroke of a deer's horn, and had brought a part of it. We implicitly believed this story then, but afterwards became convinced that it must have been a portion of the body of Belanger or Perrault.

On the following morning the tent was pitched, and Michel went out early, refused my offer to accompany him, and remained out the whole day. He would not sleep in the tent at night, but chose to lie at the fire-side.

On the 13th there was a heavy gale of wind, and we passed the day by the fire. Next day, about two P.M., the gale abating, Michel set out, as he said, to hunt, but returned unexpectedly in a very short time. This conduct surprised us, and his contradictory and evasive answers to our questions excited some suspicions, but they did not turn towards the truth.

October 15.—In the course of this day, Michel expressed much regret that he had stayed behind Mr. Franklin's party, and declared that he would set out for the house at once if he knew the way. We endeavoured to soothe him, and to raise his hopes of the Indians speedily coming to our relief, but without success. He refused to assist us in cutting wood, but about noon, after much solicitation, he set out to hunt. Hepburn gathered a kettle of *tripe de roche*, but froze his fingers. Both Hepburn and I fatigued ourselves much to-day in pursuing a flock of partridges from one part to another of the groups of willows in which the hut was situated, but we were too weak to be able to approach them with sufficient caution. **In the** evening Michel returned, having met with no success.

Next **day** he refused either to hunt or cut wood, spoke in a very surly manner, and threatened to leave us. Under these circumstances, Mr. Hood and I deemed it better to promise, **if** he would hunt diligently for four days, that then we would give Hepburn **a** letter to Mr. Franklin, a compass, inform him what course to pursue, and let them proceed together to the fort. The non-arrival of the Indians to our relief now led **us to** fear that some accident had happened to Mr. Franklin, **and** we placed no confidence in the exertions of the Canadians **that accompanied him,** but we had the fullest confidence in Hepburn's returning the moment he could obtain assistance.

On the 17th **I went** to conduct **Michel to where** Vaillant's blanket **was** left, and after walking about three miles, pointed out the hills to him, at a distance, and returned **to** the hut, having gathered a bagful of *tripe de roche* on the way. It was easier to gather this weed on a **march than at** the tent, for the exercise of walking produced a glow of heat, which enabled us **to** withstand for a time the cold to which we were exposed in scraping the frozen surface of the rocks.

Michel proposed **to** remain **out all** night and to hunt **next** day on his way back. He returned in the afternoon of the 18th, having found the blanket, together with a bag containing two pistols and some other things which had been left beside it. We had **some** *tripe de roche* **in** the evening, **but** Mr. Hood, from the constant griping it produced, was unable to eat more than one or **two** spoonfuls. He was now so weak as to be scarcely able to **sit** up at the fire-side, and complained that the least **breeze** of wind seemed to blow through his frame.

H

At this period we avoided as much as possible conversing upon the hopelessness of our situation, and generally endeavoured to lead the conversation towards our future prospects in life. With the decay of strength our minds decayed, and we were no longer able to bear the contemplation of the horrors that surrounded us. Each of us excused himself from so doing by a desire of not shocking the feelings of the others, for we were sensible of one another's weakness of intellect, though blind to our own. Yet we were calm and resigned to our fate, not a murmur escaped us, and we were punctual and fervent in our addresses to the Supreme Being.

On the 19th, Michel refused to hunt or even to assist in carrying a log of wood to the fire, which was too heavy for Hepburn's strength and mine. Mr. Hood endeavoured to point out to him the necessity and duty of exertion, and the cruelty of his quitting us without leaving something for our support; but the discourse, far from producing any beneficial effect, seemed only to excite his anger, and amongst other expressions he made use of the following remarkable one : 'It is no use hunting, there are no animals; you had better kill and eat me.' At length, however, he went out, but returned very soon with a report that he had seen three deer, which he was unable to follow from having wet his foot in a small stream of water thinly covered with ice, and being consequently obliged to come to the fire. The day was rather mild, and Hepburn and I gathered a large kettleful of *tripe de roche*.

Sunday, October 20.—In the morning, we again urged Michel to go a hunting, that he might, if possible, leave us some provision, to-morrow being the day appointed for his quitting us; but he showed great unwillingness to go out,

and lingered about the **fire under the pretence of** cleaning
his gun. After we had read the morning service, **I went**
about noon to gather some *tripe de roche,* leaving **Mr.**
Hood sitting before the tent at the fire-side, arguing with
Michel ; Hepburn was employed cutting down a tree at **a**
short distance from the tent, being desirous **of** accumulat-
ing a quantity of fire-wood before he left us. **A** short time
after I went out I heard the report **of a** gun, and about ten
minutes afterwards Hepburn called to me **in a voice of**
great alarm, to come **directly.** When I arrived, I found
poor Hood lying lifeless at the fire-side, **a** ball having apparently entered his forehead. I was at **first** horror-struck
with the idea that, in a fit of despondency, **he** had hurried
himself into the presence of his Almighty Judge, by an act
of his own hand ; **but** the conduct **of Michel soon gave rise**
to other thoughts, and excited **suspicions which were con-**
firmed, when, upon **examining the body, I** discovered **that**
the shot had entered **the back** part **of the** head, **and passed**
out at the forehead, and **that** the **muzzle** of the gun **had**
been applied so close as to set fire to the nightcap behind.
The gun, which was of the longest kind supplied to **the In-**
dians, could not have been **placed in a position to** inflict
such a wound, except by **a second person.** **Upon** enquir-
ing from Michel **how it** happened, he replied that Mr. Hood
had sent him into the tent for **the short gun, and that** during his absence the **long gun had gone off, he did not** know
whether by accident **or not.** He held the **short gun** in his
hand at the time he was speaking to me. **Hepburn** afterwards informed me, that previous **to the report** of the gun
Mr. Hood and Michel **were** speaking **to each other in an**
elevated angry tone ; **that Mr. Hood** being seated at **the**
fire-side, was hid **from him by** intervening willows, but

that on hearing **the** report he-looked up, and saw Michel
rising up from before the tent **door,** or just behind where
Mr. Hood was **seated,** and **then** going into the tent.
Thinking that the gun had been discharged for the purpose
of cleaning it, he did not go to the **fire** at first ; and when
Michel called to him that Mr. Hood **was** dead, a considerable **time had** elapsed.   Although **I dared** not openly to
evince any suspicion that I thought Michel guilty of the
deed, **yet** he repeatedly protested that he was incapable of
committing such **an** act, kept constantly on his guard, and
carefully avoided leaving Hepburn and me together.   He
was evidently afraid of permitting us to converse in private,
and whenever Hepburn spoke, he inquired if he accused
him of the murder.   We removed the body into a clump
of willows behind the **tent,** and, returning to the fire, read
the funeral service **in** addition **to the evening** prayers.

'Bickersteth's Scripture Help' was lying open beside
the body, as if it had fallen from his hand, and it is probable that **he** was reading **it** at the instant of his death.
We passed the **night in the** tent without rest, every one
being on his guard.   **Next day,** having determined on going
to the **Fort,** we began to patch **and** prepare our clothes for
the journey.   We singed **the** hair off a part of the buffalo
robe that belonged to Mr. Hood, and boiled and ate it.
Michel tried **to** persuade me to go to the woods on the
Coppermine River, and hunt **for deer,** instead of going to
the Fort.   In the afternoon, a flock **of** partridges coming
near the tent, he killed several, which he shared with us.

Thick snowy weather **and a** head wind prevented us
from starting the following **day,** but on the morning of the
23rd we set out, carrying with us the remainder of the
singed robe.   Hepburn and Michel had each a gun, and I

carried a small pistol, which Hepburn had loaded for me.
In the course of the march, Michel **alarmed us** much **by**
his gestures and conduct, was constantly muttering to **him-**
self, expressed an unwillingness to go to the Fort, **and tried**
to persuade me to go southward to the woods, where **he**
said he could maintain himself all the winter by killing
deer.   In consequence of this behaviour, and the expression
of his countenance, **I** requested **him** to **leave us and go to**
the southward by himself.

This proposal **increased his** ill-nature; **he threw out**
some obscure hints **of freeing** himself from **all** restraint
on the morrow; **and I** overheard him muttering threats
against Hepburn, whom he openly accused **of** having told
stories against him.   He also, for the first **time, assumed**
such a tone **of** superiority in **addressing me, as** evinced
that he considered us to be completely **in his power, and**
he gave vent to several expressions **of** hatred **towards the**
white people, or, as he termed us in the idiom of the **voy-**
ageurs, the French, **some of** whom, he said, had killed and
eaten his uncle and two of his relations.   **In short, taking**
every circumstance of his conduct into consideration, **I**
came to the conclusion that he would attempt to destroy
us on the first opportunity that offered, and that **he had**
hitherto abstained from doing so from his ignorance of the
way to the Fort, but that he would never suffer **us to go**
thither in company with him.   In the course **of the** day
he had several times remarked that we were pursuing the
same course that **Mr.** Franklin was doing when he left him,
and that by keeping towards the setting sun he could find
his way himself.   Hepburn **and I were not in a** condition
to resist even an open attack, **nor could** we by any device
escape from him.   Our united strength **was** far inferior to

his, and, besides his gun, he was armed with two pistols, an Indian bayonet, and a knife. In the afternoon, coming to a rock on which there was some *tripe de roche*, he halted, and said he would gather it whilst we went on, and that he would soon overtake us. Hepburn and I were now left together for the first time since Mr. Hood's death, and he acquainted me with several material circumstances which he had observed of Michel's behaviour, and which confirmed me in the opinion that there was no safety for us except in his death, and he offered to be the instrument of it. I determined, however, as I was thoroughly convinced of the necessity of such a dreadful act, to take the whole responsibility upon myself, and, immediately upon Michel's coming up, I put an end to his life by shooting him through the head with a pistol. Had my own life alone been threatened, I would not have purchased it by such a measure, but I considered myself as intrusted with the protection of Hepburn's, a man who, by his humane attentions and devotedness, had so endeared himself to me, that I felt more anxiety for his safety than for my own. Michel had gathered no *tripe de roche*, and it was evident to us that he had halted for the purpose of putting his gun in order, with the intention of attacking us, perhaps while we were in the act of encamping.

I have dwelt upon many circumstances of Michel's conduct, not for the purpose of aggravating his crime, but to put the reader in possession of the reasons that influenced me in depriving a fellow-creature of life. Up to the period of his return to the tent his conduct had been good and respectful to the officers, and, in a conversation between Captain Franklin, Mr. Hood, and myself, at Obstruction Rapid, it had been proposed to give him a reward upon our arrival at a post.   His principles, however, un-supported by a belief in the divine truths of Christianity, were unable to withstand the pressure of severe distress.

On the two following days we had mild but thick snowy weather, and as the view was too limited to enable us to preserve a straight course, we remained encamped amongst a few willows and dwarf pines, about five miles from the tent.   We found a species of *Cornicularia*, a kind of lichen, that was good to eat when moistened and toasted over the fire, and we had a good many pieces of singed buffalo hide remaining.

On the 26th, we resumed our march, which was very painful from the depth of the snow, particularly on the margins of the small lakes that lay in our route.   We fre-quently sunk under the load of our blankets, and were obliged to assist each other in getting up.

Next day we had fine and clear but cold weather. We set out early, and, in crossing a hill, found a considerable quantity of *tripe de roche*.   About noon we fell upon Little Marten Lake, having walked about two miles.   The sight of a place we knew inspired us with fresh vigour, and there being comparatively little snow on the ice, we advanced at a pace to which we had lately been unaccus-tomed.   We encamped within sight of the Dog-rib Rock, and from the coldness of the night and the want of fuel, rested very ill.

On the 28th we rose at daybreak, but from the want of the small fire that we usually made in the mornings to warm our fingers, a very long time was spent in making up our bundles.   This task fell to Hepburn's share, as I suf-fered so much from the cold as to be unable to take my hands out of my mittens.   We kept a straight course for the Dog-rib Rock, but, owing to the depth of the snow in the valleys we **had to cross,** did not reach it till late in the afternoon.   We would have encamped, but did not like to **pass a second** night **without** fire, and though scarcely able to drag our limbs after us, we pushed **on** to a clump of pines about a mile to the southward **of** the rock, and arrived at them in the dusk of **the evening.**   During the last few hundred **yards of our march, our track lay over** some large stones, amongst **which I fell down** upwards of twenty times, and I became at length so exhausted that I was unable to **stand.   If** Hepburn had not exerted himself far beyond his strength, and speedily made the encampment and kindled a fire, I must have perished on the **spot.**   This night we had plenty of dry **wood.**

On the 29th we had clear and fine weather.   We set **out at sunrise and** hurried on in our anxiety **to** reach the house, but our progress was much impeded by the great depth of the snow **in** the valleys.   Although every spot of ground over which we travelled to-day had been repeatedly trodden **by us, yet we got** bewildered on a small lake, and **fancied that we saw the rapid** and grounds about the Fort, **although they were still far distant.   Our** disappointment **when this illusion was** dispelled, so operated on our feeble **minds as to exhaust our** strength, and we decided on encamping ; but upon ascending a small eminence to look for a clump **of wood we** caught a **glimpse of the** Big Stone, a well-known rock upon the **summit of a** hill opposite to the Fort, and determined upon proceeding.   In the evening we saw **several** large herds of **reindeer ;** but Hepburn, who used to be considered a **good** marksman, was now unable to hold the gun straight, **and although** he got near them all his efforts proved fruitless.   **In passing** through a small clump of pines we saw a flock of partridges, and he succeeded in killing one, after firing several shots. We came in sight of the Fort at dusk, and it is impossible to describe our sensations, when, on attaining the eminence that overlooks it, we beheld the smoke issuing from one of the chimneys. From not having met with any footsteps in the snow, as we drew near our once cheerful residence, we had been agitated by many melancholy forebodings. Upon entering the now desolate building we had the satisfaction of embracing Captain Franklin ; but no words can convey an idea of the filth and wretchedness that met our eyes on looking around. Our own misery had stolen upon us by degrees, and we were accustomed to the contemplation of each other's emaciated figures ; but the ghastly countenances, dilated eye-balls, and sepulchral voices of Mr. Franklin and those with him were more than we could at first bear.

Weary and starving, Franklin and his companions had toiled on to Fort Enterprise ; but who can depict their feelings of dismay at finding the houses in ruins and neither food nor Indians ? Still there was a faint hope that aid might arrive in time. A note from Mr. Back informed his commander that he had gone to seek the Indians, and to his energy, bravery, and perseverance, the final deliverance of the remains of the Expedition is mainly due. Regarding his own condition while looking for the Indians, Mr. Back said :—

I was now so much reduced, that my shoulders were as if they would fall from my body, my legs seemed unable to support me, and in the disposition which I then found myself, had it not been for the remembrance of my friends behind, who relied on me for relief, as well as the persons of whom I had charge, I certainly should have preferred remaining where I was, to the miserable pain of attempting to move.

Lieutenant Franklin and those with him at Fort Enterprise kept themselves alive by using skins which had been thrown away during their former wintering there, old bones, and scanty supplies of *tripe de roche*. Franklin undertook the cooking, but being too weak to pound the bones, one of the Canadians agreed to do that in addition to the more fatiguing work of collecting wood. The other two were so debilitated and depressed in spirits that they kept their beds, and scarcely ceased from shedding tears all day.

' We had even to use much entreaty,' wrote Franklin, ' before we prevailed upon them to take the meals we had prepared. Our situation was indeed distressing, but in comparison with that of our friends in the rear we considered it happy. Their condition gave us unceasing solicitude, and was the principal subject of our conversation. We perceived our strength decline every day, and every exertion began to be irksome; when we were once seated, the greatest effort was necessary in order to rise, and we had frequently to lift each other from our seats; but even in this pitiable condition we conversed cheerfully, being sanguine as to the speedy arrival of the Indians.'

Thus terminated a month of unparalleled horrors, endured in patient resignation to the will of God and firm faith in His mercy. Misery and want still encompassed them, but friendly sympathy and mutual aid went far to alleviate their distresses and lengthen out their days, till the Indians, the messengers of life, sent by Mr. Back, arrived.

CHAPTER XII.

FORT ENTERPRISE—DEATH OF THE CANADIANS SEMANDRÈ AND
PELTIER—THE WHOLE PARTY RAPIDLY LOSE STRENGTH—
CONSOLATION FROM RELIGIOUS SERVICES — THEIR MENTAL
POWERS BECOME WEAK—THE INDIANS ARRIVE WITH RE-
LIEF—REACH SLAVE LAKE—LETTER TO MRS. RICHARDSON
—PROCEED TO YORK FORT—THEY ARRIVE IN ENGLAND.

1821-1822.

DR. RICHARDSON immediately began to clear away
the filth which had accumulated in the house, and
aided by Hepburn cut and brought in the wood,
while Mr. Franklin, who was too weak to aid in
these laborious tasks, was employed in searching
for bones and cooking. On November 1, Hepburn's strength was found to be so rapidly failing,
that he was advised by the officers to give up
attempting the pursuit of deer, but try to kill a
few partridges for the Canadians Peltier and
Semandrè, the former of whom died that evening,
the latter early next morning, leaving only one of
the voyageurs in a low and despondent state. In
Franklin's journal are the following affecting en-
tries at this time, which illustrate the courage,

faithfulness to each other, and firm trust in God which carried these brave men through all their trials :—

On the 3rd, the weather was very cold, though the atmosphere was cloudy. This morning Hepburn was affected with swelling in his limbs ; his strength, as well as that of the doctor, was rapidly declining. They continued, however, to be full of hope. Their utmost exertions could only supply wood to renew the fire thrice, and on making it up the last time we went to bed. Our stock of bones was exhausted by a small quantity of soup we made this evening. The toil of separating the hair from the skins, which in fact were our chief support, had now become so wearisome as to prevent us from eating as much as we should otherwise have done.

November 4.—The Doctor and Hepburn, exclusive of their usual occupation, gathered some *tripe de roche*. I went a few yards from the house in search of bones, and returned quite fatigued, having found but three. The doctor again made incisions in Adam's leg (the remaining Canadian), which discharged a considerable quantity of water, and gave him great relief. We read prayers and a portion of the New Testament in the morning and evening, as had been our practice since Dr. Richardson's arrival, and I may remark that the performance of these duties always afforded us the greatest consolation, serving to reanimate our hope in the mercy of the Omnipotent, who alone could save and deliver us.

On the 5th, the breezes were light, with dark, cloudy weather, and some snow. The Doctor and Hepburn were getting much weaker, and the limbs of the latter were now greatly swollen. They came into the house frequently in the course of the day to rest themselves, and when once seated, were unable to rise without the help of one another, or of a stick.   Adam was for the most part in the same low state as yesterday, but sometimes he surprised us by getting up and walking with an appearance of increased strength. His looks were now wild and ghastly, and his conversation was often incoherent.   I observed that, in proportion as our strength decayed, our minds exhibited symptoms of weakness, evinced by a kind of unreasonable pettishness with each other.   Each of us thought the other weaker in intellect than himself, and more in need of advice and assistance.   So trifling a circumstance as a change of place, recommended by one as being warmer and more comfortable, and refused by the other from a dread of motion, frequently called forth fretful expressions, which were no sooner uttered than atoned for, to be repeated perhaps in the course of a few minutes.   The same thing often occurred when we endeavoured to assist each other in carrying wood to the fire; none of us were willing to receive assistance, although the task was disproportionate to our strength.   On one of these occasions, Hepburn was so convinced of this waywardness that he exclaimed, 'Dear me, if we are spared to return to England, I wonder if we shall recover our understanding.'

The long-looked and often prayed for relief at last came.   Mr. Back, after much toil and suffering, found the Indians, and a party left Akaitcho's encampment, on November 5, with a small supply of provisions to enable them to travel quickly. They reached Fort Enterprise on the 7th, bringing deliverance to the faithful band who had long looked together into the valley with the dark

hadows, and, bound together by the endearing
ies of mutual suffering and sympathising aid, were
henceforward to be constant friends and loving
brothers.

The tender nursing of the Indians, and the
powerful medicine of hope, long deferred, at last
realised, enabled them, on November 16, after
having united in prayer and thanksgiving,' to set
out for the hunting ground of the Indian chief,
and to reach Fort Providence, Great Slave Lake,
on December 11. At that post they were kindly
received by the traders of the Hudson's Bay
Company, and had also the happiness of joining
Mr. Back. 'Our feelings,' says Franklin in his
narrative, ' on this occasion can be well imagined.
We were deeply impressed with gratitude to him
for his exertions in sending the supply of food to
Fort Enterprise, to which, under Divine Providence, we felt the preservation of our lives to be
owing.'

The following letter from Dr. Richardson to his
wife is dated Great Slave Lake, April, 1822:—

We left our quarters at Fort Enterprise on the 4th of
June last, and after travelling upon the ice until the beginning of July, embarked on the Coppermine River, and
reached the sea on the 18th of that month. Here the
Indians left us, no promise or hopes of advantage being
sufficient to induce them to encounter the privations and
dangers attendant upon a journey along the coast. Not
withstanding this desertion, we launched our bark canoes

on an icy sea, and commenced our voyage with only fourteen days' provisions. This scanty stock, however, with the
addition of a few deer which **we** killed, and with some
little fastings, lasted until the **25th of** August, when its
total consumption **and the broken state** of the weather
compelled **us to quit the** sea and attempt to cross the
Barren **Grounds. We did** tolerably well, living on the
casual **products of the** chase, until September 4, when we
were surprised **by** the premature appearance of winter, and
from **that day we had** to traverse a country deeply covered
with snow **and** destitute **of** wood. **I** shall not attempt to
describe the miseries we endured in **this** journey, for no
description can convey an adequate idea of them, and the
bare detail would be too harrowing to your feelings. The
deer fled to the south before the unusual inclemency of the
season, and half our party perished through cold, famine,
and fatigue. **The** survivors were found by the Indians on
November **7, and these** savages (as they have been termed)
wept on beholding the deplorable condition to which we
were reduced. They nursed and fed us with the same tenderness they would have bestowed on their own infants,
and, finally, on December **11, conveyed** us to Fort Providence, the nearest **post.**

Let them give thanks **whom the Lord** hath redeemed.
I bless the Almighty Protector **of the universe** that He was
pleased to comfort me under every **trial by the** consolation of
religion. The consciousness of being constantly under His
all-seeing eye, **and for ever an** object of His paternal **care,**
conjoined with His glorious declaration that ' all things work
together for good **to** those **who love** Him,' supported me
under every **trial, and produced** a calmness of mind and
resignation to **His will,** under the prospect of approaching
death, **that I** could not have previously hoped **for.**

We returned to the Coppermine River, nearly opposite Fort Enterprise, about the end of September, and attempted to cross it upon a raft of willows, but wanted the means of impelling it to the other side. To supply this defect, I undertook to swim across with a line, at a time when the temperature of the air was far below freezing point; but my thin, emaciated, and exhausted frame could not withstand the effect of the cold, and I sank before I reached the other side, through an entire loss of power in all my limbs. My companions drew me to the shore with the line, and through their care I was restored to life; and I now mention this circumstance only for the purpose of telling you, that as the waves closed over me, and I was losing the sight of the light of day, as I thought for ever, your happiness and that of my mother was my principal concern, and the last moments of recollection were spent in breathing a prayer for the temporal and eternal welfare of two so deservedly dear to me.

Through the protection of God, I have escaped from still greater dangers than this, and when I reflect upon the astonishing support I received from the habit of addressing myself to Him in every difficulty, I feel that I can never, by the utmost devotion of my future life, sufficiently express my gratitude for His kindness in permitting my heart to be touched with a sense of my duty. If it were possible that any man could remain an infidel in such a situation, how dreadful would his suffering be!

Since my arrival at this post, I have, through plentiful fare, become fatter than ever I was before, and have recovered from every painful effect of my late sufferings; but you must be prepared to behold traces of age upon my face that have been impressed since we parted. This, however, is the common lot of humanity, and I have only taken

I

a sudden **start of you by a** few years ; hereafter I hope **we** shall grow **old together.**

I trust that the navigation **will** open about the end **of** next month, when **we shall proceed to York** Factory, **to** wait for the annual ship, which may be expected in August. The exact time **of** our arrival in England, depending on the weather, is of course uncertain, but it is possible that it **may be in** October, and I trust it may not be protracted beyond the **first week in** November. On **the** subject of where we are to **meet, I** shall write to you **fully in my** first English letter.

Write to my mother **and to my friends in** Edinburgh, and say I am in the land of the living, as I have written to no one but yourself. **May the** God of mercies bless you.

The party remained at Fort Providence about **five months,** awaiting **the** coming **of** spring to **enable** them to **proceed by** Fort Chipewyan to **York Factory, which they** reached on July 14, **1822, having travelled in America, by** land and water, **including the voyage** on the Arctic Sea, a distance of 5,550 miles.

In the month of **October they arrived in** England, **and were** received by **all classes of the** people **with the** enthusiasm which **awaits** conquering heroes, **and with** the **outbursts of** grateful joy which come **from** loving hearts when those dear to **them** have returned from distant wanderings, after having for **a long time** been **given** up and **mourned for as** lost.

CHAPTER XIII.

LETTER FROM MR. HOOD'S FATHER—DR. RICHARDSON'S REPLY
—THE PRAYER OF THE PRINCESS ELIZABETH OF FRANCE—
SPENDS THE WINTER IN LONDON—VISITS DUMFRIES.

1822–1823.

WHEN the expedition arrived in London, Dr. Richardson enjoyed the happiness of meeting his beloved wife, from whose affectionate society he had torn himself within a year of their union.

The touching story of the privations and sufferings which had been heroically endured, during the retreat through the Barren Grounds, from the shores of the Arctic Sea, and at the ruined Fort, deeply moved the hearts of the British people; and the singular generosity of character displayed by Dr. Richardson, combined with his perseverance and success as a naturalist, drew to him many attentions from high quarters.

One of the most grateful recognitions was received from the Rev. Dr. Hood, of Bury, Lancashire, in a touching letter, dated October 22, 1822 :—

Will you permit the father of poor Robert Hood to address you as a friend, and from an overflowing heart retur

I 2

you his most grateful thanks for your extraordinary kindness to his dear son. I am quite overwhelmed with the greatness of my loss and with the suddenness of the manner in which it was communicated to me from a newspaper. Alas! I feared that his frame was not sufficiently robust to encounter the appalling hardships attending on Captain Franklin's expedition, but he would engage in it. To you, my dear sir, I am indebted far more than I can express, for remaining at your own great hazard with my poor Robert along with the faithful Hepburn, and supporting him when his strength failed, and especially for reviving in his mind those principles of religion, which I trust he had never entirely forgotten. From what I understand, I fear that at the time when that abominable villain deprived my poor boy of his precious life, he was so far exhausted as not to have been able to survive until the arrival of relief, even had not that dreadful event taken place. I shall be obliged to you to inform me if this opinion be correct. The dreadful sufferings which he must have endured during the return from the sea-coast made me shudder to think of. In a letter which he wrote me in July 1821, at the mouth of the Coppermine River, he says, that he has no apprehension of want if obliged to return, because Indians were appointed to collect provisions in various parts for the supply of the expedition. Permit me to ask why this did not take place.

Poor fellow, he informed me two years since that 'Dr. Richardson was a very acute and good man.' He little suspected, at that time, how truly good you would prove to him! Oh, sir, my loss is very great, and I am nearly broken-hearted. My dear, dear Robert, the pride of my little family, to whom I looked as a chief source of consolation in my declining years, is lost to me for ever in this life.

But God's will be done! Through the extraordinary kindness of Dr. Richardson, I trust that he will not be lost in the next.

May God bless you and yours, and repay you that for which I am utterly bankrupt.

Your sincere friend,
RICHARD HOOD.

To this letter Dr. Richardson replied :—

October 29, 1822.

REV. SIR,—I received your affecting letter this morning, and sit down immediately to reply to the queries contained in it. My departed friend, I firmly believe, had never suffered the principles of religion to be absent from his mind, and we were throughout the whole course of the expedition deeply indebted to Captain Franklin for the excellent example he set us in the strict and regular performance of his religious duties. But it was during our perilous march across the Barren Grounds that we unbosomed ourselves to each other, and our conversation tended to excite in us mutually a firm reliance on the wisdom and beneficence of the decrees of the Almighty. Our sufferings were never acute during the march, the sensation of hunger ceased after the third day of privation, and with the decay of strength, the love of life also decayed. We could calmly contemplate the approach of death, and our feelings were excited only by the idea of the grief of our relatives. It was of you that your talented son thought and spoke in the latter weeks of his life. When obliged to abandon everything else, he carried a Prayer-book, from which the Service was daily read; and I may add, as every anecdote of such a son is interesting to a father, that he delighted in repeating the beautiful little prayer appended to one of Fénelon's works, the exact title of which I forget, but it is a series of short meditations or homilies for every day in the month.

The grievous disappointment we experienced in not finding the supply of provision at Fort Enterprise, solemnly promised to us by the Indians, arose partly from the natural fickleness of that people, which renders them expert in finding reasons for changing an arrangement however important, but principally from two of their hunters having been drowned by the oversetting of a canoe. As usual on such an occasion, the rest threw away their clothing, broke their guns, and thus by their mode of expressing their grief curtailed themselves of the means of procuring their food.

The extraordinary ability of your now blessed son must appear from every page of Captain Franklin's narrative. His talents shed a lustre upon the expedition. For such a loss I can offer no consolation, but my prayer shall be directed to Him who alone is able to pour balm on the broken heart. With much esteem, I am, reverend sir,

Your very sincere friend,
JOHN RICHARDSON.

The prayer referred to as that which Lieutenant Hood delighted in repeating, is said to have been one of the Princess Elizabeth of France, appended to a work of Fénelon, which, amongst others, had been presented by a lady before the expedition left England. Through the kindness of Mrs. Roe, sister of Mr. Hood, we are able to insert it:—

What may befall me this day, O God, I know not. But I do know that nothing can happen to me which Thou hast not foreseen, ruled, willed, and ordained from all eternity, and that suffices me. I adore Thy eternal and inscrutable

designs.   I submit to them with all my heart through love
to Thee.   I accept all, I make unto Thee a sacrifice of all,
and to this poor sacrifice I add that of my Divine Saviour.
In His name, and for the sake of His infinite merits, I ask
of Thee that I may be endowed with patience under suffering and with the perfect submission which is due to all
which Thou willest or permittest.

Dr. Richardson spent the winter in London,
preparing the papers for Captain Franklin's narrative of the expedition, which was published
early in 1823; and after spending the month of
May with Captain Franklin's friends in Lincoln
and Nottinghamshire, returned to Scotland.

CHAPTER XIV.

DR. RICHARDSON'S RESIDENCE IN EDINBURGH—THE ZOOLOGICAL
APPENDIX TO THE NARRATIVE OF CAPTAIN PARRY'S SECOND
VOYAGE—FRIENDSHIPS—LETTER TO HIS SISTER, MRS. CAR-
RUTHERS—APPOINTED SURGEON TO THE DIVISION OF MARINES
AT CHATHAM.

1823–1824.

TOWARDS the end of November 1823 Dr. Richardson took up his residence in Edinburgh, but few
particulars are known regarding his quiet family
life and occupations during this season of retirement from public duty. In his study he was
actively engaged with the preparation of the
'Zoological Appendix to the Narrative of Captain
Parry's Second Voyage of Discovery, made to the
Polar Seas during 1821, 1822, 1823.' This work,
descriptive of the mammalia and birds, was begun
at the close of 1823 and published early in 1825.
He was also looking forward to another botanical
excursion to America, and lost no opportunity of
making progress in the various branches of natural
history.

One of his nearest neighbours at this time, and

a friend of congenial spirit, was Mr. Francis **Boott**, then studying **medicine at** Edinburgh University. He obtained **his** degree as **doctor in 1824, and** shortly **after settled in London, where** he died **on** December **25, 1863. Dr. Boott** was **a native of** Boston, in **the** United States, where he was born in **1792. He** was an **able physician, but** early retired from practice **to devote himself to his** favourite pursuit, **the** study **of botany. His** 'Illustrations of the Genus Carex' is **a** beautiful **and** valuable work. The friendship formed in Edinburgh between Dr. Richardson **and Dr. Boott was only interrupted** by death. **The sacred** bond **also included Robert** Brown, **the** greatest botanist **of his age, kind of** heart, genial **in** his feelings, **and purely benevo-** lent in his disposition ; **and Sir William Jackson** Hooker, **the** promoter **of** science **and** all **that is** good and enlightening, and many others **remark-** able for **their** learning **and uprightness. On** January **23, 1824,** Richardson **wrote** to Boott :— 'Many thanks, my dear sir, for **the valued** profile of our mutual friend Brown. **It is not** more prized by me as a faithful **resemblance of a man** whom I admire than **as a** memorial **of the kindness and** friendship **of the donor.'**

Mrs. Boott, referring **to the time when the two** families lived opposite **each other in** Edinburgh, says of Dr. Richardson : **'His modest,** unpretend- ing bearing **would** have **led one to infer** that his fame had never extended **beyond his own** doorstep. From the first hour my husband knew him, he was impressed with feelings of deep respect and high admiration, which he continued to cherish through life.

'The Lauriston home was a pleasant, happy, tranquil one, where pleasant and social little parties often assembled. There we met Professor Jamieson and other agreeable people.' Mrs. Boott describes Mrs. Richardson as 'a most gentle, amiable, but very delicate lady, presiding over her house with an attention to all that could render it neat and attractive.'

On December 16, 1823, in announcing to his mother the death of a relative's wife, while her husband and father-in-law were absent in London on business, he adds: 'On how frail a tenure mortal life depends, and with what assiduity ought we to prepare ourselves for our appearance before that Judge who may summon us into his presence to-morrow! "Deep crieth unto deep." I was mourning little Janet's death, and now a dear friend and a mother snatched from a numerous family calls for the most heartfelt sympathy.'

Little Janet was a sister's infant child, the wife of Mr. Charles Carruthers of Mousewald Place, in Annandale. A few days previously he had written to her the following letter :—

My dear Sister,—I sit down to condole with you on the loss of our dear little Janet. The melancholy intelligence came very unexpectedly upon us. I had hoped, indeed, from the last accounts we got, that the poor little innocent was recovering. The sweet-tempered thing was dear to us all, but God in his merciful dispensations often interferes to prevent our relying too much on earthly happiness. He has left us to mourn our loss, but we ought at the same time to adore His goodness. He has taken to Himself a guiltless being, who had experienced only the happy dawn of existence and undergone none of the sorrows which arise in after life from broken affections and still more from the sins which beset the best of us. 'Suffer little children to come unto me,' says our blessed Redeemer, and we should not repine that He has called our darling to the realms of everlasting happiness. Although the decrees of God may, to our finite understandings, be inscrutable, yet we know that the Almighty loves us as a father loves his children, and that He who gave His only begotten Son as a ransom for us, will not afflict us beyond what is good for us.

On January 11, 1824, he wrote to his mother :—

I hope in the course of another year to receive an appointment for collecting objects of natural history in America. The purpose of this appointment, if I succeed in obtaining it, is to enable me to give a full account of the animals and plants within the limits of the Fur Trading Posts, and will be unattended with any hazard. If I go out I shall be absent from this country for two or perhaps three years, but will be resident during all the winter at one or other of the principal posts in the Fur Country, and have to travel in quest of plants only in the summer, and then merely from post to post. The arrangements, however, are not agreed upon, and as they may not eventually take place, I do not wish that my proposal should become public.

He had even then **formed the plan of his** great work, 'The Fauna Boreali—Americana,' and was anxiously longing for an opportunity of completing **the collections necessary** for that undertaking.

In the spring of 1824, the situation of surgeon to **the division of Marines at Chatham** became vacant, and **the prospect of** being appointed to it gave him great **satisfaction,** especially as leave of absence **would be granted for the** necessary time to allow him **to accompany the** contemplated Arctic expedition. He had just returned from a short visit to Dumfries when this occurred, as we find him writing to his mother, from **Edinburgh, on** April 20.

I arrived safely at home and found a notification of an appointment as surgeon of the marine division at Chatham. I shall proceed **in** the course of ten days to London, in **consequence, and enter** immediately upon my duties. The **emoluments are a guinea a-day,** with a house, coals, candles, **and a field-officer's** allowances. **It is a very** good appointment, and **is, I** hope, the earnest **of further** promotion on the staff.

Sir John Barrow's letter must have been, in no ordinary degree, gratifying **to Dr. Richardson.**

Admiralty, **April 17, 1824.**

DEAR SIR,—I have the pleasure to acquaint you that Lord **Melville has** appointed you **to the** Chatham Division of Marines, **and that it** will **not prevent** you from accompanying Franklin, **if so disposed, as** the business may **in your** absence **be done by deputy.**

I am, **dear Sir,** very faithfully yours,

JOHN BARROW.

He lost no time in setting out to his new sphere of duty. On May 4 he is in London, and at the grand fête given by Captain Parry, on board the 'Hecla,' to nearly 500 people of fashion, before beginning his third voyage of discovery. The festivities are described in the Memoirs of Sir W. E. Parry : 'Both ships were gaily dressed out, and the proceedings varied by a concert on board the "Hecla." Several of the best performers of the day, Madame Pasta among the number, had volunteered their services, and seemed to their delighted hearers as really inspired for the occasion, beyond their usual powers of pleasing. As the twilight closed in, a novel and brilliant effect was produced by coloured lamps hung amongst the rigging and along the bulwarks of the vessels.' 'It certainly was,' writes Captain Parry's sister, 'a beautiful sight, and under other circumstances we should have thoroughly enjoyed it.'

A few days later, Dr. Richardson began his duties at Chatham, and for some time was so busily engaged as to have little time for writing letters.

CHAPTER XV.

1825.

CAPTAIN FRANKLIN's **plan** for **his** second expedition, **as laid** before **Government, was** to proceed
to the mouth of the Mackenzie River, and thence,
by sea, along the coast to the north-western extremity of the American continent, on the one
hand, and from the Mackenzie to the Coppermine
on the other. The plan **was** approved, and he
received **orders to** make **the** necessary preparations and **take the** command. Associated with
him **were his** friends Dr. Richardson, Lieutenant
Back, and **Mr. E. N. Kendall,** who **joined** the
party as assistant-surveyor. Mr. Thomas Drummond was assistant naturalist. In addition **to** his
duties as surgeon **and** naturalist, Dr. Richardson
was appointed to survey the coast between the
Mackenzie and Coppermine Rivers, **while** Captain
Franklin was endeavouring to reach Icy Cape.

Every precaution was taken to prevent a recurrence of the disasters which befell the first expedition, and the party sailed from Liverpool for New York on February 12, 1825. From the experience formerly gained, Captain Franklin and the promoters of the journey had been enabled to make arrangements for travelling as rapidly as possible and obtaining sufficient supplies. The position of affairs in the fur trading countries had also assumed a most favourable character.

The Hudson's Bay Company had now amalgamated with the North-West Company, and were carrying on a peaceful commerce throughout the length and breadth of the Fur Countries. The Indians, well-treated and happy, acquiesced in the absence of the 'fire-water,' which was no longer carried to the north, and were beginning to listen to the missionaries, as well as becoming gradually more amenable to the influence of the traders, which has always been beneficial when not perverted by commercial rivalry.

From Liverpool, Dr. Richardson wrote: 'I have only time to inform you of my safe arrival here on Saturday night, and that we sail this morning at ten o'clock, in the "Columbia," New York packet, an excellent vessel with every accommodation. The merchants of Liverpool have paid us the utmost attention, and seem to regret that our stay here is so short that they are not able to show us more.'

After a favourable voyage of twenty-seven days they arrived at New York, and found the season so early and the spring so far advanced as to give them the prospect of a pleasant journey through the interior. The following interesting account of the reception which the party experienced at New York, and of the journey to Great Bear Lake, is in Dr. Richardson's own words :—

At New York we were received with much hospitality, and I may say kindness, by the upper class of citizens. We spent a very agreeable week with them, and in the manners and characters of the friends and acquaintances we made could trace no resemblance to the portraits of the national character drawn by travellers who have lately given their observations to the world. I suspect that few of these flying visitors had an opportunity of studying the habits of the class of people to whom I refer, for although the leading men are accessible enough in their public capacities, the distinction of ranks seems to be preserved in private intercourse more tenaciously in the republican United States than in monarchical Britain. The pride of birth reigns in full sway on this side of the Atlantic, tempered however by good sense and concealed by the veil of good breeding. The higher orders have in fact inherited many feelings from their English ancestors more suitable to a monarchical than to a republican form of government, and possess, particularly the Federal party, a liking to English measures and men which might easily be cherished into a strong attachment.

We left New York in a steam-boat, and proceeded up the River Hudson to Albany, landing, by the way, at West Point, to visit the Military Academy established there on a large scale. The Hudson is a magnificent river, and much of its scenery possesses a grand, almost Alpine character. We were entertained by the Governor of the State, General De Witt Clinton, a polished gentleman of great scientific attainments, and by Van Ranselaer, the proprietor of a county which bears his name. We accompanied the governor to church, and the clergyman, the Rev. Dr. Christie, a presbyterian, prayed in express terms for the success and safety of the expedition.

At Albany, we hired three coaches with four horses each to convey us to Lewistown, a distance of about 420 miles. Our party consisted of five officers, four marines, and Mr. Buchanan, the British consul, who came with us from New York, and accompanied us during our journey through the United States and Upper Canada, facilitating our progress greatly by his intimate knowledge of the route, modes of travelling, and manners of the inhabitants. The American horses are spirited animals, and the coaches very light vehicles, with accommodation for nine passengers in each, so that we had some spare room; but as our luggage was heavy, and the roads extremely deep from the recent breaking up of the winter, it was necessary for the sake of expedition to travel as we did.

Accustomed as we had been to the luxury of an English inn, we found those in the United States inferior. They are, however, equal or superior to the general run of inns on the continent of Europe, and we never suffered from the intrusion of people not of our party, but had always a sitting-room appropriated to our use and separate bedrooms, the size of the inns on this line of route admitting of this accommodation. After we struck off, however, from the great western road to Buffalo, in order to go to Lewistown on the Niagara, we found, as might be expected from the smaller thoroughfare, less accommodation for so large a party.

K

We arrived at one of the smaller inns about midnight after the family had retired to rest, found the door on the latch, and walked in, but experienced some difficulty, as it was a frosty night, in getting the inmates to quit their warm beds to provide us with supper. Mr. Buchanan, however, hit upon an expedient which answered admirably. He sent our Highland piper into the long passage leading to the bed-rooms, and he had not marched twice along it to the tune of the 'Gathering of the Clans,' before the landlord, his wife, and five or six female attendants, hurried forth. They took all this in good part, said it was delightful music, cooked some ham for our supper, with their usual expedition, and spread clean sheets on the beds which they had left, and which on our retiring to them we found still warm. The bed-rooms we got were the best in the house, and the good people, in resigning them to us, most probably shifted but poorly themselves for the remainder of the night. In travelling through the newly-settled States, particularly in the spring, ham is almost the only article of provision that can be got. It has the advantage, however, of being cooked in a very short time. The moment we arrived at an inn, the spacious frying-pan was placed on the large wood fire, and we never had occasion to wait above twenty minutes for dinner or supper.

At another inn we witnessed a rather amusing display of that boisterous attachment to equality which is so often mistaken for liberty by those who have nothing at stake and who know nothing about the matter. After we had taken possession of our seats in the coaches and were about to drive off, a man made a show of seating himself beside us, but was told by the driver that they were not stage coaches, being hired for the sole use of the party that occupied them. One of the dram-drinkers, of whom there are always several lounging at the door of an inn, observed that in a free country we had no right to engage more seats than we could fill, nor to prevent a citizen from taking a vacant one. This observation was not made directly to us but to one of the bystanders, who answered that if we were extravagant enough to pay for what we did not use, no person in a free country had a right to prevent us. This produced a rejoinder, and when we drove off they seemed inclined to decide by blows the cause of liberty of opinion.

In the meantime, the gentleman who wished to ride with us had quietly taken a seat beside the driver. As this was done without permission, Mr. Buchanan desired him to come down. He did so, and approaching the coach door, said to the Consul in a humble tone, ‘Governor, will you permit me to go only twelve miles to see my wife and family?’ His request was now complied with, but on reaching his destination he walked off without even bidding us good night.

From Lewistown we crossed the Niagara to Queenstown, on the Canada side, and went about seven miles up the river to visit the celebrated falls. Many have endeavoured to describe them, and I think with very little success. I shall not make a new attempt, but merely remark that notwithstanding all I had read on the subject, and the various drawings I had seen, the grandeur of the scene far exceeded my previous conceptions of it. On comparison with this all the other cataracts which I have seen dwindle into perfect insignificance. It is a stupendous monument of the power of the Creator of the universe, who wields at will an element that mocks the utmost strength of man.

From Niagara we proceeded to Fort George, situated on Lake Ontario, at the influx of the river, and crossing the lake landed at York, the capital of Upper Canada. After spending twenty-four hours at this place, we proceeded in carts by miserable **roads** and through a **thinly** settled country to Lake Simcoe, which we crossed, and descending the Natawasaga River **to Lake Huron, arrived in** a few days at Penetanguishene, a naval depot, situated **in** one of the bays of the lake. The most advanced Canadian settlements approach Penetanguishene, but the cleared spots are mere **patches in the** desert, and the roads **by** which they communicate are only in some instances passable for horses, being for the most part **only to be traced by an** Indian or experienced backwoodsman. **It is in** this quarter that the Canadian Company have purchased from Government the **reserves,** and I have no doubt **but** that through their exertions it will be completely settled in a few **years.**

At Penetanguishene we were joined **by** twenty-four Canadian voyageurs from Montreal, and on April 23, the whole party embarked in two large canoes, which, together **with some stores,** had been forwarded from Lower **Canada the** preceding season. In these canoes we coasted Lakes Huron and Superior, and arrived **at** Fort William on May **10,** having suffered **a few days' detention,** partly from **ice** but principally from high **winds.**

Fort William, previous to the union with the Hudson's Bay Company, was **the** principal depot of the north-west traders. Here we exchanged our large canoes for four smaller ones adapted **to river** navigation, and separating into two parties, Captain Franklin and I pushed forward in a partially laden canoe, whilst Messrs. Back, Kendall, and Drummond followed with the stores. We arrived on **June 15 at** Cumberland House, which was our wintering quarters the **first year** on our former journey, and it **was** also the residence, during last winter, of our seamen, who, with three boats and some stores under their charge, **left** England **in June 1824, in the** Hudson's Bay ship.

They resumed their voyage this season **on June 2,** and we overtook them on the 29th of the same month, **in** time to assist them in reaching and crossing the height **of** land which **separates the waters flowing towards Hudson's** Bay from those which fall into the Arctic **Sea. Owing to** the unusual dryness **of the** season, we experienced **much** difficulty in launching **the boats through the small streams** leading to and from this portage, which is named the **Methy** carrying-place, and particularly through **the small Methy** River, which is nearly thirty miles **long, and, this season,** nowhere offered sufficient **water to float the boats, ex-** cept in small pools **with** long almost **dry fords inter-** vening. **We had, in** consequence, **to carry the cargoes** nearly the whole way, either partially or entirely **through** swamps, from which at every step the mosquitoes assailed us in myriads. The carrying-place itself is **twelve miles** long over a high ridge **of** sand hills, and here the boats **were** partly carried on men's shoulders **and** partly **launched the** entire distance. Having completed this tedious and labo- rious operation, during which a considerable number of men **were disabled by swellings** of the legs, we descended **the** Athabasca River, and **reached Fort Chipewyan, on the** Lake of the Hills, on July 15. **By referring to** Mac- kenzie's Voyages, you will **perceive that it was from** this post that that enterprising **traveller set out** on June 3, 1789, on **that** memorable **voyage to the Arctic** Sea, in which he discovered and **navigated the river** that bears his name, and opened up **to the** fur trade **a** large tract of productive country.

It was necessary for Captain Franklin to remain at Fort Chipewyan until the **arrival of Mr.** Back, in order that he might discharge such **of the** Canadian voyageurs as were to **return to Canada** this **season, and** to make other arrangements; but that the boats, which were now four in number, an additional one having been borrowed from the Company and heavily laden with upwards of two tons of pemmican besides other stores, might be no cause of delay after the arrival of the canoes, I went on with them on July 21. The canoes, under Messrs. Back and Kendall, arrived at Chipewyan on the 23rd. Drummond was left at Cumberland House, to enable him to botanize on the Saskatchewan. On the 25th, Captain Franklin, having sent back a canoe with the voyageurs whose services were no longer needed, set out after me with the remaining three canoes. The boats reached Slave Lake on July 26, only two days later than we arrived at the same place, on the second year of our former journey, in canoes: a difference in speed attributable solely to our acquaintance with the route and mode of travelling and the previous arrangements so carefully made by Captain Franklin. After passing two days under the hospitable roof of Mr. McVicar, who was so kind to us after our former sufferings, I set out again, and coasting the southern shore of Great Slave Lake, entered the Mackenzie. The current of this stately river swept us rapidly along, and on August 3, we arrived at Fort Simpson, situated on the influx of the River of the Mountains, and at seven in the morning of the 6th, landed at Fort Norman, about 200 miles farther down. These two posts are thirteen days of winter travelling apart. At Fort Norman I left a portion of the stores, a boat and a select crew for Captain Franklin, and going on with the remainder ascended the current of Bear Lake River, which joins the Mackenzie about thirty miles below Fort Norman. Bear Lake River has a rapid current, the voyage down it being performed in eight or nine hours, while its ascent occupies three or four days. It is seventy-six miles long. We arrived at Fort

Franklin, then in progress of erection, on August 10. Mr. Dease, a chief trader of the Hudson's Bay Company, who had come down with a party of men in the month of June to make preparation for us, did not expect to see us before September 25. Captain Franklin and his party reached Fort Norman the day after I left it, and sending Mr. Back up with the canoes and stores, he and Mr. Kendall proceeded down the river in the boat with a crew of seven men, including the Esquimaux interpreter. On the third day they passed Fort Good Hope, in latitude 67° 28′, the last of the Company's posts, and in three days more reached the sea. The river flows into the sea through many channels, separated by low deltas, which are mostly covered by spring floods. Whale Island of Mackenzie, the limit of his voyage, is one of the outermost of these deltas, but it is surrounded by the fresh water of the river, and it was not until the boat had approached Garry's Island, thirty miles seaward, that the clear salt water was perceived, separated from the muddy waters of the river by a well-defined line. Captain Franklin landed on Garry's Island exactly six months from the date of sailing from England, and it will excite the sympathy of his friends to learn that he then displayed for the first time a silk flag sewed by his lamented wife in her last illness, and delivered with a presentiment, alas too true, that they were never to meet again in this world. Garry's Island lies in latitude 69° 29′ and longitude 135° 41′ west, and from its summit they saw many white and black whales and seals.

After remaining a day for the purpose of making astronomical observations and enjoying the contemplation of a sea clear of ice, they set out on their return, and arrived at Fort Franklin on September 6. During their absence we had given that name to our winter abode. They saw several Esquimaux encampments recently deserted, but were not so fortunate as to find any of the people of that nation. Presents, however, of iron work were left at their huts, and we have had the satisfaction of learning in the course of this winter, through the medium of the Sharp Eyes who frequent Fort Good Hope, that these presents were found by the people for whom they were intended, and have inclined them strongly in our favour. The expedition travelled, from the date of our leaving New York, March 26, till our reunion at Fort Franklin on September 6, including a survey of the north side of Bear Lake, which I made in Captain Franklin's absence, 5,160 miles, of which 596 were through the United States and the settlements in Upper Canada. We shall resume our labours as soon as the rivers are clear of ice, which will be towards the end of June. At present the whole party are in good health and high spirits, and sanguine as to their expectations of success.

CHAPTER XVI.

THE EXPEDITION AT PENETANGUISHENE, ON LAKE HURON—
TIDINGS OF MRS. FRANKLIN'S DEATH—AN EARLY SEASON—
MANNER OF TRAVELLING—NUMBER OF THE PARTY—THE MAC-
KENZIE RIVER—WINTER AMUSEMENTS AT FORT FRANKLIN—
DOG-RIB INDIANS—A WOLF—BIRTH OF A CHILD—DINNER ON
THE OCCASION—A BALL.

1825–1826.

WE have given Dr. Richardson's lucid account of the progress of the party until they settled down for the winter at Fort Franklin, on Great Bear Lake. A few extracts from letters which he wrote from the stations at which the expedition halted, supply additional information. On April 22, 1825, they are at Penetanguishene, on Lake Huron, and he writes :—

This is the most advanced naval post on the lakes, and the establishment consists of a lieutenant, assistant-surgeon, and five men, with a military detachment of an officer and twenty men. The assistant-surgeon and military officer are married to English ladies, who reside here amongst the woods. The most advanced settlers, in Upper Canada, are within a few miles

I had written thus far when an express arrived with letters for Captain Franklin, conveying the melancholy tidings of Mrs. Franklin's death. Although this event was in some measure expected, it has cast a gloom over the party, and it will be long before Captain Franklin regains his usual flow of spirits. He bears his great loss with Christian resignation, but he will feel it more acutely when he returns to his desolate mansion in Devonshire Street. The exertion necessary for carrying on the expedition will occupy his mind for the present.

From Fort William, Lake Superior, he wrote :—

Every exertion is being made in the interior to provide abundance of provision on our route, and all the accounts we have received are highly satisfactory, so that, compared with our last journey, this promises to be a party of pleasure. The season is unusually early, and we have arrived here more than a month sooner than canoes loaded like ours have ever done, and nearly a fortnight before any of the light canoes for thirty years past. This gives us great hopes of arriving in very good time at our winter quarters.

Of his companions he remarks : ' Mr. Back you know already ; Mr. Kendall is an exact picture of Captain Franklin, in size, face and temper ; Drummond is the most indefatigable collector of specimens of natural history I have ever seen.'

From Lake Winnipeg, on June 6, 1825, he mentions that he and Captain Franklin were pushing forward in order to overtake the boats sent out from England in 1824, and adds :—

As it may be amusing to you to know something of our mode of travelling, I shall note down some of the details.

At two o'clock, or half-past two if the morning is dark, Captain Franklin or myself call the guide, who, if the weather will permit him to proceed, awakens the men. They are on their legs in an instant, and every man marches to the beach with his blanket under his arm. Part of them put the canoe into the water and load her, whilst others take down our tent, and roll up the bedding, in which operation we assist. In twenty minutes, or at the longest half an hour, we are all embarked; and the men, after their morning dram, which on this voyage we have always had in our power to give them, strike up a cheerful song and paddle away vigorously at the rate of about four miles an hour. Every half-hour they lie on their paddles for about two minutes to rest a little and light their pipes; hence these pauses are termed by them *pipes*. At nine o'clock, we put ashore to breakfast. My occupation is to strike a light, and I therefore jump ashore at once with my fire-bag in my hand. Captain Franklin brings a handful of dry twigs, or grass, or a piece of birch-bark. Two of the men fetch dry wood; a fire is speedily kindled; our servant, who in the meantime had been filling the kettle, hangs it to the *trépied* or tripod—three sticks, which another man has by this time tied together and set up. Others of the party are employed in landing the canteen and basket, containing the cold meat, bread, tea, sugar, tea-cups, plates, &c., and a piece of painted canvas being spread, every thing is put in order. In about a quarter of an hour after landing, the kettle boils and the tea is made. Another quarter suffices Captain Franklin and myself to swallow it. The guide and servant, who have been employing their mouths as well as their hands, drink a sip of tea, wash the dishes, and pack them up again. The whole business is generally finished in three-quarters of an hour. Whilst we are at breakfast the cook of the day warms the men's pemmican, and they generally use so much greater despatch, as to get a two minutes' nap in the sun.

After breakfast we proceed as before, paddling and alternately singing and smoking. At three o'clock a *pipe*, somewhat longer than usual, affords the men time to take a mouthful or two of pemmican, and we lunch. At eight o'clock, we put ashore for the purpose of encamping, and use the same despatch as at breakfast. Whilst the crew are unloading, Captain Franklin and I light the fire. As soon as the baggage is secured and covered with painted canvas, the canoe is landed and turned up. Some of the men bring wood, and others pitch the tent. For supper, we have tea, cold meat, eggs, cheese, butter, &c., according to the state of our larder. The men also boil their kettle and chat a little while they are waiting for it. After supper, we spread our beds, the servant makes a good fire, hangs on a kettle with provisions for the morrow, and retires to rest. The men's kettle is hung up at the same time, and if the night is likely to prove rainy they sleep under the canoe; if fine, on the softest turf that is near. After a hard day's work they are all asleep within little more than an hour from the time of landing. As we sleep sometimes in the canoe during the day, we do not go to bed till ten or eleven. Sixty miles is considered a good day's journey, but two days ago we travelled about eighty, having paddled all night. This is frequently done when crossing a lake, as the men rest when detained by wind.

From Fort Chipewyan he wrote, on July 20 :—

The gentlemen of the country have everywhere exerted

themselves in providing for our party, and we have found at the different posts various luxuries set aside for ourselves.

The present crews of the boats are eighteen men. Mr. Dease, the gentleman employed in building our winter residence and laying up provisions for us, has fourteen more, exclusive of his wife and four children, the interpreter, his wife and children, so that, with the officers and their servants, our party, during the winter, will consist of fifty souls. For even a larger number the lake furnishes an abundant supply of fish. We expect to reach Bear Lake about August 18 or 20—in ample time to commence the autumn fishery and make ourselves snug before the setting in of the winter. We have hitherto come on well and pleasantly, and our prospects for the future look bright. This letter will be sent by a return canoe, and may perhaps reach you this season. My next, written from Slave Lake, is not likely to come to hand before next autumn, so that you have a long interval of silence to look forward to. It is nothing, however, to the anxiety and delay I am doomed to suffer, for your letters written within a month of my leaving England cannot reach me till the beginning of next summer, and your reply to this will meet me on my return.

At Fort Norman, a few miles from the junction of Great Bear Lake River with the Mackenzie, he wrote :—

The Mackenzie River is a magnificent stream, deep enough to float a first-rate man-of-war, and from one to ten miles broad, according as it is free or crowded with islands. The current is very rapid and we descend it cheerily. As far as we have come the country is pleasant, in some spots picturesque, and everywhere well wooded. Our winter

quarters this year will not be so far north as Fort Enterprise, and every account we have received represents Bear
Lake and its environs as abounding in fish and game. Two
of our men who went with Mr. Dease this spring and have
come down to meet us, state that, at the time they came
away, from 100 to 500 fish of good quality were taken in
the nets daily.

From their winter quarters at Bear Lake, he
wrote to his mother, on September 6 :—

I have the satisfaction of informing you that after six
months of constant but pleasant travelling, we have arrived
here, by the blessing of God, in perfect safety and with a
large stock of provisions and stores.   Our house was nearly
completed on our arrival, and as we have plenty of carpenters and smiths it will shortly be put in excellent order.
Our fishing yields daily thirty or forty large trout weighing
from twenty to fifty pounds each, and we have abundance
of venison at a short distance, so that we look forward to
good cheer throughout our stay in this quarter.   There
are five officers of us, including Mr. Dease, the Hudson's
Bay gentleman, who had charge of our men previous to
our arrival, so that we do not want for society. The greater
part of our men, amounting in all to twenty-five, are
Scotchmen, and very well behaved.   To amuse them we
have a bagpiper and a violin, and intend to be merry as
well as comfortable.   The kindness of my Chatham friends
provided me with a fine large blanket of worked worsted,
which I have got safe here, and find quite a luxury.   Margaret's bottle of pickles and that of Cayenne pepper have
also crossed all the carrying-places in safety, and I intend
to open them, together with a bottle of cherry brandy from
Chatham, on Christmas Day.

I have been about 200 miles along Bear Lake since my arrival, found plenty of rein-deer, and came back to the house with a boat-load of provision. Captain Franklin, with another party, has been down to the sea, which is about eight days' journey from this. There were many deer on the coast, some of which he killed, and he saw no ice. He returned yesterday. Everything has favoured us in our progress hitherto. We have met with much attention at the different posts, and the country where our winter residence is fixed is well wooded and abounds in provision. From what Captain Franklin saw in his journey, he is in high hopes of success next season, so that perhaps we may not see each other after parting next summer till we meet in England. If he reach the ship sent out to meet him in Behring's Straits, it is not likely that he will return to this station. I hope to hear from you by the Hudson's Bay ship which sails in May, although the letters will not reach me till spring; and trust that they will bring intelligence of the health and happiness of all the family. Give my kind love to them all and to Mr. and Mrs. Carruthers. The latter I hope will write and give me a detail of the doings in her neighbourhood—how the farmers thrive, and whether the miller's wife rejoices in the clack of the mill—what enterprising young man of her acquaintance has not thriven because his wife would not let him—in short, all the gossip of Mousewald. If she would add a little spice of the transactions on the high road to Caerlaverock so much the better, as I do not find my correspondents in that quarter over communicative. Do not let her or any of the family who are kind enough to favour me with a few lines stand upon the punctilio of being first written to. It was only to-day that Captain Franklin decided to send a despatch with an account of his discoveries. **The** messenger departs to-morrow, and as I have official letters to write, **I** have not time for many private communications, and must make one letter serve for **several.**

His letters from Fort Franklin are full of cheerful sayings for the loved ones at home, whose hearts were **beating anxiously lest the** disasters of the former **journey should be repeated.** The second **expedition, however,** was **not marred by** misfortunes or **privations. Mrs. Carruthers,** from whom **he hoped** to get all **the** harmless tittle-tattle of the agricultural parish **of Mousewald,** in Annandale, and **some account of** the family at Rosebank, his mother's residence, **was** the sister Margaret whose pickles and Cayenne pepper were to season their white-fish dinner at Christmas.

The following **letter** to her **not only** gives a **glimpse of the** life **at Great Bear Lake,** but of the **kindly, loving, and cheerful disposition** of his mind :—

Fort Franklin, February 6, 1826.

MY DEAR SISTER,—I received your letter of May **1,** 1825, **on the 1**6th of last month, and am much obliged by your kind **remembrance.** Intelligence from home is most gratifying **in this remote quarter,** and **the disappointment of** not having **tidings** by **every** opportunity proportionately severe. Your letter was a great gratification **to me.**

Before leaving London, Captain Franklin's portrait and **mine were** taken by Mr. Philips, one of the first artists in **that** city, and I observe by the newspapers which we have received that they have been **hung up at the annual ex-**hibition of the Royal Academy, **and much admired for** the style of painting and correctness **of the likenesses.**

The people in England seem to be going **mad about** railroads, **tunnels, steam-engines, air-engines, mines, and** diving-bells, **and I suppose the mania would extend to** Scotland, **if there were cash** enough in that —— country to play the fool with. **Fill up the** blank which I have left according to your taste, **as I could not, on the spur of the** moment, **hit upon an epithet that at** once expressed the romantic **attachment which a** Scotchman, **in his wanderings,** feels towards the land of his birth, conjoined _with_ the canny wisdom which prevents **her from following the** vagaries of her flaunting sister of the **south.   An English**man, 'foul fa' the loon,' has the impudence **to call the land** of the mountain and flood, a 'beggarlie **countrie,' which** puts me quite **out of** humour and ends my theme, **and I** do not know what **subject to turn to next.   Take a few of** our occurrences.

On the 26th ultimo, **the party of Dog-Ribs that have** been encamped **for some time on the borders of** the lake, struck their huts and moved off in search of a better hunt-ing-ground.   Nothing remarkable occurred upon this move-ment except that the women, owing to the late scarcity of provisions in the **tribe, had not above two hundred** weight each to drag, **and that none of the men made** their wives **drag them, although the sledges were so light,** and only **three feet of snow on the land.   The women** per-formed the march well, and with **very** little beating. When the party set out, **it** was observed that the **young** and beautiful lady of that distinguished leader, Long-legs, remained behind.   This highly-accomplished female arrived **as the** party were encamping in **the evening,** dragging her

L

sledge, and bearing on her back a son and heir of her illustrious lord, of whom she had safely delivered herself in the morning. **Mrs.** Long-legs, with her usual activity and adroitness, erected the lodge for her lord and master, cut the fire-wood, and made the fire before the other females had accomplished their tasks.

On Sunday last, a large black wolf caught a beautiful silver fox in sight of the Fort. He was instantly pursued by two Esquimaux on snow shoes, but notwithstanding the hue and cry was duly raised, the felon escaped.

This day an audacious robbery was committed at noon by a wolf, perhaps the villain whose misdeed we have mentioned, and who has been observed prowling in the purlieus of Fort Franklin for some days. He attacked the fish sledge drawn by two dogs, which had been daily in the habit of coming from the fishery without a driver. He took out fourteen fish, nine of which he ate upon the spot, but the remainder, which he hid amongst the snow, were recovered. He did not molest the dogs. It is conjectured that this robbery was committed under the pressure of hunger. The 'Gazette' of this evening offers a reward for his apprehension, and we have no doubt of our very active police speedily giving a good account of him.

We are glad to learn that the fisheries established on Great Bear Lake proved tolerably productive last season. During the months of July, August, September, and October, 18,256 white fish, weighing on an average two and a half pounds, were caught, and 1,843 trout, from fifteen to forty pounds each. The daily rations of the establishment of Fort Franklin amount to 220 white fish.

Last Tuesday, the lady of Peter Warren Dease, Esq., chief trader of the Hudson's Bay Company, resident at Fort Franklin, was safely delivered of a daughter.

A party of friends met to celebrate this event. They sat down in the grand hall of the **Fort** to a sumptuous entertainment, comprising all the luxuries of the season. At the head of the table, there was a large dish of white fish excellently boiled; at the bottom, a dish of equal magnitude, of white fish, roasted; and on each side a tureen full of white fish soup. Owing to the mice having eaten the flour, no **bread was** sported on this joyous occasion, but the place of that unattainable luxury and of vegetables of every description was amply supplied by a bottle of delicious bird-peppers. The travels of this bottle might furnish an interesting article.

During the long winter, the spirits of the party were kept up by cheerful amusements and regular employment. Here is an amusing description of a ball :—

We had a ball on the Monday after Christmas, and another on the second day of the New Year, attended by all the rank and fashion of Bear Lake. First in dignity shone the lady of Peter Warren Dease, Esq., chief trader of the Hudson Bay Company and superintendent of the Post; next came Madame Savante, her sister, the lady of Felix, the voyageur; and thirdly, Wabisca the Fat, who styles Boileau the Interpreter, lord and master. These three, alike in manners and in grace, were the matrons of the feast. The two lovely, though little, Misses Dease and Miss Boileau also graced the ball with their presence. There were also some Indian dames, decorous spectators of the scene, their raven hair dripping with unguents prepared from the marrow of the reindeer, and their expanded countenances ornamented with twin rows of ivory teeth, gracefully contrasting with their lovely bronze features whereon streaks of lampblack and rouge were harmoniously blended.

Nor were the beaux, of whom thirty figured in the dance, less worthy of renown. There were who came from the farthest Shetland, where the Romans heard the sun hiss as he set in the sea; and her sister Orkney also sent forth her hardy sons, along with the red-haired Celts from Ross, Inverness, and the Island of Isla, the eastern and western extremities of the Highlands; Caithness and Sutherland contributed their quota, and the lowlands and borders did not want representatives there. The sons of Chalk-girt Albion also came; from coaly Northumbria, and southern tin-producing Cornwall, they came; from Yorkshire, skilled in horses; Cheshire, renowned for cheese; and Lincoln-shire for fens; from Kent, the land of hops; Bedford, of lace; and Leeds, town of smoke, they came. Canada also sent forth her children; the descendants of the light-heeled race of France; and the red sons of the desert, and seal-pursuing Esquimaux, stayed not away. Such and so various were the nations that came, and

> Much we marvelled Bear Lake's strand
> Could marshal forth such various band.

And many times we plyed the flagons filled with odorous punch and rosy wine, until the head growing heavier than the heels, we retired to needful repose.

Playfully he requests his sister not to send any niggardly sheets of Bath post, but a full flowing sheet of foolscap, written in a close, neat hand, and crossed with red ink if she pleased.

Tell me who has got married, who is to be married, and

who ought to be married in Annandale, for, although I
hate scandal, there is nothing so amusing as a gossiping
letter; it brings to remembrance so many persons and
things of bygone times.

Adieu, my dear Sister,
Ever yours affectionately,
JOHN RICHARDSON.

P.S. The wolf has been killed, and I intend to send its
skin home to the British Museum.

CHAPTER XVII.

PREPARATIONS FOR THE SUMMER EXCURSIONS—THEY DESCEND
THE MACKENZIE—CAPTAIN FRANKLIN ADVANCES TOWARDS
ICY CAPE—DR. RICHARDSON PROCEEDS EASTWARDS TO THE
MOUTH OF THE COPPERMINE RIVER—THE PARTIES RETURN
TO BEAR LAKE—ENGLAND.

1826–1827.

WITH the approach of summer, everything was
got in readiness for another advance towards the
Arctic Sea. On June 12, the Doctor wrote to Mrs.
Richardson :—

This spring has been unusually fine, and fully a fortnight
earlier than it was at Fort Enterprise in 1821. We have
been abundantly supplied with provisions of late, and have
a good stock in store for summer use. Another excellent
boat has been built here, in addition to the three brought
from England, so that I shall have two boats with me in the
summer excursion. Captain Franklin and Mr. Back go to
the westward with a party of thirteen men, also in two
boats, one of which is the new one. They hope to meet
Captain Beechy, in the 'Blossom,' at Behring's Straits, or
even on this side of Icy Cape, in which case they will return
to England by China and the East Indies. If they do not
see the 'Blossom,' or do not get to Icy Cape before a certain
date, they will return to this post and to England in the

summer of **1827. Mr.** Kendall **and I go to the** eastward towards the Coppermine **River,** and if **the Indian report of** Captain Parry's ships wintering in that **quarter be correct,** we shall **most** probably enjoy **the great** gratification **of** meeting them, **and shall** then return to the Mackenzie **River,** where we **will leave them** and proceed **home by way of** Hudson's **Bay or Canada,** wintering either **at** this **post or** Great Slave **Lake. If we do not see** Captain **Parry, we** shall come to Fort Franklin **by way** of the Coppermine River; and that we may travel as comfortably **as** possible, a party of Canadians and **Indians are** appointed to meet us at the other **end of this lake, which** is within two days' march **of the** Coppermine, **and reach** England **in October,** 1827, **with** Captain Franklin, if **he** come this **way.**

We **have** everything which **we could desire to render** our voyage agreeable. The **men** are **in high** spirits **and** eager to set out. **My party** are all English, except Uligbuck, an Esquimaux. Captain Franklin **has two Canadians in** his crew, and Augustus, the Esquimaux, who formerly ac-companied him. The boats are excellent of their kind and completely equipped. **In short,** we can never be sufficiently **grateful to Providence for the** favourable **aspect** of **our** affairs. **Both parties are** instructed to commence **their** return **on or before August 15th or 20th to avoid any** hazard **whatever.**

Vegetation **is** making **rapid strides at present, as well it** may at a **season** when **the sun** scarcely sets. **We see his** beams over the trees at half-past **ten** in **the evening, and I can** lie in bed at midnight and read the smallest print by the light which passes through our parchment **windows.** Many plants are already **in** flower, and the mosquitoes become troublesome. **I set out to-morrow to** examine the tracks on the borders of Bear Lake **River.** Captain Franklin follows with the boats and the rest of the party on the 22nd. We shall be three days at Fort Norman, taking in provisions and making other arrangements, and will stop a day at Fort Good Hope in our way down the river, the date of arrival on the sea-coast being settled for July 5th or 6th, when we hope the ice will be breaking up. Everything wears a favourable aspect, and trusting in the all-powerful protection of the beneficent Ruler of the Universe, who has hitherto sustained us, we hope to return successful and in safety. May the same Omnipotent Being guard and protect you, my dearest Mary, shall ever be the prayer of your affectionate husband.

On June 25, the expedition reached Fort Norman, and, after having taken in additional stores, set out for the sea. At the expansion of the Mackenzie River, where the different channels branch off, Captain Franklin encamped to make the necessary arrangements for the separation of the parties. The evening was spent in kindly intercourse with each other.

'We felt,' says Franklin, 'that we were only separating to be employed on services of equal interest, and we looked forward with delight to our next meeting, when after a successful termination we might recount the incidents of our respective voyages. The best supper our means afforded was provided, and a bowl of punch crowned the parting feast.

'By six in the morning of the 4th, the boats were all laden and ready for departure. It was impossible not to be struck with the difference between our present complete state of equipment and that on which we embarked on our former disastrous **voyage**. Instead of a frail bark canoe, and a scanty supply of food, we were now about to commence the sea voyage in excellent boats, stored with three months' provision. At Dr. Richardson's desire the western party embarked first. He and his companions saluted us with three hearty cheers, which were warmly returned; and as we were passing round the point that was to hide them from our view we perceived them also embarking.'

Captain **Franklin** despatched Dr. **Richardson** on this special **service, in accordance with his instruc**tions from **Earl Bathurst, and before setting out** to the **westward, delivered to him a letter in which** he says :—

I am directed, if I should have been able to accumulate at the mouth of the Mackenzie River stores and provisions sufficient, to despatch Dr. Richardson with Mr. Kendall and five or **six** men in one of the boats to examine the intermediate coast between the Mackenzie and Coppermine Rivers.

The present amount of stores and provisions happily affords me the means of fulfilling his lordship's directions ; and as there might be some insecurity in a party going in one boat along this portion of the coast, and it would not contain sufficient provision for the voyage, I have caused another boat to be built at Bear Lake in anticipation of being able to furnish two for this service.

You are therefore hereby directed to **take under your** charge Mr. Kendall and the ten men appointed to accompany you, and to proceed in the ' Dolphin ' and ' Union ' to examine the coast between the Mackenzie and Coppermine Rivers; and on reaching the latter, you are to leave the boats and proceed with **your party to the** Portage road, which communicates with that part of Great Bear Lake that you visited last autumn and named **Dease** River.

Captain **Franklin** proceeded westward as far as Return Reef, more than a thousand miles distant from Fort Franklin. Dr. Richardson's party, doubling **Cape** Bathurst and Cape **Parry,** and passing through **the** Dolphin and Union **Strait,** between **Wollaston Land and Cape** Krusenstern, reached the Coppermine River, **thus** connecting the discoveries made during the former expedition, to **the** eastward in Coronation **Gulf,** with those of **Captain** Franklin, on this occasion, **to** the westward of the Mackenzie. These surveys, conjoined **with** Captain Beechy's, defined the northern outline **of the** American Continent from Behring's Straits eastwards, through sixty degrees of longitude, with **the** exception of 160 miles adjacent to Point Barrow, **which** remains unexplored.

Dr. Richardson's party **arrived** at the mouth **of** the Coppermine River, **on August 8, and** the following day ascended **as far** as Bloody Fall, where **the** boats were drawn up and abandoned. They **then commenced their** march along **the** bank of **the river to its bend** at the Copper Mountains, and **thence** straight across the **hills in the** direction of **the mouth of** Dease River, **which was** reached on August **18. 'On** Sunday, **the** 20th,' says Dr. Richardson, 'prayers were read, and thanks returned to **the** Almighty **for** His gracious protection and the success which had attended our voyage.'

Several days of anxiety were passed here, the party from **Fort Franklin** not having arrived **with** the boat, **and to walk round** Great Bear **Lake,** a distance **of 300 miles, would have entailed much** fatigue **and suffering, and could not have been** accomplished **in less than three weeks.   On the** evening **of the 24th, the boat and several** canoes made their appearance, and the expedition reached the Fort on September 1, **having travelled, by** land and water, **1,980** statute miles **in** seventy days.

The western party **arrived** on September **21,** having travelled 2,048 statute miles, of which **610** were through parts not previously known.   Meantime Dr. Richardson, eager **to** extend his geological researches, as far as the season would permit, had gone in a canoe **to the** Great Slave Lake, after having written a **despatch for** Captain Franklin :—

Fort Franklin, Great Bear Lake, September 4, 1826.

Sir,—I have the **honour to acquaint** you that **in** pursuance of your order, I proceeded **with** a detachment **of** the expedition to examine the coast **between the Mackenzie** and the **Coppermine Rivers.**

After separating from you **on** July 4, we pursued **the** easternmost channel of the Mackenzie until the 7th **of that** month, when finding that **it** distributed itself by various outlets, of which the more easterly were not navigable **for** our boats, we chose a middle one, and that night got into brackish water with **an** open **view of the sea in** latitude 69° 29′ north, and longitude 133° 24′ **west.**   On the **11th, in** latitude 69° 42′ north, **and** longitude 132° 10′ west, the water was perfectly salt, the sea partially covered with drift ice and no land visible to seaward.

We experienced considerable difficulty in crossing the estuaries of several rivers, which we deemed to be the outlets of the shallow channels of the Mackenzie, that we had left to the eastward, and suffered besides some detention from ice and bad weather, and it was not until July 18 that we got entirely clear of the widely-spreading mouths of the Mackenzie and of a large lake of brackish water which seemed to receive one of the branches of that river. The navigation across these wide estuaries was rendered embarrassing from extensive sandy flats, which compelled us to go occasionally nearly out of sight of land, yet left us exposed to a frequently dangerous surf, in boats too slight to venture out into deep water, amongst heavy ice, in stormy weather, and we gladly exchanged it for a coasting voyage of the open sea.

We subsequently rounded Cape Parry in latitude 70° 18′ north and longitude 123° west, Cape Krusenstern in latitude 68° 46′ north and longitude 114° 45′ west, and entered Coronation Gulf by the Dolphin and Union Strait, which brought us within sight of Cape Barrow and two degrees of longitude to the eastward of the Coppermine, our sea voyage terminating on August 8th, by our entering that river.

With the exception of a few hours, on two or three days, we had contrary winds the whole way, and latterly were delayed and compelled to round every inlet of a deep bay, by thick ice driving in from seaward and packing closely on the shore; but our crews, taking every advantage of wind and tide, cut a passage with the hatchet, and by four days of hard labour cleared this obstacle, the most troublesome that occurred during our voyage along the coast.

Although we saw much heavy floe ice, some of it aground even in nine fathoms water, yet none of it bore marks of being more than one season old, and from the heights of land we could discern lanes of open water outside, so that a ship, properly strengthened for such a voyage, could make way through it with a favouring breeze.

Throughout the whole line of coast we had regular tides, the flood setting from the eastward, and the rise and fall from twelve to twenty inches. In the Dolphin and Union Strait the current in the height of flood and ebb exceeded two miles an hour. We found drift timber everywhere, and a large portion of it on many parts of the coast lay in a line from ten to fifteen, and in some places upwards of twenty feet above the ordinary spring tide water mark, apparently thrown up by a heavy sea. The coast, in such places, was unprotected by islands, and one would infer that in some seasons at least, if not every year, there exists a long fetch of open water.

We met several parties of Esquimaux, and had friendly communications with them. One numerous horde that we fell in with at the mouth of the Mackenzie, encouraged by the smallness of our numbers and the apparently distressed situation of the boats grounding on the flats of the river, endeavoured to seize and plunder the 'Union.' But the steady courage and humane forbearance of Mr. Kendall, and the cool determined conduct of both crews, frustrated the attempt without injury to the natives; and we afterwards made presents and bartered with some individuals of the same party, who had not engaged in the affair, and signified their disapproval of the conduct of their countrymen.

At the first rapid in the Coppermine, we abandoned the 'Dolphin' and 'Union' with their remaining cargoes of provision, iron-work, beads, &c., to the first party of Esquimaux that should chance to pass that way, and on August 10, set out by land with ten days' provision, and our personal luggage reduced to a single blanket and a few spare moccasins, that we might travel as lightly as possible; and further to reduce the men's loads, the tents were left behind, and Mr. Kendall carried the astronomical instruments. We reached the eastern end of Bear Lake, at the influx of Dease River, on the 18th, and remained there until the evening of the 24th, before the boat arrived to convey us to the Fort. Boileau the Interpreter, whom, as the most trustworthy man, and partly at my own desire, you had directed to take charge of the boat and canoe for that service, was sent off from the Fort on the 6th of the month with supplies of everything needful, and the strictest injunctions from Mr. Dease to use diligence in getting to the river. From a vague belief, however, that we should never return, that he would make a needless voyage and remain long waiting for us in vain, he loitered by the way, and in consequence, when the 20th of the month, the latest day appointed for his arrival, had elapsed, I judged it prudent to distribute the crews into hunting and fishing parties to procure subsistence. In these operations they were successful, and we also obtained supplies from a party of Indians, so that we had abundance; but I was not able to collect all my party again until the evening of the 28th. We then embarked in a large canoe, and reached the Fort on September 1, after an absence from it of seventy-one days, the whole party in perfect health, and more fit, with regard to bodily strength, to undertake a similar expedition than they were at setting out. . . .

I have the honour to be, Sir,
Your most obedient servant,
JOHN RICHARDSON.

On September 28, he wrote to his wife :—

I am now on my way to Slave Lake, with the intention of wintering in the hospitable mansion of my kind friend McVicar. The trees have assumed the livery of autumn, and the leaves are falling fast; but the scenery in its present dress looks delightful, and the fall, as it is termed, is in fact the only season of the year when, from the absence of mosquitoes and other winged pests, travelling in this country is pleasant. The weather, though occasionally cold, continues fine in this quarter till the middle of October, when the rivers and lakes are generally bound up in ice for the winter.

From Fort Resolution, on Great Slave Lake, he wrote to his mother, in November :—

It will give you pleasure to learn that I am now in perfect health, and on my return home, after having accomplished all that was expected of me on this expedition. We have experienced no privations; on the contrary, from the previous judicious arrangements, and the present good disposition of the Hudson's Bay Company's officers, we have been supplied with everything necessary for our comfort. I am at present living under the roof of my hospitable friend Mr. McVicar, from whom I experienced much kindness on the former journey.

The expedition has this year surveyed the coast of the Arctic Sea, from the mouth of the Coppermine River to the 150th degree of longitude, and but little remains towards the complete discovery of the north-west passage. Tempestuous weather, fogs, and much ice, the usual impediments to navigation in the Arctic Sea, added to the peculiarly inhospitable and dangerous nature of the coast now surveyed, and the numerous hordes and turbulent disposition of the Esquimaux who inhabit it, rendered the voyage so hazardous that the breasts of every member of the expedition can be filled with but one sentiment of gratitude to the Supreme Disposer of events, who graciously conducted us in perfect safety through all the dangers which environed us.

To his wife he wrote :—

You will experience pleasure in learning that our friend Captain Franklin has returned with his party in good health, from a voyage full of peril and difficulties, but more successful than could have been hoped under such circumstances. He got more than half way to Icy Cape, and although he has not completed the North-west Passage, yet he has left so small a portion of the coast unsurveyed, that if Captain Beechy gets round Icy Cape he can scarcely fail in completing it. The search has extended over three centuries, but now that it may be considered as accomplished, the discovery will, I suppose, be committed, like Juliet, to the tomb of all the Capulets, unless something more powerful than steam can render it available for the purpose of mercantile gain.

From Great Bear Lake, on September 21, Captain Franklin wrote :—

MY DEAR RICHARDSON,—You can well imagine the heartfelt pleasure I received on arriving here this morning and finding that you had executed your part of the service in such an expeditious and very able manner. We unfortunately missed Boisverd, and consequently I have not yet got your own account of the voyage; but Mr. Kendall has shown me his journal, so that I am in possession of all the material circumstances as to your proceedings. We were saluted in a somewhat similar manner to you by the Esquimaux, though more roughly, and by at least 250 men, a portion of the inmates of upwards of seventy tents.

We got out of the Mackenzie on the 7th of July, and on the 9th were stopped by ice, unbroken from the shore, and followed it up, as the separation took place, till August 4, being often unable to advance a mile a day, and never more than eight miles. In this tedious way we proceeded as far as the 141st degree. Beyond that the ice had removed so as to admit of a passage for the boats, but we were visited by constant fogs, and detained eight days at one spot by a gale of wind, and so dense an atmosphere as to obscure every object more distant than a few hundred yards. The coast, too, was so low and flat as to be unapproachable nearer than two or three miles, and we could only effect a landing in one point, though we frequently attempted it by dragging the boats through the mud. At all other times, we were compelled to put up on the naked reefs in front of the coast, sometimes without water or wood. In such a situation we were placed on August 16, 17, and 18, about half way to Icy Cape, being detained by a heavy gale.

The crews were now suffering from exposure to wading in the water (whenever we required to land), which was generally about the freezing point, while the temperature of the air seldom exceeded 36°. It became, therefore, necessary to revert to the clause in my instructions as to returning, if there was a doubt of our getting to Kotzebue Sound. There was certainly every room for doubt as to our getting to that place before the severe weather set in. The coast, too, was an extremely hazardous one for navigating under any circumstances, and especially so in the foggy weather we almost invariably had; and when we launched

M

from one place, we could form no idea when we might again be able to find another, on which, by any effort, we could land. The icy gales, too, were beginning to set in, and both Mr. Back and myself considered that further perseverance would be unpardonable rashness. But the necessity of returning gave all of us the deepest concern, for our boats were in perfect order, the crews very zealous, and we had abundance of provision. Subsequent events justified the propriety of this determination, for we had scarcely turned before we had a succession of stormy weather. In the meantime, the Esquimaux were gathering again about the Mackenzie, and between them and the Indians I much fear some serious misfortunes would have befallen the party, had we been even two days later.

Ours has been a voyage of increasing anxiety, and ever since we entered the Mackenzie we have suffered in no small degree from having heard of the disposition evinced by the Esquimaux to attack you; and on arriving at Fort Good Hope, we heard a report of the chief having been killed, and of course concluded it was you. Thank God, all is now well, and I feel convinced that the British public will be perfectly satisfied with what has been done. I am in hopes Beechy will pass round Icy Cape. If so, I shall consider the passage as ascertained. As for Parry, the ice we saw precludes every hope of his success, and in fact westward of the Mackenzie, there is but one harbour into which a ship could safely enter.

In the month of December, Dr. Richardson set out for Carlton House, where, on April 5, 1827, he was joined by Mr. Drummond, the assistant naturalist. The collections which the latter had made on the mountains during the absence of the expedition in the north, amounted to nearly 1500 species of plants, 150 birds, 50 quadrupeds, and a considerable number of insects. From Carlton Dr. Richardson proceeded to Cumberland House, where Captain Franklin arrived, on June 18, and the friends had the pleasure of meeting again after a separation of eleven months. The Esquimaux interpreter, Augustus, also came to this post, in order to gratify a desire which he had of seeing the doctor once more before he left the country. Having accompanied them to Norway House, where he was to wait to see Captain Back, the faithful creature shed tears at parting, which, 'I have no doubt,' says Captain Franklin, 'proceeded from a sincere affection—an affection which, I can venture to say, was mutually felt by every individual.'

After a pleasant journey through Canada and the United States, Captain Franklin and Dr. Richardson reached New York, and sailed for England on the 1st of September, arriving in Liverpool on the 26th, after an absence of two years, seven months and a-half. Captain Back, Lieutenant Kendall, and Mr. Drummond, with the rest of the British party, returned by Hudson's Bay, and arrived at Portsmouth on October 10, bringing the sad news that one excellent man had died from consumption, and another had been drowned while trying to save one of the boats which was rushing down the Pelican Fall in Slave River. With the exception of these losses, the gallant and indefatigable band of explorers returned in safety, having added extensively to the geographical knowledge of the North American coast, made important experiments in magnetism and the effects of the Aurora Borealis on the needle, and secured large collections of natural history, especially in the department of botany.

CHAPTER XVIII.

DUTIES AT CHATHAM——MELVILLE HOSPITAL——PROPOSES ANO-
THER EXPEDITION TO NORTH AMERICA——DEATH OF MRS.
RICHARDSON——PLAN OF SEARCH FOR CAPTAIN JOHN ROSS——
THE GOVERNMENT DECIDES NOT TO SEND A SEARCHING
PARTY.

1827–1832.

ON September 29, 1827, Dr. Richardson arrived
in London, where he resided for a short time while
preparing his portion of the narrative of the
expedition and the scientific appendices to it, consisting of topographical and geological notices,
meteorological tables with remarks, and observations on solar radiation.

In 1828, he had returned to his official duties at
Chatham, and every spare hour was devoted to his
great work, 'The Fauna Boreali-Americana, or
Natural History of the Arctic Regions.' There was
little time for writing letters, and it is only occasionally that glimpses of his life, at this period,
are obtained. Meantime, Melville Hospital had
been erected at Chatham, and he became chief
medical officer. On June 30, Mrs. Richardson
wrote :—

The new Hospital is at last finished, and the patients were moved in yesterday, but we shall not be able to take possession of our house for four months. It is much larger than the present one, and in a more retired situation. Our neighbours will consist of the purveyor, his wife, and the assistant-surgeon, so I think that within our gates we shall be able to make a very snug party for the winter evenings.

The cares connected with bringing the new hospital into working order did not, however, lead him to relax his scientific and literary work. The first volume of the 'Fauna' appeared early in 1829.

The autumn holidays of this year were spent pleasantly. After a steam-boat voyage to Leith, several happy days were passed in Edinburgh with relatives and old friends, followed by a visit to Professor Hooker of Glasgow, who was busy with the 'North American Flora.' With his mother, amidst the scenes of boyhood's bright days, the time which remained glided swiftly away.

Referring to Dr. Richardson's visits to his father, Dr. Joseph Dalton Hooker of Kew says :—

Having read the narrative of both journeys during my recovery from a serious illness, and having every particular of them impressed on my mind, I regarded him as something more than man. I used to follow him all over the house offering my services in opening his boxes and carrying his bundles of plants, so a mutual understanding sprang up between us. If we did not converse much, it was not because I had not much to say to him, but he was naturally reserved, and the subject on which I longed to **cross-question** him, *Michel's death*, had been interdicted to me by the strict injunctions of my parents. He did **give me** various little **insights** into canoe voyaging, hunting **and camping**, and told me some good **stories**, as how **his** hardy botanical collector, Drummond, **had** frightened away a grizzly bear by shaking his tin botanising box full of stones under his nose when it was about to hug him.

On September **21, Dr.** Richardson arrived again in London, accompanied by **his sister** Josephine, Mrs. Richardson **meeting them there,** to enjoy a few days' **sight-seeing, previous to resuming his** scientific studies **and the routine duties of Mel-** ville **Hospital.**

The **difficulties, which prevented Sir John** Franklin, **in the** summer **of 1826, from completing** the survey **of the** Arctic **coast, westward of the** Mackenzie **river, did not seem to Dr. Richardson** to be insurmountable. **In 1830, he brought the** subject under the **notice of Mr. Hay of the Colonial** Office, and offered **his services if the Government** should resolve **to send out another expedition.**

'The details **are very simple,' he wrote : '** two officers with twenty men would **travel from Canada to Bear** Lake in one **summer.** They **could there winter and build boats,** and the **second** summer would suffice, **not** only **to enable** them to complete the examination **of the coast,** but **to make** such progress on their return as would **ensure their** reaching England by the Hudson's Bay ships the **following** year. If greater economy be required, the party may be reduced one-half, for by using certain precautions in the construction of the boats, and a light defensive armour sufficient to turn an arrow, any hostile attempts of the natives would be frustrated. Indeed I have practically shown that ten men are sufficient to navigate two boats along an equal extent of Arctic coast, and I have in this instance considered the larger number to be preferable, solely because it would be sufficiently imposing to prevent any unpleasant collision whatever, and do away with the necessity of repressing the natives by violence.'

To this proposal, Mr. Hay replied, 'If any expedition of the description to which you refer should be set on foot, the Secretary of State would naturally apply to you, but at present, I see no prospect of such a project being undertaken by the Government.'

In 1831, dark clouds began to break over him. He had left his parental home so early that of all his brothers, Peter, who was near the same age, only had been a companion and very dear to him. In the month of August, he died suddenly in Edinburgh.

Mrs. Richardson began also to droop, and though a change to Tunbridge Wells was to some extent beneficial, she gradually lost strength. On the evening of Christmas she died, at the early age of thirty-six. 'Her character was marked by a sincere and humble but cheerful piety—a faithful discharge of her duties, a meekness of demeanour and purity of thought and conversation, combined with firmness of purpose, and by the constant exercise of Christian charity and kindness to all.'

In 1832, great fears began to be entertained for the safety of Captain John Ross. Accompanied by his nephew, he had sailed, in 1829, in a small vessel called the 'Victory,' which through the munificence of Sir Felix Booth he had been enabled to fit out, with the intention of seeking a passage through Regent's Inlet, but no tidings of them had reached England.

Dr. Richardson's sympathy was aroused, and he endeavoured to stimulate the Admiralty and the public to take some interest in their fate. The appeal was in vain. He then wrote a letter to the Secretary of the Geographical Society, which, after the lapse of several weeks, was read, along with some other communications on the same subject, and excited attention. The Admiralty and Colonial Office were applied to, but the Secretary of the Admiralty said that nothing could be done, as the 'Victory' must have gone to pieces, and all her crew perished during the first winter.

Not willing to be baffled in his humane attempt, and having been made acquainted, in confidence, by Sir Felix Booth with the route which Captain Ross intended to pursue, he addressed a letter to Mr. Hay, the Under-Secretary for the Colonies, soliciting the Government to send him out with a relief-party. The proposal was at first entertained, and he began to make the necessary preparations. He selected twelve marines, **who were** blacksmiths, carpenters, **or** other **artisans, and could** all pull an oar.   **One of them had received a good** education, and **was an able** draughtsman.   **John** Hepburn was **to go out to take charge** of the winter house.

Writing to his mother, on May 20, he says :—

You **will no doubt be** a little alarmed **at the** idea of my **again** leaving home, **but there** will **be** little hazard, and my **route lies** through **a** country with which **I am well ac- quainted.**   Besides **I** go out **under much more** favourable **circumstances** than **I** did before, having now the command of the party, which will **be** well equipped **and** amply fur- **nished** with provisions by the Hudson's Bay Company.   **I am busy** making preparations, as the ship in which **I go** sails from Gravesend **on the 9th** of June.   We touch at Stornaway, in the island of Lewis, **so that I** shall have an opportunity of writing **to you from that place.**

On May 23, he experienced **the** disappointment **of being informed by the following** note from the Treasury **that the Government had** given up all idea of sending the **expedition :—**

Mr. Ellice desires **me to inform you that** he has had a **farther** discussion with **Sir James** Graham, and Lord Althorp, on the subject of your proposed Expedition ; that they **consider all** chance of saving any **of** Captain Ross's companions hopeless ; and that they **do not see** in the other objects of the Expedition sufficient public grounds to war- rant the **risk and expense.**

Notwithstanding official opinion, Captain Ross and his men **were saved, but by** God's help and their own bravery.

We know, from various sources, that the opposition to the sending of a searching party came from the Admiralty. In a letter to Dr. Richardson from the father of Commander James Clark Ross, who accompanied his uncle in the 'Victory,' he says :—

I have had a communication with Sir James Graham, and seen Mr. Barrow on the subject, without the least prospect of any assistance being obtained from the Admiralty. It is indeed only through the Hudson's Bay Company that I have any hopes of receiving intelligence of them, in the event of their having met with any serious accident, which is now too much to be apprehended.

At this time, Dr. Richardson was requested by the Lieutenant-Governor of the Hudson's Bay Company to give his opinion as to the most eligible route of an expedition from the trading posts. He recommended that by the Great Fish River, as combining the utmost economy with the best chance of obtaining intelligence of Captain Ross, and unfolded in detail the plan of search.

Though a season was lost, the attempt to ascertain the fate of the missing seamen was not abandoned. A public subscription was begun and pushed forward with great zeal by Captain (now Rear-Admiral Sir George) Back, who was appointed to command the expedition with the concurrence of Government, which eventually gave pecuniary aid also.

Captain Back descended the Great Fish River in

1834, and surveyed the coast on both sides of its estuary, touching a point of the Arctic Sea, thirteen degrees of longitude eastward of Sir John Franklin's Point Turnagain. Having received an express from England, informing him of the safe return of Captain Ross, he had only geographical research to plead for extending his voyage further, and this the advanced and stormy season, and the condition of his boat, rendered inexpedient. .

The 'Victory' had been set fast in the ice, and finally abandoned, in Victoria Harbour, near the seventieth parallel of latitude, and on the opposite side of Regent's Inlet to the Strait of the Fury and Hecla. Three winters were spent in the vessel and a fourth on Fury Beach, after abandoning her. The party at length escaped in good health, in 1833, in their boats, and fortunately reached a whaler in Lancaster Sound. On returning from his long absence Captain John Ross received the honour of knighthood. The efforts which Dr. Richardson made to stir up the Government and people of Great Britain to send out a searching party were fully justified.

CHAPTER XIX.

MEDICAL DUTIES—SECOND MARRIAGE—JOHN FRANKLIN BORN
—LETTER FROM MRS. OPIE TO MRS. RICHARDSON—LETTER
TO CAPTAIN BEAUFORT ON THE NORTH-WEST PASSAGE—
CAPTAIN BEAUFORT'S REPLY — APPOINTED PHYSICIAN TO
HASLAR HOSPITAL — HOSPITAL REFORMS — INSPECTOR OF
HOSPITALS—MRS. RICHARDSON'S DEATH.

1832–1845.

DR. RICHARDSON had no time to brood over his
disappointment at having failed in his efforts to
induce the Government to send him in search of
Captain Ross and his companions. Scarcely had
his preparations for the expedition been suspended
when cholera appeared in the barracks of the
Marines at Chatham, keeping him closely confined
to his official duties, and requiring both skill and
energy to check its progress. So unremitting was
his attendance at Melville Hospital, while the
epidemic continued, that the medical officers and
nurses said they thought he never slept, for he was
in and out at all hours by day and night. Towards
the end of July, it had so far abated that he
wrote: 'In the course of ten days I mean to
take a change for a few weeks, most likely into

Lincolnshire, to visit Captain Franklin's relations, who have kindly invited me.'

While on this visit he became engaged to Mary Booth, the only daughter of John Booth, Esq., of Stickney, Ingoldwells, a niece of Sir John Franklin. Their union was looked forward to with much pleasure by all the relatives, and especially by Sir John Franklin, who thus wrote from Patras, where his ship, the 'Rainbow,' was lying in September :—

I cannot fully convey to you the very deep interest and pleasure which your letter gave me. There is no person for whom I have so great a regard as yourself, and none, except my dear wife and child, whom I love more affectionately than my niece Mary Booth. The prospect therefore of your being united to her gives me very true happiness. By some mistake the last packet came without letters from any member of my own family. The intelligence therefore contained in yours came most unexpectedly upon me, and even drew tears of delight as I read your letter. I instantly put up a prayer to the Almighty for his blessing on your mutual wishes. Often, indeed, have I sighed for the enjoyment of that calm retirement and course of piety which you have already had, and have the prospect of living in. The hurry and bustle of mixed society and the round of visiting into which I was plunged will never return, as both my dear wife and I hope, and we shall have on our return the happiness of your united society and of others of similar tastes and pursuits. May God grant that we may each live to enjoy the happiness that seems to be promised to us !

The marriage was celebrated early in 1833. On February 8, he wrote to his mother from Oxford:—

If you received a Lincoln paper which was addressed to Josephine, you will know that I had the happiness of receiving the hand of my dear Mary on Wednesday week at Ingoldwells. She desires to use the privilege of her new relationship to you in uniting with me in kind love to yourself and all my sisters, and to the husbands and families of the married ones.

The quiet life at Chatham, and the medical duties of Melville Hospital, present few incidents worthy of record. When not officially engaged, his time was occupied in preparing the 'Fauna,' or in other scientific studies.

On November 5, a little boy was born, and named John Franklin.

In his wife he found a cheerful companion, deeply imbued with the same spirit of piety. Scarcely had she recovered from the long illness which followed the birth of her child, when she wrote to one of her sisters-in-law: 'I am so well and happy I can scarcely help jumping for joy. I have been to take up my district, and intend to be as active as possible in it, whilst God allows me so much health and strength.'

The summer holidays, this year, were spent in Scotland, where, at the meeting of the British Association, in Edinburgh, they met with Arago, Mrs. Opie, and others distinguished in science and literature.

The following **letter**, from Mrs. Opie to Mrs. Richardson, dated September 12, 1834, is characteristic of the writer :—

I am sorry indeed **to think that I shall** not see thee and thy dear kind **husband** again in Edinburgh, but I will **not imagine** for a moment that **we are not to** meet again somewhere on this side the grave,—**and as I** know where **to find you, depend on it** I shall **make my** appearance at Melville Hospital *un de ces jours*, **that is, if I** live and do well, and visit London **as usual next spring.**

In the meantime, to remind you **of one who** can never forget you nor the obligations which **she owes** you, **I** intend to desire my publishers to **send thee my** last work,—a **little** volume of ‘ **Lays for the Dead.’ I** think they may suit thee, because, if I **read thee right,** thy mind is seriously and piously **disposed, and relishes the** things of eternity full **as much as those of time. Is it too much to** ask to hear from thee when **you are once more settled at** home and delighting **yourselves in your dear child's** winning ways ?

Farewell ! never on so short an acquaintance did I say farewell, a long farewell, with so much reluctance.

Thy ever obliged and attached friend,

AMELIA OPIE.

Early in 1836, Dr. Richardson addressed a letter **to Captain** Beaufort, the Admiralty hydrographer, **on the subject of** the North-west Passage, and the survey of those parts of the **Arctic** coast of America which remained unexplored :—

To those **who meet** every generous undertaking with the question *cui bono?* **it may** be replied (said he) that the dis**covery of the continent of** North America, pregnant with consequences beyond **human** calculation, the Hudson's Bay

fur trade, the Newfoundland cod-fishery, **and the** Davis'
Straits whale-fishery, nurseries for seamen, are **the direct**
results **of** expeditions which sailed in **quest of a north-west**
passage.   But it is not on the existence of this passage that
my argument **for new expeditions of discovery rests; for**
were it even proved that, contrary to **the opinions of the**
ablest officers who have **sailed the** polar seas, no **practicable**
channel **for ships can be found, still I hold it to be the duty**
of those who **direct the councils of the British** Empire **to**
provide for **the** exploring of every **part of** His **Majesty's**
dominions.   **This** would be merely an act of justice to **the**
various tribes that have a claim on England for protection.
The deadly feuds between the Esquimaux and the neighbouring Indians can be terminated only by **the** extinction
of one of the parties or by European interference ; and
should our repeated visits to those remote coasts **be the**
means of carrying thither the blessings **of peace and shed-**
ding the light of Christianity on the benighted inhabitants,
it would, in my opinion, be an ample recompense for **all**
the exertion which England has **made and** all the expense
she has **incurred.**

Having **shown how small an extent of** coast
remained **to be explored, he pointed out in** what
manner **it could be done by a party wintering** at the
east end **of Great Bear Lake, and descending** the
Coppermine **River in June.   In mentioning the**
principal **points to be attended to, he added, ' I**
have not said that it is necessary to obtain **the**
concurrence **and cordial co-operation of the** Hudson's Bay **Company, since that enlightened body**
has never **failed to lend its powerful and indis-**

pensable assistance to an enterprise patronised by Government and having science for its aim.'

Captain Beaufort replied :—

My dear Richardson,—I am exceedingly obliged to you for your very beautiful ' Fauna,' and only regret that, having got to the end of your labours and no great probability of your seeking for fresh materials, your pen, which has conveyed so much knowledge and pleasure to the world, will now be allowed to moulder away in idleness.

I have to thank you also for your excellent letter to me about the *Arctic terra incognita.* I carried it forthwith to the Geographical Council, where it was read and admired, and ordered to be printed—and I had it read again at the evening meeting. Sir John Franklin made a good speech upon the subject, and I have just been urging him to write a letter on the same plan and let it be printed with yours.

A committee has been formed in order to report on the best means of doing something, and Sir John Barrow says he will do his best to forward the affair with government, though I am much afraid we shall have his warm support only as far as the North-West Passage.

Among the select number of friends whose society they enjoyed at this time, were Dr. Davy and his wife, who came to Chatham in 1835, and resided in Fort Pitt. This intimacy was kept up as long as Richardson lived, and was the source of much mutual enjoyment during the latter years of his life, when they dwelt only a few miles apart.

On June 5, 1836, another child was born, and named Josephine Fanny. A few weeks later their joy was changed into mourning by the death of little Franklin. **They** resigned him to the Lord in faith; yet, long after, the yearnings of their hearts were towards the darling so early taken.

In the month of August, they visited **Mrs.** Richardson at **Dumfries,** travelling **by way of Bir-**mingham and the Westmoreland lakes. Many of the dear ones **who sat** around their mother's table in 1834, had been **removed by death, and** the family meeting **brought with it sorrowful** remembrances. The **visit, however,** was one **of real enjoyment. His** ' Fauna **Boreali**-Americana,' the **labour of many** years, **had been** finished, **and there was time for a** season of recreation.

Early in 1838, the Admiralty appointed him Physician to the Royal Hospital at Haslar, **near** Portsmouth. '**I** congratulate you very sincerely,' the Director-General of the Medical Department of the Navy wrote, ' and hope the appointment will be agreeable to yourself, as I am sure it will be beneficial to the service.'

He promptly entered on his new duties, which kept him quite as much occupied as those **at Mel-**ville Hospital. **At this** time, Dr. Joseph Dalton Hooker was preparing to accompany Sir James Ross on his voyage of discovery to the Antarctic Regions, and frequently visited Dr. Richardson at Haslar.

' I daily accompanied him,'says Dr. Hooker, ' **in** his hospital **rounds,** and was greatly taken by his manner towards his patients. His words of accost, whether of recognition, sympathy or congratulation, were wonderfully few and pithy, and he had a clever way of questioning, that drew from the patient much more information than he apparently sought, and from which he could judge how far his orders had been attended to by his subordinates. In his family circle he was very genial and gentle.'

His efforts to induce the Admiralty to introduce necessary reforms in the Hospital management were unwearied. Dr. Gray, of the British Museum, says :—

It was chiefly to his exertions that the great and beneficent change made in the treatment of lunatics in the Naval hospitals was due. He had made, I believe, several earnest reports to the Admiralty on the desirableness of introducing the milder mode of treatment, which was steadily making its way in county and private asylums, into the Naval Hospital at Haslar, but without success.

While on a visit at my house, I proposed to him to go and inspect the Middlesex County Asylum at Hanwell, then under the able superintendence of Dr. Conolly. During our examination, we made the acquaintance of Mrs. Macfie, matron of the establishment, and received from her a variety of interesting details, relative not only to the success of the treatment, but to the number of keepers employed, the expenditure, and other particulars which afforded him great assistance in drawing up a new report in which he showed that the milder system was not only the most efficient, but that it could be carried out at less expense. The consequence was that the Board of Admiralty gave directions for its introduction, and every one who has witnessed the difference in the appearance and behaviour of the patients, cannot fail to regard the change as one of great importance, not only in a medical, but in a humane point of view.

Dr. Richardson established and adhered to the rule that the medical officers should visit and prescribe for the patients before breakfast, making them comfortable as early as possible, and keeping the nurses and assistants on the alert. He was ready for family prayers at half-past eight o'clock, and generally made the seasons of exercise subservient to some kindly purpose of visiting an invalid friend, or prescribing for persons whose means did not allow of their having regular medical attendance. Much of the time devoted to scientific pursuits was gained from the night, or the days when his official duties were lighter than usual. His life was varied, from time to time, by visits to scientific friends in London, attending the meetings of the British Association, and a summer or autumn ramble in the country.

On August 22, 1840, he was promoted by the Admiralty to the rank of Inspector of Hospitals, to be attached to that at Haslar.

After the completion of the 'Fauna,' he produced in succession, 'A Report on North American Zoology,' 'The Mammalia of Captain Beechy's Voyage to the Pacific and Behring's Straits,' 'A Paper on the Frozen Soil of North America,' 'Observations on Solar Radiation,' 'Plates of Rare Fishes,' and, in 1843, 'The Ichthyology of New Zealand.'

Meantime, the family circle has been enlarging, John, Beatrice and Willingham having been given to them in addition to Josephine.

During 1844, Mrs. Richardson's health, which had never been very good, began more visibly to decline, and after the birth of a little boy, named Edward, in February 1845, she never rallied. A severe attack of fever followed her confinement, leaving her in a state of extreme weakness, and on April 10, God took her to Himself to receive the reward of perseverance in well-doing and faith in her Saviour.

The character of Mrs. Richardson was estimable in the highest degree. Though often an invalid, she was ever cheerful and contented. Self-denying care for her husband's comforts and hearty interest in his labours, affection for her children, attention to her household duties, charity to the poor, compassionate helping of the sick, above all, firm faith in the Saviour, and love to the ordinances of religion were conspicuous during her married life.

Mrs. Davy, of Ambleside, who knew her well, thus writes :—

It was in the year 1835 that I first became acquainted with Mrs. Richardson at Chatham, where our husbands had medical appointments in the service of the army and navy respectively. I well remember the first day Mrs. Richardson and I met, which was soon after our arrival from abroad. We had a pleasant bond in our previous acquaintance with, and high regard for, her honoured uncle,

Sir John Franklin, and in the strange land, as to society, that Chatham was then to me, I can hardly say how attractive I felt her sunny countenance and cordial greeting. We soon became intimate friends. Each of us had little ones concerning whom we had much to say. She had a quick understanding, and was remarkably ready in giving and receiving sympathy. She had no fastidiousness or exclusiveness as to society. These, I believe, her genial nature would, in any case, have hindered, but she doubtless felt them forbidden by her strong Christian faith and the large charity it tends to foster. To the poor she did not merely give alms but loving-kindness. She experienced much of the trial of infirm health both before and during the time we lived near to one another, and sorrow visited her home in its saddest form by the death of two young children, one an infant, the other a boy of nearly three years, who was very precious to the hearts and hopes of both his parents. Her acceptance of these sorrows was tenderly instructive. I have never known so entire an acquiescence in the will of God amidst trying dispensations, or any one whose cheerful return to the business of life, after having been sorely stricken, seemed so natural. Entirely happy in her wedded union, she rejoiced over it, not only with affectionate but grateful joy. As neighbour friends, we parted in the spring of 1838, when the Richardsons removed to Haslar, and I did not see Mrs. Richardson again, but we often exchanged letters, and hers were so like herself that they were always welcome to me and much missed when they came no more.

CHAPTER XX.

1845–1848.

IN June, 1845, Dr. Richardson went to Cambridge, to be present at the meeting of the British Association, and read a paper on the Ichthyology of the seas of China and Japan.

Somewhat later, the 'Eclair' arrived at Portsmouth, from a cruise on the coast of Africa, with a malignant type of fever raging on board, and all his energies were put forth for the relief of the sufferers. Instead of confining them within the narrow limits of the infected vessel, he recommended the sick to be removed to a wing of the hospital, in hopes that fresh air and proper treatment might restore them to health. In his despatch to the Admiralty, he said:—

Notwithstanding the extraordinary mortality that has swept off so large a proportion of the crew of this vessel, I entertain no fears of her being the means of introducing epidemic disease into this country, and were the sick placed in well-ventilated wards with fresh bedding and the other means of cleanliness afforded by an hospital, I anticipate no farther risk to the attendants, than would occur in wards set apart for cases of typhus fever.

Meantime, at the suggestion of Sir John Barrow, the Earl of Haddington, First Lord of the Admiralty, applied to the Prime Minister to obtain for him the honour of knighthood, in acknowledgment of his services as an Arctic explorer and naturalist. In reply to a letter from Sir John Barrow, Dr. Anderson of Haslar wrote, that Dr. Richardson, who had been attacked with spasms of the heart, had resumed his duties, adding: 'The honour which is intended to be conferred on him, will, I am sure, be most gratifying to every officer in the medical department of the naval service; and the circumstance of the distinction having been proposed by yourself, who are so capable of judging of his merits, will greatly enhance the value in the estimation of us all.'

In his Autobiography, Sir John Barrow says :—

I may mention an incident which marks an amiable stamp on the character of the individual in question. While the title was in progress, intimation was conveyed to me that Dr. Richardson had been attacked with severe paralysis. I wrote immediately to Haslar Hospital to in-

quire after him ; the answer was that it was only a fainting
fit, occasioned by stooping too long, and that he was then
quite well.   It turned out that he was employing himself
in stooping to plant flowers and ever-greens round the
grave of his late wife, whom he had recently lost. Another
trait may be mentioned.   Having himself made no application nor expressed any desire to be knighted, Lord Haddington asked me if I was sure it would be acceptable.
' That,' I said, ' shall be ascertained.'   On seeing him,
I asked if knighthood would be agreeable, provided it
could be obtained.   His answer to me was, ' As a mark of
approbation from the Government, for my services, it could
not be otherwise, but it would have been much more so,
had it been granted in the life-time of my beloved wife.'
These are pleasant traits of strong domestic affection, and
correspond, as I have been informed, with the whole tenour
of his life.

He was knighted by Her Majesty on February
11, 1846, and in August, 1850, was made an ordinary member of the military division of the third
class, or Companions of the Bath.

In the month of April, 1846, Sir John Richardson pointed out, in a despatch to the Director-
General of the medical department of the navy,
the inconvenience of having the hospital at Haslar
governed by a Captain-Superintendent, and the
necessity of leaving the entire control, as at Melville and other hospitals, in the hands of the chief
medical officer.   He showed that both efficiency
and economy would be thereby gained.   The post
of Captain-Superintendent, however, was not abo-

lished; but he had the gratification of learning that Sir Edward Parry, a man of congenial mind, was to fill it; and during the whole time of his command they cordially co-operated in improving the establishment.

Early in 1847 many began to feel anxiety regarding the expedition under Sir John Franklin, and the Admiralty lost no time in consulting those best qualified to judge of the dangers to which the crews might be exposed, and the proper steps to be taken in case of disaster. Sir John Richardson's opinion was asked, and given with precision and judgment. In a letter to Sir Edward Parry he says :—

Sir John Franklin's plans were to shape his course in the first instance for the neighbourhood of Cape Walker, and to endeavour to get to the westward in that parallel, or, if that could not be accomplished, to make his way southwards to the channel discovered on the north coast of the Continent, and so into Behring's Straits. Failing success in that quarter, he meant to retrace his course to Wellington Channel and attempt a passage to the northwards of Parry's Island. And if foiled there also, to descend Regent's Inlet and seek the passage discovered by Dease and Simpson.

With respect to the strong apprehensions that have been expressed in regard to the safety of the expedition, I agree with you in thinking that they are premature. The expedition was prepared to pass two winters in the Arctic Sea, and until next November shall have passed without tidings, I see no well-grounded reason for more anxiety than that which was naturally felt when it sailed from this country, as an enterprise of peril, though not greater than that which you have repeatedly encountered yourself, and on one occasion for the same length of time, and returned in safety.

The case will, however, be very different if the next winter sets in without satisfactory tidings of the expedition, and in contemplation of the possibility of such an event, it may be advisable to take some precautionary steps this season.

I concur in the opinion that it would be useless and hazardous to send anything short of a second well-appointed expedition to trace the course of the missing ships, and I can suggest no plan superior to the one you have purposed of encouraging the whalers, by an adequate reward, to examine the shores of Lancaster Straits and Wellington Sound.

The boat expedition from Hudson's Bay to the Welcome and bottom of Regent's Inlet, now in progress, will procure intelligence of the ships should they have visited that neighbourhood.

There remains the contingency of the ships having penetrated some considerable distance to the south-west of Cape Walker, and having been hampered and crushed in the channels of the Archipelago, which, there is every reason to believe, occupies the space north of Wollaston Islands and south of Bank's Land. Such accidents are seldom so sudden but that the boats of one or both ships with provisions can be saved, and, in such an event, the survivors would either retrace their way to Lancaster Straits or make for the Continent according to their nearness, and Sir John Franklin and his officers are fully aware of the localities where they might best seek relief from the Indians or servants of the Hudson's Bay Company.

It is possible, however, that the shipwreck may be so complete as to leave the party, or such of them as escape to the shore, without the means of crossing to the main, yet with provisions thrown upon the beach sufficient to support them for a season. Or a few might escape and associate themselves with the wandering hordes of Esqui-- maux. To rescue such individuals or to obtain tidings of the lost ships—Wollaston Land, Victoria Land, the neigh- bouring islands and channels, might be visited by boats. Under no circumstances could this be effected, even in part, earlier than August 1848, and then only through arrange- ments made immediately with the Hudson's Bay Company and the aid of a favourable season.

He then unfolded, in his letter, a plan of relief by an expedition descending the Mackenzie River in boats, and searching the line of coast to which the ship-wrecked crews would naturally endeavour to make their way; during the second summer, if the weather and ice permitted, exploring also the channels between Wollaston and Victoria Lands.

While many had gloomy forebodings, Sir John Richardson clung tenaciously to the hope that his friend would return. To his mother, who was on her death-bed, he wrote in April : —

I fear that you must have heard of a paragraph in some of the papers mentioning my being appointed to conduct another Polar expedition. There are no well-grounded apprehensions for the safety of Sir John Franklin, but the Admiralty have thought it advisable to take some precau- tions, and I am busy preparing a quantity of pemmican and other provisions to be sent out to Hudson's Bay in

June, and forwarded through the country in boats. **Should nothing be heard of Franklin's Expedition** in the winter, I shall go out next spring, not for the purpose of making discoveries, but to follow our former **tracks** and carry the provisions to the **ships, if** on the north **coast** of the American continent.

On June 15, 1847, the Hudson's Bay Company's ships sailed from the Thames, carrying the boats, men, and stores for Sir John Richardson's expedition to the shores of the Arctic Sea, during the following summer, if, before spring, no news of Sir John Franklin reached England. He cherished the hope, however, that there would be no necessity for going in search of his friend, and thus wrote :—

I really do not feel the anxiety and excitement which would be inseparable from the certainty or even great probability of my having to look for them in another quarter of the globe; but God orders all for the best, and whatever be the result, in this case I shall consider as a plain indication of my line of duty. I did not put myself forward or make the offer from any prompting of vanity ; but my opinion was sought for, and my offer to go followed as a part of the plan which I thought to be most advisable. Should Sir John Franklin not return this autumn, the circumstances will be greatly altered; and a strong desire to contribute to his relief and that of his party (which I do not at present feel, because I do not think their safety to be compromised) will then stimulate me to exertion, and make my going a much inferior evil to what my lingering at home and shirking such a duty would be.

His marriage with **Mary, the** youngest daughter
of Archibald Fletcher, **Esq.,** of Edinburgh, was celebrated in the church at Grasmere on August 4th ;
after which he spent **some** time on the Continent,
examining especially **Pastor** Fliedner's Institution,
near Dusseldorf, for **the** training of **nurses, in**
which he **was much interested.**

They returned **to Haslar in the first** week of
September.

At this **period, Sir Edward Parry** was Captain
Superintendent of the Hospital, **and the many**
points **of** interest which he and Richardson **had in**
common, especially their knowledge **of Arctic**
affairs, and affection for Franklin, made **the** intercourse between the two families most cordial **and**
intimate, while **their** influence as **chiefs of the**
administrative and medical departments was most
beneficial to the establishment.

A few days after his mother's death, which occurred **at** the end of **October,** he visited Mrs.
Fletcher **and** Mrs. Davy **at** Lesketh How, near
Ambleside. He was meditating **on** Franklin's
return, and **in one of** his letters from that lovely
spot says, ' We may soon expect **the** first **of the**
whalers of the season, and, about **the** middle of
November, Sir John Franklin in their rear.'

The last of the whalers came **without** bringing
any tidings of the ' Erebus ' and ' Terror.' Apprehension for the safety of their **crews** increased,
and Sir John Richardson felt it necessary to com-

plete the preparations for his journey. The merry group of children, too young to realise what was before them, except as an exciting adventure, of which 'finding uncle Franklin' was the end, had gone to bed, one evening, after listening as usual to an amusing tale read by their father. When all was quiet, he communicated to his wife, in a low and touchingly mournful voice, the almost certain necessity of his departure, which made her conscious that she would indeed be unworthy of the confidence reposed in her, were she to increase the load that pressed on his heart by any expression of weakness which it was possible to conceal, and the burthen was in some degree lightened to both after the worst had been made known.

Towards the close of the year, Sir John Richardson recommended the appointment of Dr. John Rae, a chief trader of the Hudson's Bay Company, to be second in command. He had lived long in Rupert's Land, knew how to turn the natural products of the country to advantage, was a skilful hunter, 'quick in devising expedients for tempering the severity of the climate, an accurate observer with the sextant and other instruments usually employed to determine the latitude and longitude, or the variations and dip of the magnetic needle, and had just brought to a successful conclusion, under circumstances of very unusual privation, an expedition of discovery fitted out by the Hudson's Bay Company, for the purpose of exploring the limits of Regent's Inlet.'

On reading in the *Times* newspaper a letter from Dr. Rae describing his journey, Sir John Richardson said, 'I have found my companion, if I can get him.' He was immediately communicated with, and at once expressed his willingness to go as second in command. Lord Auckland, the First Lord of the Admiralty, had also discovered Dr. Rae's ability. A ready assent was therefore obtained to the proposal that Dr. Rae should accompany him.

The choice was altogether a happy one. Dr. Rae not only possessed the highest qualifications for the duties to which he was appointed, but was a most congenial companion. His soul was in the work. Six winters after the crews of the 'Erebus' and 'Terror' had perished, he was destined by Providence to find the relics of the deceased, which satisfied the Admiralty that the members of the Franklin Expedition had all died, and obtained for himself and party the 10,000*l*. promised to any one who should find and relieve the missing mariners, or bring correct intelligence of their fate.

The following letter to Mrs. Fletcher, written by Sir John Richardson, on January 14, 1848, contains a statement of his motives for undertaking the search :—

o

I cannot allow your birthday to pass without congratulating you on the event, and expressing a wish that the
yearly recurrence of the day may witness your enjoyment
of all the blessings which, in the expansive benevolence of
your heart, you so warmly desire for others.   Since the last
anniversary of your birthday, I have had the happiness of
becoming connected with you, and acquired the privilege
of expressing a deeper interest in your welfare than one
who was bound to you by a less important or less valued
trust. . . . .

The prospect of our temporary separation is very sad to
me, and I do not like to dwell upon it; but my going is a
point of duty which I cannot conscientiously evade, unless
I were convinced that another person could carry out
my plan of search in the way that I have conceived it.
But there is no one now alive who is acquainted with the
track but myself; and no one who is so bound by the ties
of friendship and affection to do his utmost to find Franklin,
if he should unhappily be in a situation in which he and
his party cannot help themselves.

About the middle of February, he, along with
Lady Richardson, were the guests of Lady Franklin, then living in Charlotte Street, Bedford Square.
Here he received a note from the Admiralty, dated
February 21, acquainting him that up to September 27, 1847, no intelligence of Sir John Franklin's
expedition had reached the Sandwich Islands, and
all hope of tidings of the missing ships by way of
the Pacific came to an end.   Mrs. Fletcher was
also in London, and her Journal contains the
following entry :—

We dined with Lady Franklin on February 24, to meet the Richardsons who were staying with her. A larger party assembled in the evening, among whom was Thomas Carlyle, whom we were glad to meet again. He was sitting close by me, and chatting pleasantly, when Dr. Boott came into the room and advanced towards me, with even more than usual brightness in his fine countenance, saying: ' Louis Philippe has fled, and France has declared herself a Republic.' There was a dead silence. Carlyle threw himself back in his chair, clasped his hands, burst into a loud laugh, and left the room. We did not see him again. The rest of the party gathered round Dr. Boott to hear every particular which he had collected from the evening papers.

On March 2, the Richardsons, accompanied by Mrs. Fletcher, returned to Haslar, and as the preparations for the journey were by that time nearly completed, Sir John was able to be much in the family circle, though the serious illness of his children's faithful nurse occupied much of his time and thoughts. Mrs. Fletcher has noted down in her journal: ' It is only necessary to see the invariable cheerfulness and goodness of Sir John Richardson in his own house, and his attention to those most dependent on his kindness, to form a true value of his admirable character. I saw him at a time of great excitement, just about to leave his happy home and part with all he most loved on earth, to fulfil what he considered a sacred duty.'

March 25 was fixed as the day of sailing from Liverpool, and early in the morning of the 20th he left Haslar, to the sorrow, and with the blessings of all around him. We pass over the affecting scene of parting with her who had so recently cast in her lot with his, and the children on whom he fondly doted. To his sister Mrs. Wallace he wrote : 'I pray God to bless you and your large family. If you bring them up in the fear of the Lord, you do more for them than if you left them a fortune. Let religious instruction be a main employment with you. A few clear words on that subject from a mother are remembered in after years, and may by God's blessing be the means of saving an immortal soul.'

After a few days he was on the broad Atlantic, eager to reach the Arctic Sea and examine, during the brief polar summer of that year, the coast between the Mackenzie and Coppermine Rivers, and the south coast of Wollaston's Land, in hopes of aiding his long absent friend and the crews of the ' Erebus ' and ' Terror.'

CHAPTER XXI.

1848.

ON May 19, 1845, **the** 'Erebus' and 'Terror,'
under the command of Sir John Franklin, sailed
from England, **and** reached Whalefish Islands,
near Disco, **early in** July. They were seen, for the
last time, by **the** 'Prince of Wales,' whaler, on
the 26th of that **month, making for** Lancaster
Sound.

A year and a half later, fears for the safety of
Franklin began **to be** expressed, and the Admiralty, at **the** close **of** 1847, despatched vessels to
meet him with **supplies at** Behring's Straits; two
ships were sent **in 1848 on Franklin's** route, and
Sir John Richardson **was** despatched through Rupert's **Land to** the coast of the Arctic Sea.

These were the beginnings of a series of searching expeditions, persevered in, year after year, until tidings were obtained.

Sir John Richardson and Dr. Rae landed at New York on April 10, and after having ascertained the rate of the chronometers, they started for Albany and Troy, proceeding by way of Lake Champlain to Montreal, where the canoe-men, engaged for them by Sir George Simpson, had been ordered to rendezvous. From Montreal, the route lay through Lakes Ontario, Erie, St. Claire, and Huron, to Sault St. Marie, where, being in advance of the season, they were detained for several days by ice at the outlet of Lake Superior.

When off Halifax Harbour, on April 7, he wrote to his eldest daughter :—

Forty years ago, on this very day, I entered the navy, and I have had a varied and arduous course by sea and land in the progress of my long service. It will gild the evening of life if I see my children growing up around me, beloved by their connections, acquiring knowledge steadily, and above all, devoting themselves unreservedly to the service of God. Be sure, my dearest Josephine, that there is no peace unless the heart be right with God, and as love to Him is incompatible with any self-indulgent feeling, He tries those whom He loves, in various ways, until He has brought them wholly to Himself. It is my prayer that you may meet Him and co-operate with His Holy Spirit in this gracious work. God bless you, my dear daughter, and may you set a good example to your younger sister.

To his little daughter, six years old, he thus wrote, from Buffalo, Lake Erie, on Good Friday:—

My dearest Beatrice,—I am now travelling on the great American Lakes, and have reached the town or city of Buffalo, not far from the mighty Falls of Niagara. I intend to continue my voyages on these lakes, till I reach Fort William on Lake Superior, and shall then have gone over one quarter of the circumference or round of the earth. The earth, my dear little child, turns once completely round in twenty-four hours, presenting each spot in succession to the sun. If the circle it makes, in turning, be divided into twenty-four parts, each part is equal to an hour of time; or, if it be divided into 360 degrees, each hour includes fifteen degrees, and six hours are equal to ninety degrees, which is the longitude of Fort William west of Greenwich. When it is four o'clock in the afternoon with you, it is ten o'clock in the morning there.

You are not old enough to understand this, but Josephine will comprehend it, and endeavour to explain it to you; and should you have access to a globe, mamma will show you, by turning the globe round from west to east towards a candle, how each spot on the earth is lightened by the sun in succession. You will perceive by this, my dear child, that the light of the sun, powerful, brilliant, and warm, is not everywhere present at once, but comes to us in succession, and alternating with night; but God, the Creator of the sun and the earth, with all its inhabitants, and of the entire universe, is everywhere present at the same instant of time. His eye sees every action and thought, as clearly in the night as in the day, and not a withered leaf can fall from a tree in the pathless forests of this vast country but by His permission. Unless your papa was under the constant guardianship of His providence, his long journey would be a wild and vain attempt; and as He bids us pray regularly for assistance from His Holy Spirit, not only for ourselves, but for all that are dear to us, and for all mankind, I beseech you, my dear child, never to forget to pray, morning, evening, and at noon-day, for your papa.

You, mamma, Josephine, John, Willingham, and Edward, are constantly in my thoughts, and are always objects of my prayers. May the all-kind God grant my petitions and yours, if agreeable to His will. This letter is to be for Josephine as well as you. Be kind sisters one to another, and love your brothers.

From Hudson's Bay House, Michipicoten, Lake Superior, he wrote to his eldest son, John, on May 7 :—

My dear Boy,—This being the largest piece of fresh water in the world, is frequently called the King of Lakes. It occupies nearly as much space as the whole of England. At present it is not much frequented, except by straggling tribes and families of Indian hunters, and the fur traders passing to and fro between their posts, which are generally as far distant from each other as London is from West-moreland. To speak more correctly, this was the case a few years ago, but owing to the discovery of copper on both sides of the lake, its waters are now more frequently navigated. Two small steamboats now come up in the summer to the American mining stations on the south side of the lake, and on Grand Isle, or to the Canadian mines at Mamainse Point, which we passed yesterday at noon.

It is more than 100 miles from the spot at which I now write, which is in Michipicoten Bay.

We travel in two canoes, each manned by eight voyageurs, that is, travellers or sailors. As soon as the day begins to break, the guide, that is, the chief voyageur, who directs the others and points out the route, summons the party to rise, and we are all instantly on foot, every one engaged in rolling up his blankets, and trudging as quickly . as possible to the beach, from our sleeping place.

The guide and another man, called the ' gouvernail,' or helmsman, in the meantime put the canoe into the water, and as soon as all the luggage is properly stowed, we embark and paddle away. If the weather be fine and the wind moderate, the voyageurs begin to sing, and enliven their labour in that way, one man singing, and the others joining in a chorus.

At the present time of the year, it happens to be light about half-past three in the morning, and we are generally away from our encampment by four o'clock. We continue on our route till about eight or nine, when we put ashore on the first favourable spot that occurs, land the canteen, containing the tea-kettle, plates, knives, and spoons, teapot and teacups, make a fire with wood, which abounds everywhere, cutting down three or four trees for the purpose, and having cooked and eaten breakfast, we again embark and proceed on our voyage. The time allowed for breakfast is one hour.

At two o'clock we again put ashore, for half-an-hour, to dine, this time eating cold provisions. At seven, or half-past seven, we encamp for the night. The whole of the lading is brought to shore, and the canoes themselves are taken out of the water, to be dried and repaired, if necessary. A tent is pitched, and if the ground be uneven, the floor is laid with small flat branches of Canadian fir, which make a fine elastic carpet. This is covered with an oil-cloth, and our beds, rolled up, are placed for seats.

In the meantime, some of the party have cut firewood for the night, and placed the kettle in a proper situation. The fryingpan is made ready, and, in about an hour, we have tea, ham and eggs, with biscuit and butter; no bad fare after a long day's voyage. Supper being ended, we enjoy ourselves a little at the fireside, talking to the voyageurs, or to one another, and one of the men, whose business it is, unrolls the beds, and we retire for the night, after having read or written what is necessary.

I carry my Bible and Prayer-Book with me, and also an excellent book by Bishop Wilson, which I find a great help to my devotions; and, my dear son, I can assure you, from experience, that every care or danger is easily borne, when we acquire the habit of recurring to God for aid, and every pleasure sweetened, when we acknowledge that we owe it to His bounty. In our own strength we can do nothing, and it is only by His permission that we succeed in any attempt that we make.

The whole of the country bordering the lake is thickly covered with wood, and much of the land is rocky and unfit for agricultural purposes. It seems, however, to be a remarkably rich mineral district, and this may be the means of bringing a considerable population to some parts of its shores in a few years. If any of my accounts of my journeys should give you a desire to see these wild coun-tries, and try this mode of travelling through them, re-member that your desire will be most likely gratified by becoming an engineer. Some of the Royal Engineers are generally employed surveying or making observations on the confines of Canada, and a party of them, under Captain Lefroy, are established at Toronto, the capital of Canada West, for that purpose.

I have little chance of receiving your letters, my dear boy, till I am on my return home, but I shall be glad to meet them as harbingers of welcome on my way back. Adieu. I commend you to the protection of your Heavenly Father, beseeching Him to take you into His tender care.

On the ice breaking up at the outlet of Lake Superior, they resumed their journey, arriving at Fort William on May 12, and the water-shed of the St. Laurence and Winipeg Valleys on the 18th. The season was cold and wintry, and on reaching Norway House, Lake Winipeg, he thus wrote to Lady Richardson on June 5 :—

Our detentions and the wintry weather have been by no means pleasant, but I have endeavoured to repress all impatience to advance faster than circumstances permitted, and try to submit to the will of Him who orders all for the best. My companion, Mr. Rae, is the same cheerful person that I considered him to be at first; but, to equalise the lading, we travel in different canoes, and our days are consequently solitary. The many hours I spend alone will, I trust, be of vital service to me in bringing me into closer communion with God. The motion of the canoe prevents me from writing, and the weather has very generally been such that I can neither read nor write. It is a great consolation to me, at such times, to offer up petitions for you and the children, and for all my friends and connections.

I do not forget to pray for my enemies, though I am not conscious that I have one.

They reached Cumberland House on June 13, having travelled 2,880 statute miles after leaving New York on April 11. Deducting the time lost by ice obstructions, the journey was remarkable for speed. It was also arduous, the ascent to the summit of the water-shed between Lakes Superior and Winipeg, by the Kamenistikwoya River, being made by about forty portages, and the descent to the Winipeg by a greater number. Scenes of picturesque beauty were passed, from time to time, one of which was the Thousand Islands' Lake, which forms the funnel-shaped outlet of Lake Ontario. 'The round-backed, wooded hummocks of granite, which constitute the more than thousand islets of this expanse of water, are grouped into long vistas, which are alternately disclosed and shut in, as we glide smoothly and rapidly among them in one of the powerful steamers that carry on the passenger traffic of the lakes.'

Early in the morning of June 14, the party left Cumberland House, and two days later reached Beaver Lake. The season was now 'striding onwards rapidly, and the tender foliage was trembling on all sides in the bright sunshine.'

Cheerily they pushed on, encouraged by the tidings that Mr. Bell, who had charge of the boats and stores, though long delayed by the ice, was now making good progress.

The woods, **says Sir** John Richardson, in his 'Narrative of the Journey,' being **now in full but still tender** foliage, were beautiful. The graceful birch, in particular, **attracted** attention by its white stem, light green spray, **and pendent** golden catkins. **Willows of a** darker **foliage** lined **the** river bank, and the background was covered with dark green pines, intermixed **with patches of** lively aspen, and here and **there a tapering larch, gay with** its minute **tufts** of crimson **flowers, and young pale green** leaves. The balsam **poplar, with a silvery foliage, though** an ungainly stem, **and the dark** elder, disputed the **strand, at** intervals, with the willows, among which the purple twigs of the dogwood contributed effectively **to** add **variety and harmony** to the colours **of spring.**

On June **18 the** party reached **the Churchill** River, the boundary between **the** Chipewyan **and** Cree Indians. The navigation **was** impeded **by** portages; still they sped on, and reached Isle à la Crosse Fort **on the** 24th, to learn, with joy, that the boats and stores **were** still **four days in** advance.

At Methy **Portage, Sir John** Richardson **and** Dr. **Rae** overtook **the boats. Here an** unexpected delay occurred, owing **to the transport** horses belonging to an Indian **settler having all** died **of** murrain during the former autumn.

I had **used every** exertion, he **wrote, to** reach **the sea**coast some days before the appointed time, expecting to be able to examine Wollaston's Land this season. This hope was now almost extinguished. The portage occupied nine days from the time of Mr. Bell's arrival; but, with the assistance of horses, we could have passed it easily in three, and saved nearly a week of summer weather, most important for our future operations, besides husbanding the strength of the men. The transport of the four boats, being made on the men's shoulders, employed two days and a half of our time.

While these operations were being performed, he wrote to his two daughters on July 3 :—

My dearest Josephine and Beatrice,—I am now seated on the ground, near a small lake, about seven miles from one end of this long and, to the men, laborious portage, and four from the other. The hot sun beats through the tent and raises the temperature, while the mosquitoes crowd in at the other side, which we cannot keep shut, owing to a fresh breeze of wind which disorders the fastenings. I am, therefore, called off every moment from my pen, to remove the tiny creatures, that are increasing fast in size at the expense of the blood they draw from my veins.

God said he would send His fly to drive out the Amorites from before the people of Israel. A short experience of travel in this country teaches one how small a cause may destroy the comfort of men, and also gives the lesson, that comforts so easily destroyed are not worth the wise man's aim. The future is to be his object. The present world has its duties, which bring their reward; but the various illnesses, deprivations, and disquietudes to which we are exposed, tell us plainly, that whoever builds his hopes of happiness on any foundation but sincere love to God and His law, builds on a sandy soil. They who are constant in praying for His Holy Spirit to guide them in all their ways, are the most certain to have real enjoyment in this life.

Most of the feelings which embitter the mind arise from some petty rivalries or discourtesies, and the sure preventive is that divine spirit of love and forgiveness, which is generated by a love to God. My dearest girls, cultivate the domestic virtues. Be obedient and attentive to your mamma and governess. Write often and kindly to your brother John, and be very tender with Willingham and Edward. I shall be happy to receive minute accounts of all your doings from both of you. One of your shortest letters would be a great treasure to me at Fort Confidence, and I hope you will, from time to time, write out fully how you spend your time and of all the occurrences in the vale of Easedale.

God bless you, my dear children. Kiss your little brothers from papa.

On July 3, the whole of the baggage and the boats were brought to the banks of Little Lake, and on the 6th, everything having been carried over to Clear-Water River, the canoe-men set out on their return to Canada, and the expedition resumed their journey. They proceeded rapidly, and on the 9th entered the Elk or Athabasca River, a majestic stream, between a quarter and half a mile in breadth, with a considerable current, but without rapids, the speed attained by the boats being six geographical miles an hour. It is the most southern branch of the Mackenzie, and may be considered its source.

At the Athabasca Lake, they met the Mac- ·

kenzie River trading **boats, under** Mr. McPherson,
who informed **them** what means **he** had taken for
supplying the **expedition with** provisions during
their winter **residence at the north** end of Great
Bear Lake.

Once afloat **on the** Mackenzie, **they** pushed forward with all possible speed, **never** landing, except
to cook the necessary food; and during darkness,
fogs, or when the men required a few hours' sleep,
the boats were allowed to float with **the** current,
trusting that it would carry them clear of shoals
and low islands.   On through the Narrows, where
this magnificent **river is a** mile and **a** half broad,
and **fifty feet deep in** mid-channel, they reached
Point **Separation ; and, in** compliance with his instructions, **Sir John Richardson** buried a case **of
pemmican, with a memorandum for the** boat party
of the 'Plover,' should they reach **the** Mackenzie
from Behring's Straits. **In** September**, 1849,** Commander Pullen, with two boats **from the '** Plover,'
found **the** depôt **safe.**

Point Separation was the spot **at** which the
western exploring party, under Sir **John** Franklin,
and the eastern, under **Sir John** Richardson, sepa-
rated to fulfil **their allotted** tasks during the former
expedition, **and a slight feeling** of honest disappointment **was felt by the latter when he** thought
of the way **in which he and his** companions in
danger and daring **had been treated** by the House
of Commons.   ' In performing these duties at this

place,' he says, in his 'Boat Voyage through Rupert's Land,'—

I could not but recall to mind the evening of July 3, 1826, passed on the very same spot, in company with Sir John Franklin, Sir George Back, and Lieutenant Kendall. We were then full of joyous anticipation of the discoveries that lay in our several paths, and our crews were elated with the hope of making their fortunes by the Parliamentary reward promised to those who should navigate the Arctic Seas up to certain meridians. When we pushed off from the beach, on the morning of the 4th, to follow our separate routes, we cheered each other with hearty good will and no misgivings. Sir John's voyage fell some miles short of the Parliamentary distance, and he made no claim. My party accomplished the whole space between the assigned meridians; but the authorities decided that the reward was not meant for boats, but for ships. Neither men nor officers made their fortunes; and, what I more regretted, my friend and companion, Lieutenant Kendall, remained in that rank till the day of his death, notwithstanding his subsequent important scientific services.

On the present occasion, I endeavoured to stimulate our crews to an active look-out by promising ten pounds to the first man who should announce the Discovery ships.

The estuary of the Mackenzie was reached on August 4, when a tumbling sea drove them to leeward, and a succession of stormy weather was experienced. Here Sir John Richardson fell in with the Esquimaux, but could obtain no information of the missing ships.

P

The expedition, after a journey of 4,500 miles from New York, had now entered the field of search, which comprised the examination of the coast from the mouth of the Mackenzie to the Coppermine River, and the shores of Victoria and Wollaston Lands lying opposite.

On August 11 they entered the green sea, then coasted eastwards, endeavouring to gain information whenever the Esquimaux were seen, and depositing provisions according to instructions. In a few days packs of drift-ice were seen, and stormy head-winds retarded their progress. After almost incredible efforts to advance through the ice-floes which obstructed their way, it became apparent that the boats must be abandoned. The disappointment was great. Sir John Richardson had hoped to deposit the boats and stores up the Coppermine River, beyond the range of the Esquimaux, so as to be available for a voyage to Wollaston Land during the following summer. If left on the coast, the boats were certain to be found and destroyed.

The 1st and 2nd of September were employed in preparing to cross the country to their winter quarters at Great Bear Lake. How solemn that Sunday morning, when, after breakfasting, the party united at six o'clock, and Sir John read prayers before beginning their journey! Baffled in their enterprise, they were about to turn from the ice-bound sea, which held, firmly locked up, the secret of the missing ships and the struggle of their crews for life.

Having committed their way unto the Almighty, the party set out, carrying thirteen days' provisions, cooking utensils, hatchets, astronomical instruments, a few books, the ammunition, two nets, lines, a portable boat, and other necessaries, the load of each man being calculated to weigh sixty or seventy pounds. Wearily they marched on over hills covered with snow and through half-frozen swamps, the discomfort being frequently augmented by the freezing of their clothes, which were wet in crossing streams, a branch of the Kendall River having taken them up to the waist.

Our course, says Sir John, in his journal, was shaped directly across the country for Dease's River, and as we ascended the high grounds, the fog became more dense, so that by noon we could not see beyond two or three yards. We steered by the compass, Mr. Rae leading, and the rest following in Indian file. I kept rather in the rear, to pick up stragglers; but though we walked at a much brisker pace than usual, there was little loitering. The danger of losing the party made the worst walkers press forward. On the hills the snow covered the ground thickly ; and it is impossible to imagine anything having a more dreary aspect than the lakes which frequently barred our way. We did not see them until we came suddenly to the brink of the rocks which bounded them, and the contrast of the dark surface of their waters with the unbroken snow of their borders, combined with the loss of all definite outline in the fog, caused them to resemble hideous pits sinking to

an unknown depth. The country over which we travelled
is composed chiefly of granite; and after walking till half-
past five, without perceiving a single tree or the slightest
shelter, we came to a convex rock, from which the snow
had been swept by the wind. On this we resolved to
spread our blankets, as it was just big enough to accom-
modate the party. There being no fuel of any kind on the
spot, we went supperless to bed. Some of the party had
no rest, and we heard them groaning bitterly; but others,
among whom were Mr. Rae and I, slept well. We learned
afterwards that a clump of wood grew within a mile and
a half of our bivouac; but even had we been apprised of
its existence, we could scarcely have found it in the fog.
Several showers of snow occurred in the day, and some
fell in the night.

On the afternoon of September 15 the weary
journey was ended, the expedition having safely
reached the winter station at the north side of
Great Bear Lake, and found that Mr. Bell's
party had the houses nearly finished. On the
17th all met in the hall, and Sir John read divine service, the fishers, employed about five miles
distant, having come in to join in the Sunday
worship. These services were kept up during the
long winter, and regularly attended, even by the
Roman Catholics from Canada.

The day after the party arrived at Fort Confidence, he wrote to Lady Richardson:—

The whole party, thank God, got here safely yesterday,
but I regret to say without hearing any tidings of the Dis-

covery ships, or having it in our power to render assistance
to their crews; or rather, I hope that our not having been
privileged to do this may be a favourable omen, and that
they have either effected a passage in higher latitudes than
those we followed, or returned to England by the way in
which they came out.

We reached the sea on the 3rd of August, and were soon
afterwards beset by upwards of three hundred Esquimaux,
who were very importunate in their demands; but the
strength of our party, well armed with guns, kept them
within bounds, and we parted, after a troublesome interview
of some hours, on terms of friendship. They are the most
expert and determined thieves I ever met with, and succeeded in abstracting a few things from one of the boats
which had no officer in it. After this we advanced along
the coast, which is fully described in the 'Narrative of the
Eastern party of Franklin's Expedition,' and remained a
few days at Point Atkinson, in the neighbourhood of a
small party of Esquimaux, who were assembling there to
chase the whale. With these people we were on very
friendly terms, traded with them for sea trout, and made
them many presents; but even they could not resist the pro-
pensity to steal.

The weather continued good, and our voyage pleasant
until we entered the Union and Dolphin Straits, which
we found packed with ice, which rendered the air cold;
and on August 23, winter fairly set in, with hard frost
and much snow which remained on the ground. The
frost bound all the pieces of ice together, and we could no
longer push our way among them. On September 3, all
hope of doing so with success was abandoned, being at
that time in Icy Cove, a narrow inlet not marked on

the map, but situated about nine miles to the north of Cape Kendall.

We left the boats at this place, and set out for Bear Lake by way of the Coppermine. On the same evening we reached Back's Inlet, and made our beds under a high cliff, where we slept soundly. Next day we came to the banks of a wide and deep river falling into the inlet, and should have found much difficulty and lost much time in crossing but for the aid of a friendly party of Esquimaux, who ferried us across with their kaiyaks, two and two together. Some of these men had seen Dease and Simpson's party, and they came to us without fear. They were fine manly fellows with open countenances, indicating content and cheerfulness. Their dress was neat and clean. Their women, on the other hand, were dirty, had much inferior countenances, and looked all the worse for the extremity of their fears, which they could not or did not attempt to conceal.

Having rewarded these kind people to the extent of our power, and more highly than they expected, we resumed our journey, and next day crossed the Richardson by help of Lieutenant Halkett's portable boat, and the same evening encamped on the banks of the Coppermine. There we had hoped to be met by a party of hunters whom I had appointed to be here in the first week in September, but the bad weather which arrested our progress on the coast prevented them from leaving Bear Lake, as I have learned since my arrival. We therefore continued the ascent of the Coppermine to the Kendall, which we crossed on a raft and directed our course to Bear Lake.

The following day we had a very thick fog; and having to cross some high hills covered with snow, we found no firing, and, when evening closed in, lay down on a rock,—

Mr. Rae and I side by side on our plaids, with our two blankets, and an oil cloth over us. Under this covering we passed a comfortable night, though some of the men, whose blankets were of smaller size, fared worse. On this day the party in search of us lost their way, and did not recover their proper course for three days. We were more fortunate, and steering by compass were able to advance in weather that would stop an Indian. On the following day we came to a fine clump of wood, and were fully recompensed, by the excellence of our night's encampment, for the badness of the preceding one. We had plenty of provisions, geese, partridges, and venison, and greatly enjoyed our warm supper.

The following day we were seen by a party of Indians, more than five miles off, who raised a signal smoke, knowing, by having seen the party in quest of us, who we were. Our route was altered in order to join them, and we purchased a full supply of excellent deer-meat, besides hiring one of their number as a guide. He led us in three days more to Fort Confidence, by better, though not more direct, paths than we should have chosen for ourselves.

The whole march was thirteen days, and I thank God that I have suffered no inconvenience from the exertion, but, on the contrary, feel myself more able for a journey of similar extent than when I set out from the boats. Many instances of God's favour during the past voyage have been manifest to me, and I have had daily occasions for thanksgiving.

On the whole, I have been in a most comfortable and happy frame of mind. Mr. Rae has taken the labouring oar and managed it well. The Fall Boat, as it is called, or the boat bringing our things from Norway House, being the last of the season, has not yet arrived, and I am without further intelligence from home of a later date than that which I received at Sault St. Marie. How much I long for a few lines of your well-known hand to look upon.

Dr. Rae has kindly **supplied the** following interesting details :—

I shall pass over our journey through the inland rivers of the Hudson's Bay territory, and come at once to the boat voyage along the coast, from the Mackenzie to the Coppermine River, which was a very trying one, on account of the ice which was packed close on the shore. Whenever we had an opportunity of making observations for latitude and longitude, we found that the former survey of the coast had been made with correctness.

When we were forced to abandon our boats in consequence of the young ice, which was not strong enough to bear our weight, we were thirteen days' journey, for laden men, from winter-quarters on Bear Lake; and as we did not know, from personal experience, the quantity of game likely to be found on the route, and were aware that the men could kill nothing for themselves either with net or gun, we had to take full allowance for the whole time, and Sir John, at first, insisted on carrying a part.

When fully equipped and ready to start, he read prayers in a most impressive manner outside the tent; and our appearance, with gun on shoulder and loads on our backs, reminded me much of what I had read of the Covenanters of old, when they worshipped in the glens and on the hillsides, prepared at a moment's notice either to fight with or flee from their persecutors. The season of the year was the worst possible for travelling over a rugged country. There had been much rain, some snow and frost, but not sufficient of the latter to make the soaked ground hard enough to bear our weight, so that the labour of walking was very great.

Sir John once and only once seemed to suffer from fatigue on the journey. We had been up a hill full of half-frozen holes of water, when he was seized with spasm of the heart and with cramps, which he thought would prevent his continuing the day's walk, but he recovered in a short time and was able to proceed. Our flour being nearly expended, we had little to live upon but pemmican, which did not agree with Sir John; and he would not use the whole of the little cake which was baked for us each day by Albert, but insisted on my taking the half, and it was only by stratagem that I could get him to have any other diet than I took myself. Fortunately, we were soon able to get a few ptarmigan, ducks, and geese, and at last a deer, so that the change of food quickly restored him to perfect health.

On September 16, he wrote to his eldest daughter :—

MY DEAREST JOSEPHINE,—During the long and arduous voyage which I have now happily finished, by God's blessing, I have daily, and several times in the day, prayed earnestly that He would extend His protecting care to you and your sister and brothers. I trust He has heard my prayers and that you are all safe; and moreover that you show your sense of His continued mercy and watchful, ever-present eye, by docility and kindness to those who have the rule over you, and diligence in performing your appointed tasks. I hope, should He spare us to meet again, to give you an account of many instances of His good Providence which we experienced in our voyage; and I feel that, without His sustaining hand, I should not now be seated, at my ease, in a comfortable room, writing this brief letter to you. May God ever bless you, my dear child.

The party at Fort Confidence consisted of forty-two persons, and the Indians were certain to be attracted, in considerable numbers, to the wintering-place of the expedition. To lessen, therefore, the difficulty of procuring sufficient food, Sir John sent off eighteen of the party to winter at the fishing station on Big Island, Great Slave Lake (two of them being intrusted with letters for England), to Isle à la Crosse, where the wife of one of them resided. The resources of the Fort were considered ample to maintain the remainder, and the winter was expected without anxiety. To secure abundance, however, he thought it prudent to continue a fishery at the west end of Great Bear Lake, lest the take near the Fort should fail.

CHAPTER XXII.

1848—1849.

On September 20, Sir John received letters from his family in England, and immediately wrote to Lady Richardson :—

The Fall Boat has brought us ample supplies. In order to bring our necessities within the resources of the vicinity, I sent away half the men of our establishment, and have now received pemmican enough to put us out of the reach of want, even though the season should prove unusually bad, of which I have no apprehension at present.

Reindeer are numerous. The Indians are healthy and active ; supplies come in steadily, and we have abundance of goods to pay for them. I am thankful to God, whose providence in ordinary events can be more distinctly traced in a land like this, than in the complicated mazes of civilised life.

My public despatch and letter to you will have informed you, in brief terms, that I examined the whole line of coast mentioned in my instructions, with the exception of Wollaston and Victoria Lands, which we could not approach for ice.   Mr. Rae, with one boat, and a crew of active volunteers, of his own selection, will perform this service next summer ; and to save government farther expense, I shall myself return to England as quickly as possible, taking all the English party with me to Norway House.   I shall return by way of Canada, as it will be necessary for me to remain some days at La Chine to arrange the accounts.   I hope to take my passage from Boston in one of the October steamers.

I have a series of magnetic observations to make which will fully occupy my time during the stay here, and I intend to cross the lake, on the ice, after the snow is gone— that is, in the end of April or beginning of May.   If I keep my health as well during the comparative inactivity of winter as I have done during the voyage and overland march, I have nothing more to desire, except to find all well when I return home.

Their winter-quarters and employments are described in the following letters, written in the form of a journal, and begun on October 3, 1848 :—

Since I sent off my last letter, we have had a fortnight of unusually mild weather for the time of the year in this district.   The snow disappeared even from the hills, a considerable quantity of rain fell, and the marshes became almost impassable.   The untimely frosts, in August, cut off the usual supply of cranberries, and other fruits which this country produces.   Not that they altogether failed, but they are much less abundant than usual, and of inferior quality.

On the disappearance of the snow, the deer, which had begun to draw towards Bear Lake, returned to the northward, and our supplies of venison have consequently become scanty. Fish are also scarce.

In no part of the world does the supply of daily food appear to proceed more directly from the Almighty. The agency of man is much more limited than in civilised life, where, from the multiplicity of concurring agents, we are apt to lose sight of the good providence of God. Here, on the other hand, our supply of daily food is like the manna in the wilderness. Unless the wild beasts are driven to their usual haunts by the weather proper to the season, and the frost sets in at the usual period, the hunter's skill avails not, and we also lose what is called the Fall fishery. The petition, therefore, 'give us this day our daily bread,' is felt here in its full importance.

Indeed, if this expedition should be unproductive of public advantage, it will, I trust, produce the personal benefit of bringing me into closer communion with God. I have so many petitions to offer for you, the other dear ones at home, and the rest of my absent friends, and so much reason for thankfulness for the numerous providential occurrences of the voyage, that I must be dull indeed were my devotional feelings not rendered more fervent.

October 7.—I have been busy for the last four days in putting some instruments for observation on magnetism in adjustment, and shall have full occupation, during my stay here, in attending to them. I have had a small observatory built, in front of the house, so that I have a very short way to walk from the fireside.

I may as well give you a short descriptive sketch of our residence and routine of life, which, I expect, will be very little varied till next spring. **Fort Confidence** is situated on a rising bank, **about** thirty **feet from** the borders of the lake, **on** the north **side of the bay,** into which Dease's River falls. A large island, opposite to **the** house, divides the entrance of the bay into straits, **the** northernmost, on which the fort stands, being about three-quarters of a mile wide. The island rises gently to **the** height of **about** one hundred and twenty feet in the centre, **and is well** wooded on our side. The wood, within a mile of the **house, has** been mostly cut **down for firing** or building purposes. Dease's River is **about** three miles distant.

When Mr. Bell arrived here, in the middle of August, to prepare our winter-quarters, he found none of the buildings erected by Dease and Simpson remaining, except **a** house for the labourers, and two chimneys of the dwelling-house. **All the rest had been burnt down** by the carelessness **or wantonness of the Indians. His** first care was to build **a good-sized store-house** of squared logs, let **into** grooved **posts at the** four corners, roofed with the same, the interstices **being** filled with tempered clay well beaten in. The dwelling-house was next commenced on a ground plan of forty feet by fourteen, having a dining-hall in the centre, **measuring** sixteen by fourteen feet, and the remaining space divided **into a store-room,** and three sleeping apartments.

The chimneys are built of stone and clay, and project into the several rooms, occupying a good deal of space. We have floors and ceilings of planed boards, the walls being, like those **of the store,** of squared logs daubed with clay. Each of the **sleeping-rooms has a** glazed window, but the hall windows are **only of** parchment. We have well-made tables, beds, and convenient shelves in our apartments, and **the carpenters** are now busy framing chairs. In fact, we are provided with everything essential to comfort, including a good supply of tea-cups, plates, and cooking utensils.

The hall is not only our breakfast and dining-room, but also the place of resort of the Indians when they come to the house. This is the custom, or I should have been inclined to build a detached room for the natives. Our numbers are likely to be increased by a few old and infirm Indians, who are sure to become pensioners on the esta-blishment in the course of the winter.

November 2.—My library, as you know, is a very small one, but it is a great solace. Most of the books were chosen by yourself, and I thank you, dear, for making so good a selection, which will bear recurring to again and again. I feel the advantage of having only a few books, in that one reads with more care and deliberation. It is owing to this that I have felt Shakespere's beauties more than I ever had time to do before. I have read through the one volume copy of his plays your mother gave me, with great pleasure, since coming to Fort Confidence, and shall do so again, at least once a month, during my stay.

My after tea treat, at present, is from your copy of Bacon's ' Essays ' and Cowper's ' Task.' The return of our messenger from Fort Simpson may be described in Cowper's words, from his ' Winter's Evening on the Arrival of the Post,' with a very slight alteration :—

> He comes, the herald of a noisy world,
> With snowy boots, strapp'd waist, and frozen locks,
> News from all nations lumbering at his back.
> True to his charge, the close-pack'd load behind,
> Yet careless what he brings, his one concern
> Is to conduct it to the destined Fort ;
> But oh the important budget, who can say
> What are its tidings ?

November 4.—On Monday, two men, with an Indian, are to set out with the packet for Fort Simpson, and we shall count the days until they return. The temperature fell last night to twenty-seven degrees below zero, the sky was beautifully clear, the aurora borealis brilliant, and to-day we have a bright sun. Winter has set in without any mistake, and we want only a little more snow, to make the sledges run smoothly over rough ground, to complete our comfort in these respects.

I register the temperature every hour, the height of the mercury in the barometer, the winds and weather, and the position of the magnetic needle, from seven in the morning till midnight, Mr. Rae assisting me. This, with observations on the magnetic force, and observations of the stars to regulate the chronometers, furnishes both of us with sufficient occupation.

I am now writing after our dinner hour. The cloudless sky and the clear bright fire tell of a cold evening. A beautiful moon—the half-full—sheds a chilly light over the scene, and I think of those beloved ones, who have her light in their evening, but to whom she is now set, or setting. When I offer up my nightly prayers for you all, I hope that you are in the enjoyment of sound midnight repose, and when I repeat my petitions in the morning, you are all about your noon-day occupations. There is a satisfaction in looking at the silvery satellite which I know you must have been contemplating only a few hours previously, but my heart is most strongly drawn towards you when I pray that we may all be united hereafter in that heavenly union which fears no separation.

On October 26, Sir John Richardson thus wrote to Mrs. Fletcher :—

I requested Mary to inform those interested in my movements of the progress I was making, and I shall not therefore trouble you with a repetition of the outline of my route.

I know that you always feel a lively interest in anything relating to the welfare of the great family of mankind and its progress towards freedom and happiness; but the people by whom I am now surrounded cannot be said to have made a single step as yet on the road to civilisation. They are free enough. Every man does that which is right in his own eyes, the only restraint on his actions being the desire of standing well in the opinion of his neighbours; for I believe that the Hare Indians, of whom I write, have no religious worship; nor have I been able to learn that they have any distinct idea of a Deity, nor how far they are possessed of a conscience of right and wrong.

The men hunt or fish, and as a good hunter is esteemed by his tribe, the more generous of the young men are stimulated by a desire of excelling in the art; but, as in other communities, there are many indolent people among them also, who are content to be looked down upon, while they live by the labours of the more active. The women dress, for clothing, the skins of the animals that are slain, construct the huts or tents, and draw or carry the baggage in their migrations. One cannot suppose that their mode of life or motives of action could ever have been more rude or simple.

The traders have as yet introduced few new wants among them. Guns have replaced their bows and arrows, and in addition to the ammunition which they require and purchase with skins or meat, they procure now and then a small piece of blue or scarlet cloth or a blanket. These are actually not more useful to them than their leather or fur dresses, but they look gayer in their eyes.

They are not provident. Indeed custom prevents their being so to any extent, as a successful hunter must share his game with those in the same encampment, should they be in want. When animals are scarce they are exposed to famine, and many years seldom pass without some deaths from this cause. When they have abundance they are merry enough, are great mimics, and enjoy a joke heartily; but they are very timid, and give way to causeless alarms. A strange footstep will strike terror into a whole encampment.

An incident of this nature occurred on the lake while Dease and Simpson were residing on the spot where our house is built. An Indian, bringing a packet of letters for these gentlemen, not knowing exactly where the fort was situated, was looking for it in an arm of the lake at some distance. Several families of Dog-ribs, a section of the Hare Indians, encamped in the neighbourhood, saw the track of a southern snow-shoe, and observed the fire of this solitary man. Their fears magnified his single track into the trail of a war-party, and they fled instantly towards the fort, abandoning everything they had, and burrowing at night under the snow.

None of the Indian tribes in this quarter consider it a virtue to speak the truth. They almost invariably tell a lie at first, even among themselves, and the fact has to be gathered from subsequent communications. This habit soon causes a rumour of a trifling accident to swell into some dreadful calamity.

From what I have seen of the Indians, I am confirmed in the belief that a simple mode of living and few wants do not produce innocence, and that, as the Bible informs us, the thoughts of man's heart are evil continually, if unconverted by the Gospel. Arcadian innocence and happiness exist only in the imaginations of the poets. The missionaries have as yet not advanced farther than Isle à la Crosse, about one thousand miles to the south of this place, but the Hare Indians, Dog-ribs, Copper Indians, and other tribes in this district, are branches of the Chipewyan stock, of whom the converts at Isle à la Crosse are composed, and of whose natural disposition the Roman Catholic missionaries speak well.

Perhaps these virtues are the first-fruits of the teaching of the missionaries, and I should like to see the torch of truth carried into the dark regions of the north. The Esquimaux on the coast would, I am convinced, readily receive instruction, and I should rejoice were the Moravians to take them in hand. When I was formerly in this country, missionaries had not penetrated farther than the colony at Red River, which may be said to be comparatively on the confines of Canada, as a bi-monthly post has been established between it and the Upper Province.

Then most of the gentlemen and a large proportion of the servants were living with natives, and only a small number, when they retired from the service, took the women home with them. Now they marry, and the condition of these women has been raised. They are all sent to the schools at Red River, and are much less disqualified than formerly for taking their station in the civilised world when they follow their husbands thither.

My latest English news left you in London, on the eve of the threatened meeting on Kennington Common. I trust that it was not held, and that no riots ensued. By the return of the messenger who takes this to Fort Simpson (only twenty-five days' march off, and we look for him, therefore, in six weeks after he leaves us), I hope to hear that you travelled safely and comfortably to Lancrigg, and that Mary, with her charge, speedily followed; that you enjoy your 'Examiner' as you inhale the balmy air flowing through the open window into the pleasantest of drawing-rooms, and discuss the revolutions of Europe, as is your wont, with all the freshness of youthful hope.

Every day was teeming with events when I left England, and in January, or earlier, I expect to receive a quarter of a year's intelligence at once. You may judge of my anxiety to get my packet, but I do not look for it without fear. I have many treasures on earth and my heart strays towards them, convinced though I am that God orders all for the best, and that He sends trials to His people only in love.

Though we have none of the husbandman's hopes and fears in this region, our seasons of plenty and scarcity are no less influenced by the weather. God's providence rules it all, and He governs by his frosts and snow the migration of the deer and fish, as surely as He does the young blade of wheat by the genial weather in spring. The past summer was an unfavourable one here for vegetation. The frost and snow in August destroyed the blue-berries and other fruits. At Fort Simpson, the potatoes attained no greater size than that of small plums.

We have had snow lately, which has driven the deer into our vicinity, and the hunters have a good many laid up for us, at the distance of about two days' journey, but there is not yet sufficient snow to enable the sledge to bring them in. Meantime we have plenty. The temperature for a month past has been unusually mild for the season.

To his second daughter he wrote on Nov. 5 :—

MY DEAREST BEATRICE,—Having written to John and Josephine, I cannot let this packet go without a letter for my little Beatrice, and it has so happened that the letter is dated on papa's birth-day. Three-and-twenty years have passed since papa spent one of his birth-days on this lake, and many changes of kingdoms and families have occurred in that interval of time. It is a long period to look forward to, my dear little child, and to you, I fancy, it looks like a life-time, but I look back upon twenty-five years as a dream of the night.

So is it always. Time appears long in childhood and youth, and too short as we advance in years. It is a precious treasure, a talent committed to us by God, and it greatly concerns our eternal happiness that we make a good use of it. Yet there are none of our possessions of which we are so careless. It is given to us to prepare for eternity, and that ought therefore to be our chief care, and we ought to set apart a due portion of it to praying to God, reading the Bible, and other religious exercises.

A proper division of time to our several labours prevents waste. First pray to God, and rise early that you may have sufficient leisure to do it without interfering with the breakfast hour or other regulated occupations of the household. Then get your lessons and do your tasks. Work first, play afterwards. This will sweeten your hours of recreation. You cannot amuse yourself pleasantly if the thought of a lesson omitted is coming continually into your mind. Put everything in its proper place, and you will know where to find it again without loss of time. 'Let everything be done decently and in order ' is the advice of St. Paul; and if my little girl follows the precept, and

loves God and His Christ, she will be a good child, loved
here and happy hereafter.

I send you a little sermon, because you are a little girl ;
but you are bigger and older than Willy and Edward, and
I would, therefore, have you to be kind to them. Mamma
told me in her last letter that you intended to write to me.
Perhaps I may receive your letter by the next packet,
which will arrive in the middle of winter, and it will be a
nice Christmas gift. I am living so far to the north that the
sun does not rise here at Christmas ; but the Sun of Right-
eousness has risen for all quarters of the world, and His
glory will fill the whole earth. Adieu, my dear Beatrice.
May God bless you, is the prayer of your affectionate
father.

On January 21, 1849, he wrote to Lady Richardson :—

It is now time to seal up my letter, which is the last I
shall have an opportunity of sending until I am within the
humanities, I should perhaps say amenities, of a post-office.
I shall, however, from time to time, set down my cogita-
tions for your perusal on a wet day, such as Westmoreland
only knows, when the verdure of Easedale glows with a
brighter green under its invigorating bath. I long greatly
to have a peep at your golden fern, as it reflects the rays of
the western sun, and still more for a quiet saunter with
you along the Poet's Walk. When one strikes the key-note
of home, it has the effect of the tune of ' Lochaber ' on a
Highland emigrant.

I have sent to Lady Franklin a sketch of Mr. Rae's
intended proceedings next summer, and trust that if (which
God forbid) nothing should be heard of the Discovery
ships this year, she will be satisfied that this quarter has

been rigidly searched. Were it not for the dear ones
I left behind, I should scarcely feel myself to be an
unit of the great European family, and I could almost
fancy at times, when in my solitary room of an evening,
that I have never been anything but an inhabitant of
these wilds.

March 25.—We have received about 2,000 pounds'
weight of venison and two musk cows, so that we are
amply provided with provision for the remainder of the
season, and can minister to the wants of the Indians. The
fishery totally failed, and the Indians, who had been living
but indifferently for some time, found it necessary to move.
About ten days since they came in a body to the fort and
received rations from the store, with a supply for their
journey on the following day. Two of our fort hunters
who had left their wives at the fishery, came to take
them to their hunting-grounds, where, having been successful, they had a small store of venison.

One of these, a young and very small woman, was confined of her first child in the morning, just as the party
began to move off from their rude huts of pine-tree branches,
constructed in the snow a few hundred yards from our
house. The new-born infant was wrapped in a deer's skin
and stuck in a hole made in the snow, as the softest bed
that could be found. When the intelligence reached the
fort, one of the women went for it and dressed it by my
fire. This event delayed the mother's departure an hour
or two, when she set out, taking her infant on her back
and dragging her household goods on a sledge. She was
not even permitted to walk on the well-beaten track made
by the party who had gone before, as she would have
thereby destroyed the luck of the hunters, but had to make

a fresh road for herself in the loose snow, parallel to the other.

April **22.**—A little before one o'clock in the morning of the 12th of this **month, I** was awoke by a man coming into **my** room to **tell** me that the packet had arrived: I dressed **with all expedition, and** after returning thanks **to God** for the blessing, and praying that the intelligence might be **favourable,** was speedily engaged with your **dear** communications. **I** received, **in** addition **to** the letters by the ship, **two others** through the United States, **the latest bearing** date **June 22, 1848.** I did not go to bed again, and **by six** o'clock had read all your letters, and before breakfast had also taken the cream off the newspapers.

A party of Indians, twelve in number, arrived **three** days ago with dried **meat** from a considerable distance, their journey having occupied six **days.** They were descried afar off **by** the inhabitants of the Indian lodges near **the** fort, and **all the women** and children **came in** front of the store **to wait** their arrival.

The **first act of** the new-comers was to run **the** loaded sledges into the store-house, which was opened to receive them. The chiefs of the party were suffered to pass in with impunity; but as a young lad was crossing the threshold the women, with shouts **of** welcome, threw their arms around his neck, while one of them cut the strings of his knapsack and its edible contents were appropriated by the harpies. **All was done in** perfect good humour, and the young **fellow bore his** loss well, as it is beneath the dignity of an Indian to quarrel about meat.

The following passage, from his 'Journal of a **Boat V**oyage through Rupert's Land,' shows that there was no time for **ennui** during **the** long winter at Fort Confidence.

Two men were constantly employed as sawyers; four as cutters of fire-wood, each of them having an allotted task of providing a cord of wood daily; others were occupied in drawing it home on sledges, and four men were continually engaged in fishing.

On the Sunday, no labour was performed, the fishing party came in, and all were dressed in their best clothes. Prayers were said in the hall, and a sermon read to all who understood English; and some of the Canadians, though they were Roman Catholics, usually attended. James and Thomas Hope, who were Cree Indians, having been educated at Norway House as Protestants, and taught to read and write, were regular attendants; and James Hope's eldest son, a boy about seven years of age, who had already begun to read the Scriptures, frequently recognised passages in the lessons he had previously read.

During the winter, Mr. Rae and I recorded the temperature hourly, sixteen or seventeen times a day; also the height of the mercury in Delcroix's barometer; the degrees of the aneroid barometer, the declinometer, and dipping-needle. Once in the month a term-day, extending to thirty-six hours, was kept, in which the fluctuations of the magnets were noted every two and a half minutes, and various series of observations were made for ascertaining the magnetic intensity with the magnetometer, the vibration apparatus, and Lloyd's dipping-needle. Mr. Rae ascertained frequently the time and rates of the chronometers by observation of the fixed stars; and a register of the winds and weather and appearances of the aurora was constantly kept.

Both officers and men had their appointed tasks to perform, and enjoyed as much comfort as could be expected. It almost freezes the blood in one's veins, however, to think of an average temperature over the 17th and 18th of December of fifty-five and a half degrees below zero. During that month the sun was absent ten days, rays of light shooting into the sky at the beginning of January being the only indication of his reappearing.

If, before the setting in of winter, they had succeeded in conveying the boats and stores to a place of safety on the Coppermine, Sir John Richardson and Dr. Rae would have resumed the search during the summer of 1849, and mutually aided each other in attempting to cross over to Wollaston Land; but having now only one boat for that service, it became necessary to decide which of them should take charge of the small party it could carry.

Sir John decided to give the command to Dr. Rae, who was in the prime of life and peculiarly fitted for the duty; while, to save expense to the Government, he with as many of the men as were not required for the enterprise should return to England.

On May 1, he delivered to Dr. Rae a memorandum appointing him to continue the search in the direction of Wollaston and Victoria Lands. During the summer, Dr. Rae perseveringly endeavoured to carry out his instructions, but as

Coronation Gulf remained full of impracticable ice, every attempt to cross over was frustrated.

Sir John Richardson set out from Fort Confidence on May 7, and passed Great Bear Lake, on the ice, in five days and a half.

Referring to the winter spent together, Dr. Rae says :—

Sir John's mind and time seemed to be constantly occupied in useful pursuits, his recreation being the repeating of poetry, with which his memory appeared to be largely stored, and the study of the Scriptures.   During the latter part of the winter I observed that he became habitually more cheerful and fonder of society, as if his mind had been relieved from some great care.

The lateness of the season detained Sir John Richardson's party for a month, Bear Lake River, which flows into the Mackenzie, remaining impassible, from ice, till June 9. From Fort Franklin, or rather its site, as no vestige of their former winter home remained, he wrote :—

This is an uncomfortable atmosphere for the gipsying life which we are leading, under an old sail for a tent ; but the thaw advances, and the season for our release from Great Bear Lake comes, though with lagging pace.   The mossy ground on which we are encamped has become a wet sponge, but the soil is still frozen ; and we had to cut a trench round the tent with a hatchet, to convey the water away that flows from the melting banks of snow lying deep on the hill-side.

The red-breasted thrush, called in America the 'robin,'

the golden-headed warbler, the white-headed finch, which whistles ' O dear, what can the matter be,' and several other song-birds, now enliven the woods with their notes. They begin singing immediately after midnight, and are most silent in the heat of the day, so that they are night warblers or nightingales.

Geese, swans, gulls, and eagles are continually passing, all hasting to their breeding-places. They will return again from the north with their young in August. These periodical flights may be considered as the first and second harvests of the few Indian tribes scattered so widely over this extensive country. God deals as faithfully with them as He does with the husbandman of more genial climates.

The sun in the clear spring atmosphere has a power which equals that of the tropics, and although there is a great difference between the temperature of the air here and at the Equator, yet the direct rays of the sun act with greater force on the skin in Rupert's Land. When the snow is filled with water it looks like frosted silver in the sunlight, and every little rising is studded with innumerable polished facets, as if sprinkled with diamonds. The intensity of all this splendour soon becomes painful to the eye.

Here only, of all the countries I have seen, can I understand the deep blue skies of some of the ancient Italian masters. Two days ago I was particularly struck with the pure China-blue of the whole vault of heaven, a few soft fleecy clouds floating seemingly far beneath, and giving the appearance of immeasurable distance to the blue profound. Towards the horizon it gradually softened into grey, and blended beautifully with the snow of the distant hills empurpled by the rays of the nearly level sun. The depth of shade which marks out the low snowy waves of the lake when the sun is low would surprise a painter brought here for the first time.

The river which flows from this to the Mackenzie is now open, and the latter will be navigable ten or twelve days hence.

From Bear Lake River, he wrote on May 31:—

We have been encamped here for eight or nine days, waiting the arrival of our boat. The weather has been stormy, cold, and snowy. The snow geese are still passing in flocks, and we kill some daily, taking also fish by nets and lines set under the ice of the lake. Our meals make a break in the monotony of our lives.

On June 25 they left Fort Simpson, and arrived at Norway House on August 13. Here Sir John discharged the men who had been engaged in 1847, the Europeans being sent to York Factory to be conveyed to England in the Hudson's Bay ships.

From Norway House he proceeded to Canada in a brigade of three canoes, manned by voyageurs who were returning thither at the close of their engagements in the fur country, and arrived at Sault St. Marie on September 25. Thence he travelled by steam-boat and coach to Montreal, and after spending a few days at La Chine with Sir George Simpson, the Governor of the Hudson's Bay Company, proceeded to Boston. He landed at Liverpool on November 6, after an absence of nineteen months, twelve of them passed in incessant travelling.

Having presented himself at the Admiralty and laid before their lordships a narrative of his proceedings, he shortly after received a letter announcing their approbation of his conduct.

His arrival at Haslar is thus described by Mrs. Fletcher in a letter to Dr. and Mrs. Boott, of Gower Street, London, dated Haslar, November 10, 1849 :—

Our traveller arrived by the late train on Wednesday night. He came in while the children were dancing to the tune of 'There's nae luck aboot the hoos;' and you may believe that his entrance did not spoil our mirth, although it gave it a more subdued and quiet character. He is, thank God, in perfect health, nor could we extract from him a single complaint of the hardships and privations he has suffered.

It would do your hearts good to see with how much warmth of feeling he has been greeted by his friends, the officials in the hospital, their wives, and children. It seems to me that sailors are united, by a sense of common danger, in a closer brotherhood than men of other professions. It was touching to see Sir Edward Parry grasp Sir John's hand and say, 'My dear Richardson, how very glad I am to see you!'—his eyes being full of tears, which he tried to conceal, but could not.

In Mrs. Fletcher's Journal is the following entry :—

Although we had heard of his arrival at Liverpool, by telegram on the evening of Monday the 6th, he did not reach Dr. Gray's at the British Museum till Tuesday evening. The following morning he had to report himself at the Admiralty, where he was detained several hours by meeting Sir James Ross, who had returned from the Arctic search. As the hour for the arrival of the train approached there was much excitement in the household. The younger children were wisely set to expend their energies in dancing to the merry tunes their governess played to them, while mamma and Josephine were watching from a front window for the lamps of the fly crossing Haslar Bridge.

About eight o'clock on the evening of November 8 he was thankfully received at his happy home. We all thought him looking better and younger than when he went away, and never were more heartfelt prayers of thankfulness uttered than those he offered up with his household that night.

A succession of visitors, neighbours and friends, bidding him a hearty welcome home, poured in the following morning. Sir John did not attempt to speak, but gladness shone in his face. The letters, which would have given so much comfort to his wife had they arrived in the spring as he expected, are now daily reaching Haslar, and are full of family affection, of trust in God's mercy, and of cheerful hope.

, One of the things most to be admired in Sir John Richardson is his having devolved the command of the expedition to be pursued this season, now over, on a man whom he conscientiously believed to be better fitted than himself for the task. How difficult it commonly is for a man to think any one better fitted than himself to do what he feels competent to undertake! But, as he said, Dr. Rae is twenty years younger, with more experience of the coasts of the Arctic Sea, and having more resources at his command from the appointment which he holds in the Hudson's Bay Company. He had also had a year's experience of Dr. Rae's energetic, enterprising, unflinching temper in the performance of his duty.

It was sad to return without having obtained any traces of the crews of the ' Erebus ' and ' Terror ; ' but Sir John Richardson had the satisfaction of being conscious of having done his duty and obtained the approbation of Her Majesty's Government.

CHAPTER XXIII.

1849–1862.

DURING the winter which succeeded Sir John Richardson's return from Rupert's Land, his time was much occupied. In addition to his official duties, he had frequent consultations with the Arctic Committee, and reports and letters to write on the subject of continuing the search for the missing ships.

On January 16, 1850, he received the thanks of the Lords of the Admiralty for papers, from which valuable memoranda had been extracted, for the use of Captain Collinson, who, in her Majesty's ship 'Enterprise,' was about to set sail for Behring's Straits; and again on the 25th, for a clear and comprehensive paper relative to the probable supplies available for Lieutenant Pullin, of the 'Herald,' in making a boat voyage from these Straits to the Mackenzie River.

R

Early in March, he thus wrote to his mother-in-law :—

The report, in this morning's paper, of Sir John Franklin having made his way to Behring's Straits is unsatisfactory. One cannot help clinging to what speaks so directly to one's wishes, but Mr. Peck, from whom the information comes, says nothing of the gentleman who told him, except that he came from Kamschatka, nor how he got his knowledge, so that it may be only a whaler's report of Captains Kellet and Moore having been seen in Behring's Straits.

In the month of May, Sir John, with his family, spent three weeks at Lancrigg, the mountain home of Mrs. Fletcher, to which, in writing from Fort Confidence, he had thus referred :—

My chief object in mentioning my readings in Horace is to let you know how vividly the description of his Sabine villa has reminded me of Lancrigg. There may be much difference between the mountains in Westmoreland and the hills of Apulia, but Easedale has all the elements of rural beauty which the poet ascribes to his valley of Mandela, and I do not believe that the stream of Digentia, fed by Bandusia, is superior to the burn of Easedale nourished by its mountain tarns.

At the beginning of August, he visited the Scottish metropolis, to be present at the meetings of the British Association, and was hospitably and kindly welcomed by many friends. Professor Jamieson, who had been Sir John Richardson's earliest instructor in natural history, was still living, and able to take pleasure in meeting and conversing with his distinguished pupil. With Pro-

Lancrigg

fessor James Forbes, Dr. Alison, Mr. James Wilson, Professor Christison, and others, he had a renewal of friendly intercourse.

Mrs. Fletcher spent the winter of 1851–52 at Haslar, and her journal contains a pleasant description of one of the social parties which frequently enlivened the period of Sir Edward Parry's command :—

Sir John and Mary had invited about thirty of their friends and neighbours to an evening party, to celebrate my eighty-second birthday, on the 15th of this month. The dear hostess and poor Josephine were unhappily laid up with illness when the day came, so a cloud passed over our festivities; but our good Sir John, assisted by Sir Edward Parry, put forth his strength in acting charades for the amusement of the party.

Sir Edward had been experienced in this innocent amusement, having, during the long nights of his Arctic winters, often resorted to comic and pantomimic exhibitions to divert and cheer his ship's company amid the regions of 'thick-ribbed ice.' On this occasion, music and singing intervened between the acts, and after supper Sir Edward Parry prefaced his toast to my health by a very affecting allusion to the many mercies that had been spared to me in my long pilgrimage, such a speech as filled my eyes with tears and my heart with thankfulness.

Sir John Richardson took occasion, in thanking Sir Edward for me, to express the regret with which he, in common with all the inhabitants of Haslar, looked forward to the approaching period of Sir Edward's removal from a situation which he had filled with so much honour to himself and comfort to every one connected with the establishment. The evening was concluded by the merry dance of Sir Roger de Coverley, as a remembrance of 'Old England.'

The days pass calmly and happily on at Haslar. Everybody is kind to me. Sir John is constantly occupied with his duties at the hospital, and in 'the recreation,' as he calls it, of examining and reporting upon various bones found in mountains of ice in Behring's Straits. This curious discovery was made by one of the ships sent in search of Sir John Franklin, and commanded by Captain Kellet. He also makes time in the evening to read something aloud in the family circle, Mrs. Gaskell's 'Cranford' being the present favourite, and also to play a game or two at piquet with me, which he says is good for my eyes, and I encourage it, to rest his brain.

In the summer of 1852, the establishment at Haslar lost the paternal rule of Sir Edward Parry, who was promoted to Rear-Admiral of the 'White,' on June 4. The death of Dr. Anderson, in the spring of the following year, was another great deprivation.

At this time, an epidemic scarlatina prevailed among the crews of her Majesty's screw-steamers of war 'Agamemnon' and 'Odin,' and Sir John's efforts were vigorously and successfully put forth to stay its progress.

Early in 1855, Edward, his youngest and tenderly-loved child, became dangerously ill, and though unusually occupied with official duties, Sir John took up his station nightly beside the little sufferer's crib, and all his nervous terrors were relieved when his father was near. They had many happy conversations, and often repeated to each other their favourite psalms and hymns. The Scottish version of the Twenty-third Psalm was asked for by the little boy almost every morning. It was **Sir John's** favourite, and to the end of his life he delighted to say :—

> The Lord's my shepherd, I'll not want.
>> He makes me down to lie
> In pastures green : He leadeth me
>> The quiet waters by.

Little Edward was a great favourite with the patients in the Asylum. He used to collect all sorts of pictures and story-books, to take to the poor sailors, and writing-paper for them to scribble over.

Before the March winds had ceased to blow, his Heavenly Father took him to Himself.

The situation of Director-General of the Medical Department of the Navy having become vacant by the retirement of Sir William Burnett, Sir John Richardson applied for it, in the usual terms, to the First Lord of the Admiralty, Sir Charles Wood. After some delay, the promotion was refused on the ground of advanced age. In accordance, therefore, with a previously-formed resolution not to stand in the way of the advancement of others, he sent in his resignation, and was placed on the retired list of Medical Inspectors, having spent forty-eight years in the public service.

Many were disappointed at his not succeeding to the office of **Director-General.** He was then in his sixty-eighth year, but possessed of a vigour of constitution enjoyed by few men in the prime of life; and for ten years after, the amount of work, both bodily and mental, which he accomplished, equalled that of any similar period of his singularly active career. He was constantly engaged in literary labours, and would walk miles to prescribe for the poorest person in the valley of Grasmere who might require his aid.

On being relieved from duty, he retired to Westmoreland, and with determination of purpose and a contented spirit, set about devising some new occupation for himself. In the 'Times' of June 23 appeared a letter from his pen, claiming, what is now generally conceded, for Sir John Franklin's ill-fated expedition the merit of having completed the Discovery of the North-west Passage, though no one of the party lived to tell the tale.

The autumn was spent amidst the beautiful scenery of the Trosachs, and was a season of real enjoyment. He delighted to climb the neighbouring mountains with his two youngest children, or to lead the pony of his eldest daughter, whose health was failing, to places where she could walk with safety. He had also a considerable practice among the cottagers, who speedily found out 'the good doctor' at the manse of Achray, and never failed to show their gratitude by little unexpected gifts.

He was much struck with the intelligence of the men, and the interest which they took in the Crimean war. They often came to the manse to hear the news, or gathered round him at some turn of the road when he was reading the stirring accounts of the struggle, while his wife and daughter were sketching between Achray and Loch Katrine.

On returning from a pedestrian excursion through Glenfinlas and 'the Braes of Balquidder,' to Glencoe, Sir John had the good fortune, at King's House Inn, to meet with Professor Sedgwick, of Cambridge, and his niece, on their way to the Trosachs, and willingly joined their agreeable company in posting back to the manse, where a merry evening was spent before they proceeded to the hotel.

After attending the meetings of the British Association at Glasgow, and spending some pleasant weeks in Edinburgh, before the winter set in, they arrived at Lancrigg, their future home.

The daily round of simple duties and pleasures which henceforward occupied his time affords few materials for the biographer. In the summer of 1856, it was my privilege to be able to accept an invitation to spend a few days at Lancrigg, and I shall never forget his honest face, and the hearty manner in which he introduced me to his daughters as their 'new cousin.' During our long rambles **we** chatted freely, as if old friends, Sir John from time **to** time dropping **in** to see how some sick neighbour **was** getting **on**. Between Mrs. Fletcher and her son-in-law there existed a reciprocity of affectionate **regard,** which it was delightful **to** witness. His eldest daughter, Josephine, **was an** invalid, and watched over by her father with great tenderness.

She died on September 6, and, without a murmur, Sir John resigned the child, whom he loved very dearly, to the Father **in** whose love they both firmly confided.

In October he went to Edinburgh, to give evidence as to **the** probability of none of the crews of the 'Erebus' **and** 'Terror' being then alive. **Of** the melancholy **death of** the whole party Sir **John had no** doubt. From Edinburgh, he went **to** the neighbourhood of Hawick, **to** visit Mr. Fairholme, whose brother, **a** lieutenant in the navy, was among the lost.

At the December meeting of the Royal Society, in **1856,** Sir John Richardson was presented with one of the Royal Medals. On that occasion the President, **Lord** Wrottesley, said :—

Your Council **have** awarded **one of the** Royal Medals to Sir John Richardson. His claims **to** that honour, as **a** most distinguished naturalist and scientific traveller, will, **I** am sure, **be** generally admitted. Sir John Richardson's earliest work on zoology appeared about the year 1823, **but** his first great work was published in 1829—namely,

the 'Fauna Boreali-Americana,' in which he has described
the quadrupeds and fishes of the Arctic regions, and, with
Mr. Swainson's aid, the birds. The merits of this work,
in the very accurate descriptions of the species, in the
great amount of information on their habits and ranges,
are admitted to be of the highest order. Since that
period, Sir John Richardson has published largely on
various branches of zoology, physical geography, and
meteorology. The reports to the British Association on
the fishes of New Zealand and of China are extremely interesting under many points of view. Another report to the
same body on the 'General Zoology of North America' is
a most valuable contribution to science. His later works,
which must be more particularly considered here, are the
'Zoology of the Voyages of the Terror and of the Herald,'
in which he described the fishes and reptiles collected
during those expeditions, and gives an account of some of
the great extinct mammifers of the Arctic countries, with
very interesting observations on their ancient relations and
ranges.

He has also lately contributed to the 'Geological Journal'
a valuable paper, in which he has made known the presence
of tertiary strata, abounding with vegetable remains, in dis-
tricts now rendered sterile by the extreme cold. Altogether
I think there can be no doubt that the merits of Sir John
Richardson, as a philosophical naturalist, are of a very
high order.

It is not within our province to reward his other claims
to distinction, but all will rejoice that, in the conscientious
discharge of a delicate and important duty, the Council
have been able to bestow a medal on one who has earned
the applause of all who have watched his career, for his

patient endurance and fortitude, under incredible hardships, in his first Arctic expedition, in company with Franklin, and again for his chivalrous self-devotion in the cause of friendship and science combined, at a period of life when most men resolve to rest from their labours, or at least would hesitate to encounter the fatigues and dangers of a Polar expedition, the anticipation of which must have been more appalling to one who had bitter experience of their painful reality.

Sir John Richardson, accept this medal as a token of our respect for your scientific labours and character.

During this visit to London, Sir John had an interview with Florence Nightingale.

On December 4, he wrote to Lady Richardson :—

Yesterday, I went by appointment to the Burlington Hotel, at five o'clock, to wait on Miss Nightingale, and talked with her till seven, during all that time answering questions, and occasionally making some remarks on the present state of the public departments and hospitals. I was glad to find that our opinions were precisely alike. She wished to know the mode of conducting the naval hospitals, and how the medical officers obtained alterations, amendments, and supplies. After I had detailed my experience, she remarked that it was nearly as bad as in the army, and believed that both were branches of the Circumlocution Office. The only advantage which I could point out was, that the Admiralty are much more liberal in their supplies. There is the same difficulty in introducing the improvements of modern science, from the number of channels through which every suggestion must pass, until

the head of the office is called upon to decide regarding a
matter of which he knows nothing, all the reasons for the
change having filtered away in the progress upwards of the
proposal. 'The weary Treasury,' she says, 'is at the root
of all the evil.' Miss Nightingale is an earnest reformer of
the right sort, and fills out, I believe, the ideal picture
which your mother has formed of her, but she has not
your mother's faith in public men. She believes that the
grievous failures of the past will not produce much future
amendment. She is very like the print of her at Lancrigg,
and I should have known her at once, but has much more
intellect in the countenance. She has a most brilliant and
intelligent smile, a very pleasant and not patronising address, but always perfectly self-possessed, quick in compre-
hending a subject, and distinct in her questions, which
were calculated to bring out a correct view of the subject.

During the winter Sir John Richardson was
occupied in writing for the 'Encyclopædia Britannica' an article on 'Ichthyology,' and a 'Bio-
graphical Sketch of Sir John Franklin.' From
this little memoir, Lady Franklin has selected the
words placed on the pedestal of the statue erected
by Parliament in 1866, near the Athenæum Club,
to the memory of her husband and the crews of
the 'Erebus' and 'Terror,'—

> They forged the last link with their lives.

'This,' wrote Lady Franklin, 'is but a small
tribute of gratitude to the memory of that faithful
friend and companion who, when all had perished,
as revealed by Dr. Rae, stood up nobly and alone,

in the first instance, to claim for Franklin and his followers that meed of honour to which the priority of their discovery entitled them, but which the public did not at that time understand. The inscription in front of the present monument shows that the fact is now fully acknowledged, but it is to Sir John Richardson we owe the first manly assertion of it.'

In the autumn of 1857, he attended the British Association meetings in Dublin, and enjoyed the lovely scenery around Killarney and the wild grandeur of the Wicklow mountains.

After returning to Westmoreland, his time was occupied with the preparation of various scientific papers, the protracted illness of Mrs. Fletcher, who died in February 1858, also calling forth much of his sympathy and care. They had been long strongly attached to each other, and he watched over her last sufferings with unwearied attention.

The Richardsons spent a part of the following winter in Edinburgh, and Sir John renewed his rambles in the neighbourhood of Arthur's Seat. At this time the Centenary Festival in honour of Robert Burns was celebrated, and he took a lively interest in that outburst of national enthusiasm, delighting to recount his early reminiscences of his favourite bard.

In the autumn of 1859, Professor Huxley, of the Government School of Mines, dedicated his

work on the 'Oceanic **Hydrozoa**' to **Sir** John
Richardson, under whom he had served at Haslar.
In the preface, he gracefully alludes **to** his former
chief having quietly noted the bent of his studies ;
and when Captain **Owen** Stanley, who had **been**
appointed to command a surveying expedition **to**
the eastern coast of Australia, applied to **him** to
recommend an assistant-surgeon who possessed
some knowledge of natural history, he offered him
the appointment, thus affording a suitable opportunity of developing **his tastes.**

Another of those distinguished **men** whose literary, scientific, and philanthropic **pursuits** derived an impulse from having been **subordinate to**
Sir John Richardson at Haslar, was **Dr. Balfour**
Baikie, who went to the **Niger** in pursuit **of**
natural history, and, as a means of elevating them,
to promote trade with the natives. Though often
urged **by** Sir John **to** return, he lingered **too** long
in that fatal climate, and died of fever when
about to embark **for England.** The tidings reached
Liverpool **early in 1865, and no one** mourned **his**
loss more sincerely than **his former chief.**

The quiet family **life** at Lancrigg **was varied, in**
the spring of 1860, **by a visit to** London, where he
enjoyed the pleasure of meeting with many old
and dear friends, among whom were **Dr.** Gray,
of the British Museum ; Sir William **J**ackson
Hooker, **of** Kew ; and his son, Dr. Joseph Dalton
Hooker. Before returning **to** Westmoreland, the

Richardsons also spent a few **days** at Eton, with
the Rev. Wharton Marriott, whom Sir John had
tended, with kindness and care, during **a** long and
dangerous illness **at** Grasmere.

His eldest son, John, had for some time been
an officer **in the** Royal Artillery, and this summer,
Willingham passed **his** competitive examination
at Chelsea for Woolwich.   **Sir John** met him daily
after the forenoon part of the work, spoke to him
encouragingly **over a** substantial luncheon, and
then parted to meet, later in the day, at the
friendly **house** of Dr. **Gray,** or of the Rev. John
Philip Gell.   Six weeks **later,** the post brought
the joyful announcement that Willingham was
first **on** the list.   **The** father's loving heart was
too full for utterance, **and he** turned away to
conceal his **emotion.**

This **year, Sir** John Richardson edited a new impression of Yarrell's ' British Fishes,' adding all the
species which had been discovered **in the** British
seas since the year 1839, and prefixing **a** memoir
of the author.   He **also** contributed largely to
the ' Museum of Natural History.'   During the
winter, **his** leisure hours were chiefly occupied
in reading **for the** proposed new dictionary of the
Philological Society, under the superintendence of
Mr. Furnivall, **of** Lincoln's **Inn.**   This course of
study also led him **to take** an interest in the
publications **of** the Early English Text Society.

In the summer of 1861, he left the garden and his literary work to give his youngest son a holiday trip to Paris, where they amused themselves in learning the Parisian accent, and exploring the city and environs. The libraries and the fortifications received no small share of their attention ; but the father soon began to long for 'the hayfields, the copses, and glorious Rab,' his favourite poet, whose works he was perusing, in connection with his philological studies.

Writing to his friend Dr. Baikie, then in Africa, on August 21, 1862, he says :—

The lectures of Max Müller on the ' Science of Language' have given a great impulse to philological study, and greatly simplified the mode of ascertaining the connections existing between cognate languages. The writings of Dean Trench have been the means of founding a Philological Society, and that society has undertaken a new English Dictionary. I sent a complete index of words used by Burns, with their significations and cognates in Norse, Icelandic, or Gaelic, as far as I could ascertain them. I have also read the oldest editions of Blind Harry's ' Wallace' and Gawain Douglas's ' Virgil,' to give me a knowledge of the early signification of Scottish words. The Philological Society would be a good medium of publication of any remarks you may wish to give on African tongues.

I take an interest in these matters now, having laid aside Zoology for want of material in my retirement, but on your return, I should be glad to aid you in giving your fish to the world, if I should not be found to be *hors de combat.*

John, my eldest son, is on the eve of obtaining his captain's commission in the Royal Artillery, and the youngest, Willingham, has just got his lieutenancy in the Royal Engineers.

CHAPTER XXIV.

1862—1865.

ON October 1, 1862, the British Association met
at Cambridge, where Sir John Richardson, with his
wife and daughter, spent a few pleasant days under
the hospitable roof of the Rev. Dr. Cookson,
master of St. Peter's College, and then proceeded
to Paris by way of Folkestone and Boulogne.
From the French metropolis, they travelled to
Strasbourg, Basle, Lucerne, and, over the St.
Gothard Pass, into Italy, making the tour of
Lakes Lugano and Como, and then advancing by
Milan, Turin, and Genoa, to Florence, where six
weeks were pleasantly spent. The grand historical
monuments and collections of Art, the valuable
Libraries, and the Museum of Natural History,
were inexhaustible sources of enjoyment.

Early on November 27, the Richardsons set out

s

from Florence, and near midnight of the 29th
drove through the Porta del Popolo into the
'Eternal City.' Here Sir John commenced his
daily explorations with the ardour of youthful
student life, rather than of advanced age. Before
ten in the morning, he had arranged the pro-
gramme for the day, taking his companions to the
points of interest in a special locality. Thus three
months glided past.

The month of March, 1863, was spent in visiting
Naples, Baiæ, Pompeii, Herculaneum, Castella-
mare, Paestum, Amalphi, and Sorrento. After
witnessing the solemnities of the holy week at
Rome, they proceeded to Ancona, Ravenna, Padua,
and Venice, returning home by the Tyrol, Inns-
brück, Munich, Augsburg, Stuttgart, Brussels and
Calais. The voyage across the channel was not
longer than usual, but the sea was stormy, and Sir
John became completely prostrated.

In the journal kept by Miss Richardson is the
following entry :—

We landed at Dover, thankful beyond measure to be
in our own land again, and more especially when we had
the comfort of seeing my dear father so far restored as
to be able to enjoy a refreshing sleep. Next morning, he
was much better, and we were enabled to give heartfelt
thanks to God for His great goodness in preserving us in
all dangers during our absence from Old England.

Sir John thoroughly enjoyed the return to his

books, his flowers, and his friends in the **valley of
Grasmere. The journey had** been **undertaken in**
order **to give pleasure to others rather than to**
himself, **but he had** laid up a store of pleasant **re-**
collections, and **felt a** new interest in the future **of**
Italy.

The summer **was** pleasantly **varied by** the visits
of friends from **a** distance, and a renewal of intercourse with the **Dean** of Westminster, Dr. Trench,
now Archbishop of Dublin, **and his** family, **who**
took lodgings **in** Easedale **for** the season.

In September, the British **Association** met at
Newcastle-upon-Tyne, and Sir **John Richardson**
became the guest of **a** family who, during **a part of**
the year, resided at Grasmere. **In** reference **to**
this visit, one of that family says :—

When **Sir John** came in from **the** meetings, often, **I**
should **think, a** good deal tired, for they were long and hot,
he was most **kind in telling what had** passed, taking es-
pecial pains **to be full and particular** in the relation **to**
those members **of the household who had** been **unable to**
attend. **In** listening to **these** conversations, **I used to be**
struck with **his** care to uphold knowledge as **a trust. If**
any one threw out an unwarranted speculation, he would
say quietly, 'We do not know anything, with certainty,
there.'

He gratified the Northumbrians by the interest which **he**
took in **their** county and its very rich archæological re-
mains, and on one of the excursion **days,** walked, apparently without suffering from fatigue, for twenty miles

over part of the Roman wall and the moors that lie to each side of it.

Though in his seventy-sixth year, his vigour and activity continued uninterrupted. On November 6, in a letter to one of his nieces, he said, 'Yesterday was my birthday, and I took a holiday, and went to the top of Helm Crag, and had a survey of the valley from the 'Lion and Lamb.'

During the winter, his time was chiefly occupied in reading old Scottish authors, and some of the prophetical books in Wickliffe's translation of the Bible.

In the spring of 1864, accompanied by his wife and daughter, he paid a visit to his only remaining sister and other relations in Dumfriesshire, and took a great interest in the antiquities of the district. While visiting his brother-in-law, Mr. Charles Carruthers, near Annan, he went to see the Runic Cross at Ruthwell Manse, the inscription on which, containing a portion of a poem on the Crucifixion, had long been a puzzle to antiquarians and was first deciphered by the eminent Anglo-Saxon scholar, Mr. John M. Kemble.

In company with his brother-in-law, Mr. Hannay, and the late Mr. Trotter, sheriff-substitute of Dumfries, he also visited some remains of ancient habitations which had been discovered by the draining of a lake in Galloway. The weather was unpropitious, and the adventures of the excursion

formed the subject of much mirth, in the evening,
at the hospitable table of the sheriff, who kindly
favoured me, some time before his death, with the
following reminiscences of that day :—

I have a very pleasing recollection of the visit to which
you refer. On the morning of Saturday, June 11, 1864,
Sir John Richardson, Mr. Hannay, and myself drove from
Wigton, where we had spent the previous night, to Do-
walton Loch, which is, I think, about six miles distant.
The object of our visit was to inspect the lacustrine remains which were said to have been brought to light by
the recent drainage of the Loch ; a subject in which Sir
John felt much interest.

During our drive, the morning was lowering, and, when
we reached the Loch, it rained heavily ; but nothing could
damp the antiquarian ardour of Sir John. For about a
couple of hours we traversed the oozy bed of the newly-
drained Loch, passing to the several islands, where the
remains are found, on very rude pathways formed by loose
stones and pieces of timber thrown into the soft mud by
the drainers ; and I could not help admiring the firm
elastic step with which Sir John pursued his way, sur-
mounting all the difficulties of the route in a manner which
men much younger in years could not well have surpassed.

Unfortunately, before our visit many of the remains of
lacustrine habitations had been removed by previous explorers, but we found still the upright beams and transverse
mortised rafters, with the charcoal of the fires, and bones
of the animals, which had supplied warmth and food to the
inhabitants. Sir John was much gratified, and brought
away with him many relics for future study and inspec-
tion.

Early in the afternoon, we returned to Wigton, where we joined Lady and **Miss** Richardson, whom the inclemency of the weather prevented from accompanying **us to** the Loch, and proceeded **to** Dumfries by the way **of** Newton Stewart. The day **was most** agreeably concluded by the whole **party** dining **at my house**; Sir John as usual rendering **the** evening a charming one **by his** genial disposition, **and** the stores of information **and** anecdote with which his **long** life **of** adventure and **observation** so copiously supplied him.

Such are my recollections of **a day which I** shall long remember as one of unmixed enjoyment.

During the summer, Captain Richardson spent **some** time at Lancrigg, and Sir John, who always delighted in the **society of** the young, frequently joined **them in a rough kind** of croquet-ground which **had been formed on** the only level spot **near the** house. **It used to** amuse **as** well as please **him** to see how young ladies, in **pink,** blue, and white, appeared in the valley, as if by magic, with the flowers of summer.

In August, he thus wrote to me :—

We **go on** here precisely as we did some years ago, **when** we had **the** pleasure of seeing you. My eldest son, a Captain in the Royal Artillery, is just now at home on a **visit,** but will leave us about a month hence. The younger **is still** pursuing his studies at Chatham as a Lieutenant of Engineers, and **in** six months will have completed the course of two years and a half, which officers in that corps **have to** undergo after receiving their commissions.

The following winter was a very happy and tranquil one to the family at Lancrigg. Though the snow lay long on the ground, the weather was often light and sunny, and the birds, which came to be fed, were a constant source of amusement.

At the end of March, 1865, Sir John took part in a penny reading, for the entertainment of the Grasmere villagers, selecting for the occasion, ' The Cottar's Saturday Night,' and the address ' To my Mare Maggie' of Burns, his favourite poet.

When the wintry frosts were gone and the ground had thawed, he began vigorously to complete some improvements in the garden, which had been commenced in autumn. He was passionately fond of flowers, plants, and trees, and had a true eye for the beautiful in landscape gardening. The fine days of April and May he spent chiefly in the open air, visiting the sick in his walks, or collecting ferns for friends at a distance, who had expressed a wish for them. His evenings were devoted to Wickliffe's Bible.

On the last day of May, he accompanied his family and their guests to pay a visit to old friends at Coniston. It was a standing joke between them that Sir John never left their garden empty-handed, and that evening he carried off a plant of ' Forget-me-not,' which, late as it was when they reached home, he planted in the favourite border, before entering the house.

While walking to church, on Whitsunday, he spoke of the wonderful beauty of the expressions of Isaiah, and how glad he was that he had selected that book as part of his work for the Dictionary, having felt both pleasure and profit from the study. While partaking of the communion, his countenance seemed to have diffused over it even more than his usual reverent, inward peace.

Monday, June 5, was a lovely soft June day, and Sir John spent the forenoon in quietly superintending some work in the garden. After luncheon, he and Lady Richardson drove to Ambleside and Rydal, making their first call at Dr. Davy's and last at Fox How, where they remained for some time, as Mrs. Arnold was about to go from home. Looking out on the lovely scenery, in its fresh June beauty, Sir John remarked that he wondered they could leave it.

In the evening, he worked an hour or two at Wickliffe, and at ten o'clock read, at family worship, the seventh chapter of St. Matthew's Gospel. He then stood for a short time at the window, and said, 'We shall have the moon full, in our drive to Ambleside on Wednesday,' kissed his daughter and wished her good night, took from the table king Alfred's Anglo-Saxon version of the 'History of the World by Orosius,' lighted his candle and walked off with a firm step, which sounded along the passage as that of a man in the full vigour of life. About eleven o'clock, Lady

Richardson **went up-stairs.** He was still **awake,** and spoke of **his plans for** the next day. A long suspiration followed, and **he** passed through death to life.

Thus **calmly ended a** life of almost unexampled activity **and** usefulness, uprightness, and humble faith. **Of** him, it may be said, ' **Thy** sun shall no more go down, neither **shall** thy moon withdraw itself, for **the Lord shall** be thine everlasting light, and the **days** of thy mourning **shall be** ended.'

CHAPTER XXV.

1865.

THE call was sudden, but to one who had spent
his life in the service of God and man, and reached
a good old age without experiencing mental or
bodily decay, an end so gentle was not unde-
sirable. It was a translation, without pain, from
the duties of earth to the joys of heaven—a being
' absent from the body, and present with the Lord.'

The event, however, cast a shadow over the
valley of Grasmere, where, during the last years
of his life, he had done much for the welfare of
the people. In his death, the poor lost a friend
who had been ever ready to aid them in sickness
or in sorrow, and not a few tears were shed as the
dust was committed to the dust in the lively hope
of a glorious resurrection, in the quiet churchyard

of Grasmere, where he had so often been a humble worshipper.

One of the verses of Scripture inserted on his tombstone is from the twenty-seventh Psalm, which Franklin and he used to repeat to each other, at Fort Enterprise, when too weak to hold a book : ' I had fainted, unless I had believed to see the goodness of the Lord in the land of the living.'

A lady, resident in the valley, writing to a friend, thus alluded to the event :—

You in London, where interests are so much more widely diffused, will hardly understand how absorbing is this grief in our little community ; indeed it is one that comes home to all, for all have lost a dear friend, or good neighbour, in the high and Christian sense of these terms.

When the natural expression of deep sympathy with the sorrow-stricken family has been uttered, there comes from each one a personal lamentation. Every person has some trait of him to mention ; some deed of charity, accidentally discovered ; some act of kindness, or proof of consideration. One of our Wallers, whom I met to-day, after saying a few words, which expressed his sorrow for the loss of him ' who was always glad to help a poor man, and thought nothing of the trouble,' added, ' Ay, I have left my wife and mother at home crying, and no wonder.'

The singleness of purpose which he showed was one of the most remarkable points of his character. He always seemed to do an act of kindness without a thought beyond, and as if it were but the natural thing. We have indeed lost a good, kind friend, and the blank becomes more felt as the first shock passes away.'

The manner in which he carried Christian precept into practice is also thus referred to by another neighbour :—

Sir John Richardson was one of those rare persons, to whom any one, whether high or low, might go for advice, help, and sympathy. They were sure to have it, of the best kind, wisely, promptly, and freely given. It was quite usual, in any difficulty, to say, 'I will go and ask Sir John, who will tell me what to do.' The poor people felt this strongly, and acted on it, never doubting his willingness to help. At all hours of the day, he would see those who came, and if a case of illness was mentioned, it seemed natural to hear him say that he would call on the sick person. All considerations of distance, personal inconvenience, or favourite occupations, were passed over.

One of the most striking traits in his character was the simplicity with which his good deeds were done, not only putting aside all thought of self, but shrinking from the acknowledgments which his kindness called forth from those whom he assisted or obliged. In reply to such acknowledgments, he always endeavoured to show that he was only pleasing himself. This was, in fact, the case, for doing good was his great pleasure. He was a true follower in his Great Master's footsteps.

It was quite delightful to meet him in one's walks, ever ready with a playful allusion, pleasant remark, or apt illustration of whatever subject came under consideration. One never fell in with him without experiencing the influence of his happy state of mind, which shed its pure and bright light on all he spoke of.

Great was the sorrow which his friends at a distance felt when they knew that he had been removed from his labours—that they would see his face no more. From Lady Franklin came the tender expression of regard,—

My heart is full, for he was my husband's dearest friend, and their memories are inseparable. He was very dear to me also. I loved and honoured him, and think now, with the tenderest interest, of our last meeting at Bath, when his genial kindness went to my heart.

Sir John Richardson's courage and coolness in danger were ennobled by the friendship which he cherished towards his companions in peril, especially Sir John Franklin. Sir George Back, the only remaining officer of the First Expedition, says,—

No one could perfectly understand the admirable qualities of his nature, who had not been with him in trials of no ordinary description, even when life itself was in question. In storm and sunshine, in plenty and famine, in moments of great danger, requiring unusual self-possession and coolness, he was ever firmly balanced and collected—a fine example to others. With a keen sense of humour, quick to discern, and ready to applaud, he was ever a pleasant companion, and, better than all, a moral, good man.

I can never forget one morning (the beginning of our misery), when, crossing the Barren Lands from the sea, we found the whole country covered with snow, and Franklin so faint, from want of food, that he fell down.

Richardson drew from his scanty stores for the sick a few inches of preserved soup, and gently restored him, and then as we returned for warmth and shelter, to our blankets, it being impossible to move on, he begged us to take a few bits of gum-arabic, to check the cravings of the stomach.   Oh, how I remember that morning !

Referring to the friendship which subsisted between his father-in-law and Sir John Richardson, the Rev. John Philip Gell, writing to Lady Richardson, says,—

Well as Sir John Franklin could sometimes express himself, I do not think he could have put into words the deep regard he had for your husband's noble-hearted and devoted character, nor the happy reliance which he always seemed to place in him—the happier, perhaps, because it was so unconscious, for the most part, and so simple.

To no one, probably, in all the numerous circle of his friends, did your husband attach himself, with a more steadfast and self-sacrificing affection.   No doubt, it was founded upon what they suffered for and with each other, in the adventures of their earlier days, but it was sustained through many happy years, in sharing each other's home enjoyments and scientific pursuits.   It was touching to see it break out again, in its first form, when your husband, already entered upon old age, left his home and family to seek Franklin, already dead; and more touching still, to notice the way in which, after his return, his tenderness seemed to overflow towards my wife, for her father's sake, when he sometimes stayed with us in London.

His oldest and most intimate friend, who knew

him, in **joy** and in **sorrow, for more** than forty years, thus writes :—

In thinking over our recent loss, I do not know that I ever felt anything more difficult than to determine what were the most prominent features of his character. All things were so wisely balanced, that it was, I believe, only those who knew him best, that gave him credit for all he possessed. I often feel I could say more about a very inferior man. He was so good, so consistent, so laborious, so always thinking and acting for others, in fact, always doing great acts, though but in the ordinary demands of daily life, that the greater and more remarkable points which have been dwelt upon were really but the same abiding spirit intensified and brought out into more prominent action by the peculiar incidents of the various situations in which circumstances placed him—a child-like trusting affection was the foundation of a chivalrous courage.

I should think it hardly possible to find a more perfect man, in body, soul, and spirit—strong, deep, and true.

The **Rev. Wharton B. Marriott, of** Eton, **whom** he had attended, **with fatherly care, during a long** and critical sickness at **Grasmere, says,**—

He was one whose very aspect told much of the goodness and beauty of his character. Especially I remember being struck, on the few occasions previously to my illness on which I met him, with a calm gravity and seriousness of demeanour, as of one on whose mind the solemn realities of this world and of the other were very deeply impressed, and with this there was a calm of outward manner, that reflected, so I thought, an inward quietness and confidence of spirit—God's gift to good and faithful men—to **whom** the thought **is ever** present, that over all the changes and chances **of** this troubled world **there** is One **who changes not, who sees** and **directs to issues of** his ordaining, **the counsels of all men, and the events of all things.**

One feature of his character **impressed** itself strongly **on me, namely, the** remarkable simplicity **with** which he spoke **and acted, saying and** doing, **on all occasions,** exactly what **the occasion required, as** if **by an** intuition upon which he **acted without consciousness of effort.   He** seemed **to** me to be one **to whom the highest** principles **of action were so habitually** present, that **he** could see, with clearest percep-**tion,** where others **would have been** in doubt, and act, **as** by an inward instinct, **and without any** thought of a second cause.   **What in others would have been a** triumph of self-mastery, **or self-denial, was in him only** the following out **of the path of duty by one who** habitually was led by the Spirit **of God.**

The active Christianity of Sir John Richardson exercised a salutary influence on the young **medi-cal officers who served under him.**

Dr. Andrew Clarke, **of** Russell Square, London, **in reply to a letter from Lady** Richardson **thus wrote :—**

I cannot let a post pass **without** acknowledging your letter.   No one **knowing** anything of the inner life of my revered friend could read that letter unmoved ; and me, who in days past had the privilege of seeing deeply into that inner life, **who** took from it, insensibly, the tone of my whole life, and spoke of it, among the few to whom I could speak of such subjects, as a type of true greatness, and a living example of the manner in which Christianity may become a fruitful life, rather than a barren creed,—me it has moved most deeply.

And now, when I think of his finely balanced nature, of his earnest, truthful soul, of his large, powerful intellect, of the fitting form in which they dwelt; when I recall to mind his rare sense of right, duty, and justice, his abhorrence of falsehood and all manner of subterfuge, his love of nature and all that was real and true, his freedom from finesse and affectation, his modesty and self-denial, his generous appreciation of others, his perfect naturalness and uniform consistency,—I can see how great and good a man he was; I feel how much of the little good, which I have brought forth, is the fruit of seed which he had planted, and that now, in my maturer years, seeing him by the help of a purer and greater light, I could have loved him with my whole heart.

In Sir John Richardson, a powerful intellect, simplicity of manners, modesty, candour, and abhorrence of anything mean, were combined in a rare degree. His retiring nature did not interfere with his taking an active part in every good cause, kindliness of heart and reverence for duty always overcoming inherent shyness. His firm grasp of facts, so as to draw from them a true deduction; the clearness of his judgment, which almost intuitively formed a correct estimate, both of men and things; and, above all, his deep reverence for God, and earnest faith in the saving power of Christ and Christian truth, were remarkable.

T

Sir John Richardson never attached himself to any political party, but his sympathies were strongly in favour of progress, and he rejoiced in every step taken to improve the public departments of the State, or the social condition of the people.

In a letter to me, dated July 7, 1856, he says,—

There is no political news of great moment now. The difficulties with the American Government, which were electioneering affairs from the beginning, on the other side of the Atlantic, are in a fair way of terminating. Europe is more unsettled, and there is evidently a fire kindling in the Italian Peninsula, which may eventually shake the Austrian dominion to pieces.

Meanwhile, a social revolution is going on in our own land, silently, and therefore not heeded, but nevertheless, surely. I mean the competition for Government appointments, and the giving to talents and acquirements what was before monopolised by money and influence. The Chinese were the only people who admitted the principle, but it was in a great measure inoperative with them, from the exclusive character of their national literature, and the general corruption that prevailed throughout their country. They had the form, without the essence, of a theoretically excellent scheme. I hope that the practical character of the English people will turn the experiment to good account, put honest examiners in the chair, and turn out an efficient body of public men.

The Government, at the same time, ought to take care that no looseness of practice creeps in, and that a high sense of morality should pervade the employés. Hitherto our public men have been, as a body, irreproachable in regard to a sense of public duty and honour, notwithstanding some sad exceptions.

One cannot help glancing at the probable future of Great Britain. The improvement has been great, especially in Scotland, during the nearly threescore and ten years of my life. In my boyhood, all the men of any liberality in their modes of thought were ' black-nebs,' and shunned more carefully, by the correct multitude, than a drunkard or a thief. One cannot but rejoice in the improvement of things, and pray that the future progress may be in the right path.

Of Sir John Richardson, as a man of science, Dr. J. E. Gray, of the British Museum, says,—

The most strikingly distinguishing features in his character were his extreme caution in the verification of facts, his modesty in speaking of himself and of his doings, and his untiring energy in the carrying out of whatever duties he undertook to perform. His caution originated in his entire devotion to truth, which caused him to consider no extent of research too laborious for its acquirement, and generated a feeling of the most implicit confidence in all his statements.

His modesty was especially conspicuous in the extreme difficulty with which he could be induced to speak, either of his travels or adventures, or of his professional or scientific labours. His energy was strongly evidenced in every part of his career, in the extraordinary difficulties and perils which he encountered on his various expeditions, in his unwearied attention to his professional duties, and in the extent and importance of his scientific labours.

It would scarcely be proper for me to speak of his geographical, meteorological, **and** magnetic contributions to science. I can only vouch for his great diligence in observing, and for the extreme accuracy of all his observations. Every precaution **was** constantly taken **by** him, **that no fact** should be stated, and no inference drawn, in the accuracy of which he had not the most perfect faith, and **he** never attempted to push his conclusions beyond **what the** observations justified.

Of his zoological labours, which I have watched with deep interest, throughout the whole of his **career, I** may be permitted to speak **more** decidedly, and **to** these I will now more particularly direct my attention.

On his return from his second Arctic expedition, he published his 'Fauna Boreali-Americana,' illustrated with beautiful plates. This work at once became and still continues to **be** the standard **work on** the zoology of British North **America. The** mammalia and fishes were entirely by himself, **the birds** by Mr. Swainson, who also drew the **plates,** and the insects by Mr. Kirby ; but the whole work **was** edited by himself, and **the** care and accuracy with which he collected together both the early history of the species, and the recent facts connected **with them,** can only be estimated by one who has been **engaged** in similar investigations.

It must be remembered, **too,** that at this period our zoological collections were small and imperfect, and the materials had **to** be sought in distant and scattered localities. In very many instances **it was** necessary to send instructions to the different **fur** stations of the Hudson's Bay Company to collect and transmit specimens for examination **and description,** and eventually the specimens thus procured were transferred by the Company to the British Museum, where they form some of the most valuable and interesting additions to the national collection.

After the publication of this great work, he chiefly confined his researches to ichthyology, and from this time became, *par excellence*, the ichthyologist of England, to whose superior knowledge and excellent judgment every one referred for information on all subjects connected with fishes. At the request of the British Association, he drew up an elaborate report on the ichthyology of China and Japan, taking for the basis of his work a fine collection of Chinese fishes, presented to the British Museum by the late Mr. Reeves, and a collection of drawings, made under the direction of the same gentleman, during his long residence at Canton.

To various voyages of survey and discovery, such as those of the ' Sulphur,' the ' Terror,' and the ' Herald,' he contributed most interesting appendices, descriptive of the animals, and especially of the fishes, observed during their progress, which are illustrated by figures of several hundred species new to science, and by important observations on their characters, affinities, and habits. In that of the ' Herald,' he also described and figured a number of fossil-bone mammalia, found at the Eschscholtz Bay, on the north-west coast of America, and gave an account of the osteology of some existing American mammalia.

Many papers on the fishes of Australia and New Zealand were also published by him, in connection with different voyages, and in the ' Annals and Magazine of Natural History,' and these were followed by a beautiful commencement of a work, in quarto, in which he gave figures of a number of interesting and finely-coloured species, from drawings made in Australia, under the title of 'Icones Piscium; or, Plates of Rare Fishes.'

In an excellent article on ichthyology, in the 'Encyclopædia Britannica,' he gave a capital *resumé* of all the genera of fishes, which affords the most complete view of the present state of ichthyological science. And he superintended the publication of the second edition of Yarrell's 'British Fishes,' to which he added an essay on the generic arrangement of fishes, giving also the generic characters, which had been unaccountably omitted in the first edition, and arranging the species in accordance with the modern classification.

A complete list of his various publications, on ichthyological subjects especially, would occupy a very large space, and certainly no one in England has contributed so largely, or so accurately, to our knowledge of the fishes which inhabit almost every region of the globe. In his earlier days, Sir John paid particular attention to the study of botany, and his botanical appendix to Captain Franklin's 'First Journey' is one of the most accurate and carefully prepared catalogues of the plants of a remarkable region that has ever been published.

He wrote valuable papers on 'The Geology of the Fur Countries;' 'The Aboriginal Indians;' 'Climatology;' 'The Frozen Soil of North America;' 'The Distribution of Plants in the Territory North of the Forty-ninth Parallel of Latitude,' and on a variety of other subjects. In addition to his scientific works, there appeared, in 1851, his 'Journal of a Boat Voyage through Rupert's Land and the Arctic Sea,' in two volumes, and, ten years later, a most interesting and instructive volume on 'The Polar Regions.'

The same painstaking ability which he manifested in his scientific writings was apparent in his contributions to the forthcoming 'Dictionary of the Philological Society.' The editor, in addressing the members, on October 26, 1865, said,—

We have suffered a great loss in the death of Sir John Richardson, one of the most careful and accurate of our contributors. His last work was for the 'Dictionary.' His pen had just finished a verse from the Wycliffite version of Isaiah, when his gentle, able, and manly spirit was called to its rest.

He received the honour of knighthood in 1846, and, on returning from his expedition in search of Sir John Franklin, had granted to him the rank and privileges of the third class of Companions of the Bath. In 1862, when good-service pensions were for the first time bestowed on the Medical Department of the Navy, the Duke of Somerset, without solicitation, awarded him one of 100*l.* per annum.

Sir John Richardson was member of the Geographical Society of London, and Wernerian Natural History Society of Edinburgh; honorary member of the Natural History Society of Montreal, and Literary and Philosophical Society of Quebec; Foreign Member of the Geographical Society of Paris, and Corresponding Member of the Academy of Natural Science of Philadelphia. In 1855, the Royal Society of Edinburgh elected him into the select number of British honorary members, and, in 1856, the Royal Society of London presented him with one of the Royal Medals. The following year, he received the degree of LL.D. from Trinity College, Dublin.

His life was an illustration of high intellectual and scientific attainments being combined with an earnest faith in the Saviour and confiding trust in God's goodness. How great soever the self-sacrifice required, he performed every public and private duty with sacred faithfulness, and to show disinterested and kindly affection to those in trouble was the spontaneous impulse of his warm heart. In danger and death, he was enabled, through the upholding power of constant communion with God, to look without fear on the ' house appointed for all living ;' and when the call came, ' Arise, depart, for this is not your rest,' it found him ready ' to enter into the kingdom of heaven.'

' Blessed are the dead that die in the Lord, from henceforth. Yea, saith the Spirit, that they may rest from their labours ; and their works do follow them.'

LONDON : PRINTED BY
SPOTTISWOODE AND CO., NEW-STREET SQUARE
AND PARLIAMENT STREET

www.ingramcontent.com/pod-product-compliance
Lightning Source LLC
Chambersburg PA
CBHW021037030726
47496CB00006B/1577